TWISTED KINGDOMS

Copyright

This book is a work of fiction. Names, characters, places, and incidents either are the product of the author's imagination or are used fictitiously. Any resemblance to actual events, locales, or persons, living or dead, is purely coincidental and not intended by the author.

Published by Renegade Publishing

Cover Artwork by Lisa Fricke
Copy Editing by Ocean's Edits
Line Editing by Red Ninja Editing

ISBN (paperback): 9798394139352
ISBN (hardcover): 978-1-7367090-9-2
ASIN: B09ZBF1B1B

Also By Frost Kay

THE AERMIAN FEUDS
(Dark Epic Fantasy)
Rebel's Blade
Crown's Shield
Siren's Lure
Enemy's Queen
King's Warrior
Warlord's Shadow
Spy's Mask
Court's Fool
Prince's Poison

THE BANNISHED QUEEN
(Fantasy Romance)
Traitor of the Tides (2024)

THE TWISTED KINGDOMS
(Epic Fantasy/Fairytale Retelling)
The Hunt
The Rook
The Heir
The Beast
The Hood
The Wolf
The Pearl (2024)

DRAGON ISLE WARS
(Epic Fantasy)
Court of Dragons
Queen of Legends
Throne of Serpents (2023)

DOMINION OF ASH CHRONICLES
(Urban Fantasy)
A Spire of Lies
A Kiss of Shadow
A Touch of Mayhem

HEIMSERYA

THE WILDS
KOPAL
HEIMSERYA
AZUL
BETRAZ
HEIMSERYA
MERJERI
FIERGONE
TALAGA
Dotae
Shueshun
THE FIRE ISLES
N
Fiergone's waters
Taseri
THE HINTERLANDS

Contents

`Dedication

For the courageous ones who left their abusers behind.

History of the Twisted Kingdoms

Once upon a time... Elves, Shapeshifters, Giants, Dragons, Humans and Merfolk were all at peace—all equals. Their lands and kingdoms were prosperous, and their enemies didn't dare attack for their armies were formidable. Generations passed and the people began to forget what was most important—love, courage, loyalty.

That was their downfall—for in self-indulgent ignorance they allowed darkness to creep into the land like a thief in the night. It started out slowly.

The Merfolk let vanity take root deep in their hearts, the Dragons became greedy from the skies, the Giants grew bloodthirsty, the Humans covetous, the Shapeshifters prideful, and the Elves allowed apathy to squeeze compassion from their hearts.

It was said that the earth rumbled and cracked, shaking the core of the world. When the tremors ceased, the Jagged Bone Mountain range surrounded the Elvish kingdom, cutting the elves off from every other living creature.

The Dragons abandoned their own kingdom and made their home in the Jagged Bones, threatening all who approached their lairs—making it impossible to pass through the mountains—though the Giants tried. As if the mountains of the Jagged Bones craved blood and hatred, many lives were claimed in the senseless violence there.

Upon witnessing such death, the Merfolk retreated to their watery homes, content to bask in the beauty of the sea and their own splendor, only occasionally consorting with pirates when it amused them.

Years passed and the myths faded from the world's mind.

The Elvish kingdom became the Wilds, the Giants sequestered themselves in their own kingdom of Kopal. The Fire Isle Kingdoms were forged by mercenaries—the offspring of pirates, Sirens, and Merfolk.

For a time, the Shapeshifters of Talaga held an uneasy peace with the Humans of Heimserya. The two kingdoms needed each other to survive, that all changed with the birth of a new plant and a royal son.

An extraordinary flower—the Mimkia—was discovered in Talaga. When distilled, it was a powerful drug capable of healing any wound. It was practically magical. The applications were limitless and its worth immeasurable. In their pride, the Shapeshifters boasted of their discovery, of their brilliance.

Word reached the Humans of this new source of wealth. They coveted this new miracle plant and the temptation proved to be too much for the newly crowned king who sought to enrich his kingdom. With his greed dawned a new era of bloodshed, prejudice, addiction, and depravity.

Welcome to the Twisted Kingdoms.

Prologue

There once was a little girl who believed in fairytales.

Who loved a wolf.

She hated red and shared peaches.

But love was not enough.

The monsters invaded.

And her wolf disappeared like smoke in the night.

She was left to pick up the pieces.

Enslaved and broken.

The little girl grew.

Owned by the devil's mistress.

Swathed in blood red.

Poison and silence became her weapon.

Until her wolf came to reclaim her.

But she wasn't the girl he left behind.

She was ruined.

And he would pay.

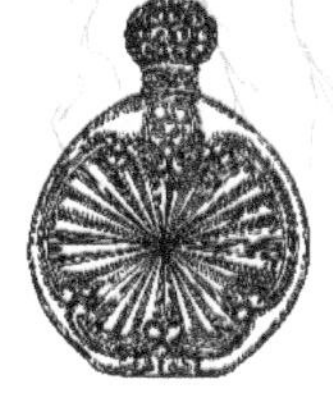

Chapter One

Scarlet

There was something about the woods that called to her.

Perhaps it was because it reminded Scarlet of her father, or that she was finally out from beneath the thumb of her horrid stepmother, or maybe just because the forest gave her peace of mind.

Scarlet peered up at the immense pines and inhaled deeply, savoring the crisp, sharp scent of the trees. For a moment, she felt safe, free, and whole.

A branch snapped in the distance, shattering her fantasy world.

Nothing in the province of Betraz was safe or free.

She stiffened as she spotted a red wolf weaving through the trees not forty paces out. Her hand slipped to the poisoned dagger at her hip. She never went anywhere without it. She pushed her blood-red hood from her blond hair and scanned the woods.

It was Tarros.

The shifter had been pushing Scarlet's boundaries in the

recent weeks, getting bolder and bolder with each turn that he didn't get caught and punished by Old Mother, the alpha and Scarlet's stepmother.

Scarlet picked up the edge of her long red cloak that marked her as the alpha's property and began hiking toward the river. The manor was closer, but she'd encounter more wolves along the way, and many would look the other way if Tarros caught her before she made it back home. Scarlet kept a sedate speed so as not to tip off her pursuer of her intentions. There were several huge rocks in the middle of the river that would offer her the refuge she sought. Tarros couldn't swim. Scarlet would stay there until her stepmother sent Bright, her stepmother's second in power, for her. She'd be punished severely for being late, but it was better than whatever the red wolf had planned.

Scarlet struggled to keep her emotions in check as she spotted the river. Wolves were sensitive beings when it came to scents. If Tarros scented her fear, it would all be over. Scarlet reached the river's edge and waded in slowly, the frigid water biting at her skin. She bent low as if looking for pretty stones and caught a flash of red fur from her right.

Time to move.

She launched herself into the deeper water just as a growl ripped through the air. Scarlet pumped her legs and arms as fast as she could through the icy river, her long cloak dragging behind her.

Almost to the boulder.

"Not so fast, little rabbit," Tarros crooned from behind her.

Scarlet glanced over her shoulder as the wolf caught the end of her cloak and yanked. She sputtered as it dug into her throat. If he got his hands on her...

Panic threatened to drown Scarlet. She tore at the clasp, ripping a few of her fingernails off. The pain barely fazed her. The clasp popped open and she swam for all she was worth, the current pulling her a little farther down before she reached the boulder. She clung to the stone, shivering in the water as she looked back at Tarros, who now held her abandoned cloak in his clawed hands.

He bared his teeth at her and growled low. "You really think that will stop me?" As quick as it came, his anger vanished, replaced by glee. Tarros lifted her cloak and ran his cheek over it, rubbing it against the rest of his body.

He'd scent marked it.

That was stupid.

Her stepmother didn't tolerate anyone touching her possessions, which included Scarlet.

Her teeth began to chatter, and she forced her muscles to work as she clambered on top of the rock. Her breath sawed in and out of her chest as she watched the deranged wolf smile back at her.

He draped her cloak over his shoulder. "So this is how it's going to be?"

Scarlet just stared back at him. He wanted her to fight, to fear him. She'd give him neither.

"Cat got your tongue?" He cocked his head, eyes narrowing. "You think you're something special because you were the daughter of the duke? You think you're too good for a Talagan male?"

This was the special side of Tarros that he kept hidden from everyone but the women he accosted. His father was one of Old Mother's betas, and that's why he got away with his crimes.

She methodically wrung out her simple dress while watching the wolf study her. He slogged out of the water and paced the shore. Now it was a waiting game. Eventually Bright would come looking for her. The sun was setting; now the challenge would be staying warm. Scarlet wrapped her arms around her body and tucked her hands into her armpits, shivers wracking her body.

"Poor little human with no fur. Come to me and I'll warm you right up," Tarros heckled.

She ground her teeth and stared right over the wolf's head like he wasn't there. He didn't like that. A feral snarl emerged from him and the hair along her arms rose.

Tarros tossed her cloak on the ground and crossed his arms. "Just remember I wanted to do this the easy way."

Scarlet blinked slowly at him and watched as he disappeared into the trees. Nothing was ever that simple with him. Ice ran down her spine as he returned a few minutes later dragging a long log.

No.

From the looks of it, the log would be able to reach her rock.

Scarlet stood on shaking legs. Tarros flashed her a triumphant smile.

"Already anticipating my arrival, Red?" he taunted.

She yanked two daggers from her sleeves and backed to the edge of the boulder as the wolf hefted the log up into the air and then down onto the boulder. Scarlet had two options. One, fight Tarros and lose. Her poison acted quickly, but not before Tarros could damage her beyond repair. Or two, jump into the river and swim for as long as she could manage.

The wolf sprinted across the log, and the vicious look on

his face was enough for her to jump.

A large hand wrapped around her waist.

“NO!” she screamed, stabbing with all her might.

Tarros bellowed, released her for a second and she leapt. The wolf grabbed a handful of her dress and toppled into the water after her. The current snagged her away from him and threatened to pull her into the depths below. She fought against the panic and didn’t fight against the river. She opened her eyes under the water and reached for the nearest roots, her lungs burning. They slipped between her fingers a moment before she slammed into a rock. Her ribs screamed and she dropped her daggers. Scarlet clung to the boulder despite the pain, breaking the surface.

She gasped for air and oriented herself. She wasn’t far from the bank. Leaning her head against the rock, she took several deep calming breaths. She could do this.

Scarlet released her rock and struggled toward the shore. Her bare feet touched sand and she slogged to the bank, falling on her hands and knees. The hair at the nape of her neck rose and she stiffened. Glancing over her shoulder, Scarlet spotted Tarros perched on top of a rock not too far away. Why would he not go away?

She scanned the other rocks. If he played his cards right, he’d be able to leap to the shore.

Tarros grinned and pointed a clawed finger at her. “I’m coming for you.”

Scarlet ripped the bottom of her dress away and got to her feet, running through the last bit of water. Her feet touched forest floor and she made it four steps before Tarros knocked her to the ground. She spun onto her back, yanking a garrote from her bracelet.

A green blur launched from the trees and knocked Tarros down. Scarlet scuttled backward on her hands and feet, blinking the water out of her eyes.

Was that a man?

Said man grabbed Tarros by the throat and lifted him like he was a twig. He gave the wolf a good shake, his green scales shimmering in the fading light.

"You think to harm a female? Have you no honor?" the shifter hissed. He slammed Tarros against the nearest tree, rendering him unconscious. The shifter dropped the wolf to the bank of the river and gave him a good kick in the ribs.

Scarlet trembled as she clutched her garrote to her chest. She stood silently and took one step back, her eyes glued to the shifter's back.

"Are you alright?" he asked, not looking in her direction, placing his hands on his hips.

She nodded, then cleared her throat when she realized he couldn't see her. "Yes," she rasped.

"You shouldn't be out here by yourself."

"You and I both agree on that." Was he a snake shifter?

He inhaled deeply. "You're from the town near here?"

"Yes."

"You're one of Old Mother's?"

She gritted her teeth and forced out another, "Yes."

"Perfect." The shifter faced her, his shocking emerald eyes locking on her. "I'm looking for a man. He calls himself the sheriff. Have you heard of him?"

Oh, how Scarlet wished she hadn't. He made her skin want to crawl. "Why do you want to know?"

The shifter grinned, flashing two wicked-looking fangs. "That is my business."

"I don't make it a habit to speak to strangers." Her stepmother had punished her for just looking in a stranger's direction in the past.

"We're not strangers any longer. I just saved your life."

Her attention darted to Tarros. But for how long? He'd be even more merciless after today. The shifter followed her gaze.

"I can make him disappear."

Scarlet blinked. "What?"

"You heard me, lovely. I can make the big, bad wolf disappear."

"Forever?" she whispered.

"Indeed. Just tell me what I need to know."

She stared hard at Tarros. It would be so easy to say yes, but did that make her any better than her stepmother? The shifter was clearly speaking about killing the wolf. "No, it wouldn't be right." The words were difficult to say.

The shifter scoffed. "What wasn't right was the way he was hunting you. That was not fun sport between the two of you. You *reeked* of terror." His upper lip curled. "Even if you don't give me the information I seek, I will not harm you, nor will I let this worthless male go without punishment."

"No one gives something for nothing."

He smiled. "You're not wrong, but I'll make an exception this time."

Scarlet's gaze darted to Tarros and then back to the shifter. He'd done her a service, and while he wasn't requiring payment, she didn't want to be in his debt. Secrets were currency in her world. She could part with one as repayment.

"You won't find the sheriff here. He's in the province of Merjeri—he's employed by the duke's son."

The shifter smiled but it was scary. "Thank you, lovely. I will not forget our encounter. Do you need assistance home?"

She shook her head no. "I'll be fine."

"Then get home. This is no place for a lady."

He didn't have to tell her twice. She ran for the river, using the rocks to help her cross. As she reached the other side, Scarlet hesitated, glancing back at the mysterious shifter as he grabbed Tarros by the ankle. "What do you plan to do with him?" she yelled.

"Make sure he can never harm a female again."

"You won't kill him?" She couldn't have that on her conscience. While Tarros was a bad egg, his family wasn't. She couldn't do that to them.

"No." The shifter looked put out. "But he'll wish he was dead."

"Thank you," she murmured.

"The only thanks I need is your silence. Can I trust you?"

"You can." She was a collector of secrets. What was one more? "Safe travels."

"Know that I have your scent memorized." The shifter dipped his head. "And that I hate liars."

A threat. She wasn't even offended.

"I'll keep that in mind," Scarlet called back as she trudged away from the river.

She'd managed to escape Tarros unscathed, but would she survive her stepmother's wrath?

Chapter Two

Scarlet

13 Years Ago

Nothing exciting ever happened. Her papa always kept her in the house and he always locked her and her mum away when they had guests. Scarlet frowned as she stared at the tangled yarn between her knitting needles. She glanced at her mum from the corner of her eye and slumped. Her mum's scarf was so perfect, so pretty, nothing like her mangled mess.

"I'm never gonna get it," she complained, dropping the knotted yarn into her lap. "I can't do it."

"That's not true, my love. It just takes practice."

Scarlet crossed her tiny arms and huffed. "I hate it."

Her mum smiled and set her scarf down on the floor and rose gracefully from her chair near the fire. She knelt down on the lush dark blue rug next to the footstool Scarlet sat on and squinted at the yarn.

"You're getting there. Look how even your rows are!"

Scarlet eyed her scarf and then her mum's. "It's not like yours, Mama."

"That's what makes it so special. Being unique is a gift. You don't want your scarf to be like mine. But if you want to *finish* your gift for your papa, you have to keep going." She ran a warm hand down Scarlet's cheek and smiled, her blue eyes twinkling. "Patience and perseverance are important, my love, even in the little things."

"Okay, Mama."

"That's a good girl. I'll get this untangled and then you can begin again." Scarlet frowned but didn't fuss. Her mum wiggled her brows. "And once papa is done with his meeting, we can sneak down to the kitchen for a sweet before bed."

Oh boy. That put a smile on her face. She loved the sweets that Dris made. She had the best biscuits in the whole world.

Her mum dropped a kiss on her forehead before standing, taking Scarlet's yarn with her. "Why don't you read a little while I get this untangled?"

Scarlet hopped to her feet and skipped over to the bookshelf along the wall that led to the door. She ran her fingers over the spines of old and new books alike. Her gaze shifted to the door. What was Papa doing right now? Who were the strangers that he talked to at night?

She peeked at her mum, who was humming a soft tune in her chair as she plucked at Scarlet's scarf. On tiptoes, she snuck to the door and turned the knob. The door cracked open without a sound and Scarlet peeked out into the hallway.

Her brows furrowed. Where were Javeh and Dadid? They always stood guard. She opened the door a little farther and squinted down the hallway. Her lips lifted into a smile as she spotted Dadid striding down the corridor toward her. Maybe he was bringing them warm milk! He often like to sneak them treats on nights like this.

A silhouette pulled away from the wall and Scarlet stiffened as the shadow crept behind Dadid. The shadow monster grabbed the guard by the head and yanked. A cry caught in her throat and tears filled her eyes as her mind struggled to understand what she'd just witnessed.

"Mama," she croaked.

Scarlet hiccupped as her mum yanked her from the door, closed it and locked it. She released Scarlet and pushed a dresser in front of the exit, the feet screeching against the stone. Scarlet shook as her mum whipped around and grabbed her by the hand, towing her to the rear of the room. Her mum pulled a blue book from the shelf and part of the bookshelf swung silently backward, revealing a hidden passageway.

"Mama?" Scarlet cried.

Scarlet flinched as someone slammed against the other door, causing the dresser to rattle. Her mum cursed and pulled Scarlet into the dark stone corridor, closing the secret door and plunging them into darkness.

Tears dripped down Scarlet's face and she began to shake. "Mama, I'm scared."

Her mum lifted Scarlet into her arms and began swiftly walking in the dark. "I know, my love. I need you to be strong and quiet for me. Can you do that?"

"Dadid..." Scarlet hiccupped again.

"I know, I know, baby. But we have to focus on getting to Papa." Her mum pressed Scarlet's face into her neck. "Take a deep breath. You're safe with me. I will never let anything happen to you."

Scarlet clenched her mum's sweater in her hands. "How can you see in the dark?"

"Special mama powers. Now we're getting close to another room. I need to put you down so I can make sure it's safe." Scarlet didn't want to let go. "I need you to be brave for me, my love. Let Mama put you down."

Scarlet released her mum. Her mama kissed her on the forehead.

"Now, keep quiet so Mama can make sure the coast is clear."

She nodded and waited, her heart thundering in her ears. She stared hard into the darkness, trying to see something—anything, wishing she had her mum's powers. A small shaft of light shone from her right and she watched with wide eyes as her mum opened a small door and held her finger up to her lips. Scarlet nodded, her bottom lip trembling as her mama slowly pushed back a curtain.

Scarlet began to shake as her mum completely disappeared. She curled up into a ball and waited, ears straining for any sound. What if the shadow monster had gotten her mama? What if her mama never came back? What if—?

The curtain lifted and her mum held out her hand. "Quickly now, Scarlet. We need to move."

Scarlet climbed to her feet, her legs shaking, and she took her mum's hand. Her mama closed the door and then led Scarlet through one of the guest quarters, toward the large door. Her mum froze as the thunder of boots echoed faintly against tile in the distance, along with a hair-raising growl.

Scarlet tucked into her mum's side as she locked the door and backed away from it. "Time to go back the way we came, love."

Her mum pulled Scarlet into her arms again and moved

back to the secret door, but her mama paused, cocking her head.

"What is it?" Scarlet whispered.

Her mum pulled away from the hidden door. Slowly she edged away, spinning in a circle. She held Scarlet tighter and rushed to the closet, opening the doors and pushing her inside. Her mum dropped to her knees and leaned away, cupping Scarlet's cheeks.

"You are so brave, do you know that?"

"What's wrong, Mama?"

"There are monsters outside, my love."

Scarlet shivered and her bottom lip wavered.

"I'm not trying to scare you but you need to be extra quiet if they find us." Her mum smiled but it was sad. "You are my whole world and I'm going to protect you with everything I have but I need you to be a good girl—you need to listen and obey me. No matter what, you do not leave this closet—no matter what you hear or see. Do you understand me?"

Scarlet nodded. "Don't leave me, Mama."

"I'm not going to leave you, my love. I'm just going to hide somewhere else so the monsters can't find you. Then I'm going to fight them." She squeezed Scarlet tightly to her chest and kissed her head. "Remember, my love, you are stronger than you know. Have courage and be kind."

She set Scarlet between the dresser and the wall before throwing a blanket over the top of her. Scarlet wiggled around until she could see out of a small hole.

"I love you."

"I love you, Mama."

"Now, remember what you promised me."

Her mum kissed her nose through the small hole in the

blanket before standing and leaving the closet. She closed the slatted doors and snuck away.

Scarlet's pulse pounded in her head, and she waited for the monsters to find them. It seemed like forever before she heard a sound. The lock rattled and her whole body stiffened. She trembled as the doors slammed against the walls, making the lanterns shake.

A beat of silence.

"No use hiding, poppets, I know you're here. I can *smell* you."

Something whistled through the air and the monster growled.

"I wasn't hiding." Her mum's voice was colder than Scarlet had ever heard it. "There's more of that waiting for you."

"Stupid mistake, wench."

Scarlet pressed her face into the blanket as a series of growls and crashes sounded from the bedroom. She jerked as her mama screamed.

No.

She leaned forward from her hiding spot and peeked out of the slats. Her mum had the monster on its back but his claws were buried in her side. Scarlet began to cry as her mum gurgled but plunged another blade into the monster's neck.

The monster snarled and tossed Scarlet's mum aside, his attention snapping toward the closet.

Scarlet snuggled deeper into the blanket, and stuffed her fist into her mouth to stifle the cries. She held her breath as her mum's gurgling stopped and heavy footsteps moved toward the closet. The doors opened with a spine-chilling creak.

Don't move. Stay quiet. Be brave.

The monster walked silently into the closet, slowly inspecting the area. She exhaled slowly, trying not to cry in fear. The hair along the nape of her neck rose as he walked past her hiding spot and paused, sniffing the air. Ever so slowly, he turned and faced her.

Quick as lightning, the monster yanked Scarlet up into the air by her arms. She screamed as he bared his teeth at her.

"Hello, poppet."

The room wavered, but her attention locked onto the wolflike ear perched atop of his head. A wolf monster. He hoisted her higher in the air and Scarlet caught sight of her mama over his shoulder.

She wasn't moving. There was too much red.

Scarlet glanced back at the monster in horror just as the world went dark.

What had she done?

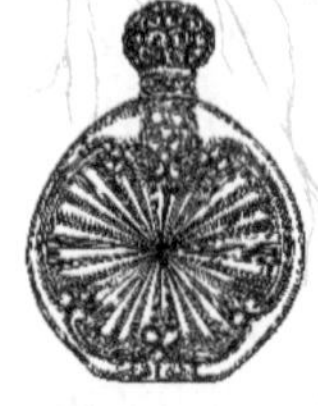

Chapter Three

Scarlet

Of all the tasks and chores thrust upon her by her stepmother, Scarlet hated gardening the least. She'd have almost enjoyed it if it weren't for the nature of the plants she was responsible for tending.

Poisonous plants.

Toxic plants.

Deadly plants.

But it was part of her job, and in any case she was largely left to her own devices while she was in the garden. The quiet time—the alone time—was something Scarlet craved. If she was doing chores in the house, there was always someone watching. It made her skin crawl even after all the years she'd been subjected to her stepmother's machinations.

She sighed and wiped sweat from her forehead, frowning at the grit she smeared against her face. Even when she was out and about, acting as a spy herself, Scarlet could not *be* herself. It was too dangerous and too much was at stake. She had to be a ghost.

But here, in the gardens, she could let go of some of the

pain and fear. Here she could dig her fingers into the damp earth and imagine a different future where no one was enslaved.

Where she was free.

She scanned the plants around her and eyed the Camas to her left with small white flowers. Death Camas. It looked like a wild onion to the untrained eye. The flower was death wrapped in an innocuous package.

Just like Scarlet's stepmother. She shivered.

With a huff, she dug the hoe back into the soil, readying it for the blood that would be tilled in among it for the benefit of the plants. She hated that part most of all; the blood filled her nostrils with its noxious iron tang and threatened to make her sick. According to her stepmother, it was essential to making the most potent, deadly plants in all of Betraz, and even Heimserya.

Death gives birth to life.

She swallowed the bile in the back of her throat. It was time to suck it up, breathe through her mouth, and retrieve the blood to complete her task.

Her gut churned violently as she glanced toward the forest.

Every day she expected Tarros to come for her.

Her escape had been lucky, and Scarlet had *never* been lucky.

She hadn't been able to think of much else in the days following Tarros's disappearance. *Disappearance,* because nobody save Scarlet knew what had happened to him, and even then she had no idea whether the deplorable shifter was alive or dead.

It was both a relief and a torment to not know what had

become of him.

A relief, for if Tarros were dead then there was a chance Scarlet would not be found responsible for his disappearance. He wouldn't be able to tell everyone what had transpired—or lie about the facts to condemn her. Scarlet would be free of his lustful, violent gaze, and there would be no repercussions.

A torment, because if Tarros did end up returning, then she would be worse than dead. And even if he *were* dead, and his body was found, there was a chance she would still be found responsible for what happened to him.

Humans were always blamed for anything that went wrong in Betraz.

Being the rightful duchess did not make Scarlet exempt from punishment.

And so every moment since Scarlet's narrow escape from Tarros was full of fear that she'd be blamed for his disappearance, and abject bliss that he was gone, as she didn't have to worry about his violent groping hands grabbing her in the dark of night.

Her fingers tightened around the hoe and she fought a shiver.

He's gone. Just breathe. No one will find out.

Scarlet had burned her red cloak to cinders of course, and with it the stench of Tarros that had been clinging to her. Keeping it would have been a sure sign that she had been involved in his disappearance, though she had feared that the *absence* of the cloak would be just as telling. It was to her immense relief when Dris, the housekeeper, had wordlessly provided Scarlet with a replacement, an identical cloak to help her avoid suspicion. Scarlet was indebted to Dris. The housekeeper had looked out for her since she was young, even at the risk of her own neck, treating the duchess as her own child.

Next, she'd scrubbed her skin with a scent-damping soap she'd created herself until her skin had turned pink and raw. It had done the trick but Scarlet still felt dirty. Even now, the taint of Tarros's touch wouldn't disappear. He'd corrupted her soul somehow.

Don't let yourself spiral. Work.

"Till the ground, till the ground," Scarlet murmured to herself in a singsong voice as the blackened, metal edge of the tool cut into the soil. Over and over, she worked the earth, sweat dampening her back and dripping between her shoulder blades. Time passed and her back began to ache. She rolled her neck and groaned, blond hair falling into her face.

With dirty hands, Scarlet adjusted the haphazard ponytail she'd tied her hair back in to keep it out of the way, then got back to work. She repeated the tilling action, over and over and over again, until she had to admit that there was no delaying the inevitable. It was past time to move on from preparing the ground to actually feeding the plants blood.

A snarl cut through the air.

The hair rose at the back of her neck and she exhaled slowly.

Scarlet knew that snarl. Knew it and feared it.

Don't let them scent your fear. Take a deep breath.

Fear excited the wolves and made them worse.

She clenched her jaw to keep her teeth from clattering and managed to slow her pulse. Scarlet tightly gripped the hoe and slowly straightened, making sure not to make any sudden movements to antagonize the Talagan male.

A sharp-clawed hand grabbed her by the hair, dragging her head painfully back. She swallowed the scream in her throat and stared up at the wolf.

Texel, Tarros's father.

He shook her roughly, pulling out some of her hair.

Tears filled Scarlet's eyes but she didn't cry out, nor did she release the hoe in her hands, even though she was desperate to tear his hands from her hair. It was her only means of protection should Texel really want to hurt her. This was just intimidation. He hadn't escalated to true danger.

Yet.

"What have you done to my son?" Texel demanded. His filthy nails scratched against Scarlet's scalp, threatening to draw blood even though he hadn't yet shifted.

She blinked slowly and stared up into his vicious amber eyes, so similar to his son's. She managed not to flinch as he growled, baring his mouth full of sharp, yellowed teeth. He wasn't far from shifting. That was the real danger.

The possibility of escape while he was in human form was low but possible. But if he shifted to his Talagan form?

He'll kill me.

Scarlet dared to minutely shake her head. "I don't know what you're talking about, my lord," she murmured, knowing the lie would not appease him. She winced when Texel's grip on her hair grew even tighter, bowing her back farther. "I haven't seen Tarros in days."

A lie and a truth.

"He's been found, useless wench," he growled, snapping his teeth closer to her cheek. "This is all because of you. *What have you done to him*?"

She hissed when he shook her once again.

Out of the corner of her eye, Scarlet noticed several shifters stepping into the garden, gathering around them to watch the drama unfold. All of them were Texel's men, loyal and fierce.

"You will tell me what I want to know."

Texel let go of Scarlet's hair and roughly spun her around to face him. She had no warning before he backhanded her across her left cheek.

Scarlet stumbled beneath the teeth-chattering blow but managed to avoid crying out, keeping her feet planted firmly on the ground. That was a lesson she learned early on. Never let the enemy knock you to the ground.

Her head spun. Her cheek throbbed and she swayed, leaning against the hoe. More shifters gathered but no one stepped forward to help. It used to disgust Scarlet, but after living under the thumb of her stepmother for so many years, she knew it for what it was.

A will to survive.

Showing mercy in Betraz was a death sentence. It was considered a weakness. She blinked hard to focus her gaze on the bristling wolf lord in front of her. Nobody was going to come to her rescue. There was only Scarlet here to defend herself.

Just as it had always been.

"I don't know what you want from me. I am happy he is okay." The lie tasted bitter on her tongue but she was proud that her voice didn't waver.

"Liar."

Texel's muscles bunched.

That was all the warning she needed.

The wolf lord launched himself at her.

That was what she'd been waiting for. She only had one shot.

Scarlet swung the hoe at him with all her might, catching him in the shoulder and the neck with the sharp end. The metal bit into his flesh and Texel grunted in pain. Quickly, she yanked the hoe back, her breathing labored as the deep wound began to bleed. She retreated several paces and clung to her meager weapon as Texel inspected his shoulder. The injury wasn't enough to kill him.

Stupid. You should have taken his head off.

Her knees threatened to tremble as silence descended around them. Even the trees seemed to hold their breath. Even if she had bested Texel, the rest of his men would dispatch her before she could utter a scream.

You're going to die either way. Fight.

Attacking one of Arwen's betas, especially Texel, would not go unpunished. Attacking a wolf lord spelled execution.

Texel focused his hate-filled mouth on her and growled menacingly.

This is it.

Scarlet's number was up, and what did she have to show for it? She hadn't done anything with her life at all. She'd acted as a puppet, bending to the will of first her father and then her stepmother, not a single thought her own.

Time seemed to slow and a sense of peace suffused her.

At least her suffering would end.

Texel growled again, breaking through her moment of peace.

A shiver ran down Scarlet's spine as the wolf lord's body

began contorting for a shift.

Death would bring peace but she wasn't going to die without a fight. Steeling her nerves, Scarlet wrapped her hands around the hoe with renewed resolve and forced herself to stand firm, ready for the inevitable.

The wind rustled her red cloak. Scarlet raised the hoe and aimed, preparing to swing again with all her might. "I don't fear you."

Texel snarled. "You will, wench."

"That's enough!" a commanding but strangely melodic voice cut through the air. "Just what is going on?"

Scarlet didn't take her eyes from the bristling wolf who held hate and death in his gaze.

From the corner of her eye, she could see the wolves around them bow deeply.

Soft footsteps approached, announcing the presence of Arwen.

Scarlet's stepmother.

Alpha to the pack of Betraz.

Old Mother to those who traded with her.

Death to those who crossed her.

And for once in Scarlet's life, she was relieved to see the vile woman.

Which was a mistake.

She was in more danger now than before.

Chapter Four

Scarlet

"I said," Arwen repeated softly, "what's going on?"

Scarlet tore her eyes from Texel and kept her gaze down, peering through her lashes at the assembly of wolves.

All had eyes turned to the head of the pack.

Arwen was dressed in her usual black silks, in stark contrast to her long, lustrous silver hair, looking elegant and beautiful and frightening in equal measure. She tapped her long black nails impatiently against her pale forearm.

"Well?" she said expectantly, sharp eyes missing nothing.

Texel hesitated, his amber gaze submissively pointed to the ground in respect to his alpha. Scarlet stiffened as he pointed a finger toward her.

"She tried to kill my son. She tried to lie about it, but I know the truth."

"Do you?" Arwen mused, cocking her head to the side and arching a haughty brow.

Texel's jaw flexed and he bowed to his alpha. "I mean no offense, my lady, in accusing your bound one. But please, test her. It is within your magnanimous power to smell the truth, my great alpha. Please grant your servant this request as it is my belief she tried to take my only son from me, and one of your loyal warriors from *you*."

Texel was physically dangerous it was true, but his real weapon were his words. Within a few sentences he'd condemned Scarlet to be a traitor to her stepmother.

She could have denied it, but no one would hear her. Plus, her stepmother had told Scarlet years prior that she should be seen but not heard, or suffer dire consequences.

So she remained silent and resolute, her expression blank as she met her stepmother's gaze and attempted to keep her heartrate as level as possible.

The woman was sharp. Intelligent. Hardly anything flew past her.

But Scarlet had been learning how Arwen worked for most of her life.

After a long moment spent scrutinizing Scarlet, Arwen nodded minutely, wearing a knowing smile. "Bring Tarros here," she ordered. "I wish to see the boy."

Texel blanched. "He isn't in good shape," he complained, genuine concern for his son paling his ruddy face. "To move him would be—"

"I said bring him here." Not a request.

Thoroughly cowed, Texel barked orders at the shifters surrounding them, and then the air was tense and still as they awaited the arrival of his son. Scarlet flexed her sweaty fingers around the hand of the hoe and fought the rising nausea in her gut. What had happened to Tarros? What condition would he be in when he was brought before her? Would he speak out against her?

Just what had been done to him after Scarlet fled?

Too many questions.

The shifters returned walking slowly, gently, carrying a stretcher between them. Scarlet kept her expression bland as they brought a covered Tarros into the garden and stopped before her stepmother and Texel.

Calm yourself.

She pulled herself together and forced herself to really, truly see what had become of the shifter who had accosted her in the forest. Scarlet's breath hitched as Texel pulled back the blanket covering his son.

Tarros was a mess. Scarlet had seen plenty of horrific things, but this was on another level entirely. The shifter's legs were mangled beyond repair, his face hardly recognizable. There were several wounds across his lower stomach and groin that implied the shifter in the forest had done worse than surface-level damage.

Images of her assault flashed through her mind. Scarlet wanted to turn away badly. Remembering what had transpired in the forest still haunted her at night. He was the monster in her nightmares. But now? He was a broken wolf lost in a feverish haze.

She couldn't turn away from the ruin of his body.

In silence, Scarlet's stepmother examined the injured shifter. She lifted an arm, turned his head to the side, and sniffed him everywhere she went.

"I can smell you on him, Scarlet," she mused quietly, but there was no hint of suspicion in her voice. "But I can also smell fear. No ... abject terror." Seconds turned into minutes as she investigated the pitiful wreck that was Tarros. Then Arwen turned to Texel and said, "These injuries aren't from a human. You know fine and well that no human could do this. They're far too severe. How could a mere girl do such a thing?"

The words were a relief for Scarlet to hear, but there was an edge to Arwen's voice that stopped Scarlet from relaxing. She knew better than to imagine she'd gotten away with this. There would be a punishment for fighting back against Tarros—her stepmother would make sure of it.

What Scarlet *could* be relieved about was that Texel knew better than to argue against his alpha. In the middle of the tilled soil, still seconds away from shifting and full of sputtering rage, he had no choice but to snarl at Scarlet before storming toward the exit, his group of shifters following quickly behind him, along with the stretcher that contained what remained of his mangled, disgusting son.

She braced herself as he neared her. Scarlet stiffen when he spat in her face. She didn't move as the spittle ran down her cheeks.

"Watch yourself," Arwen called.

Texel grunted and stormed from the garden with his posse.

Only once everyone left did Arwen saunter toward Scarlet.

This was where the real danger lay.

"Such a crude weapon," her stepmother mused. "Will you smite me with it, daughter?"

Scarlet blinked slowly as she realized she'd not yet dropped the hoe. She lowered it and bowed to Arwen. She flinched when the older woman cupped Scarlet's chin and ran her hand along Scarlet's hair. But she remained still, knowing better than to rise without permission.

"Tarros clearly touched something that wasn't his,"

Arwen crooned, the touch on Scarlet's scalp almost motherly where Texel's had been brutal. Almost affectionate. Almost kind. All lies. "So it was only karma that he should be attacked so. Stand."

Scarlet knew that wasn't the end of things. She never got off unscathed. Slowly, she rose and braced herself for the punishment that was to come. It wasn't a surprise when Arwen slapped Scarlet across her face, on the opposite cheek from the one Texel had hit. Her ears rang, teeth clacked together, and she tasted blood. She rocked back on her heels but didn't otherwise move. Arwen's predatory side was always ignited when she sensed weakness.

"What were you doing in the forest?" Arwen demanded, her face all cold angles and suspicion. "Tarros stinks of you. You were there with him. Were you whoring yourself, daughter?"

"Never, my lady," Scarlet replied softly, keeping her eyes lowered as her right one began to swell shut. "A lady should never debase herself wantonly."

"So you do remember my words."

"I remember all your words."

"Indeed. So you know how I feel about deceit." Arwen circled Scarlet, brushing a piece of dirt from her bruised cheek. "Tell me what happened."

"I was foraging," Scarlet said, which was the truth. "And then he attacked me." This was also the truth. But here was where Scarlet had to lie, to a woman who could not really be lied to. But if there was one thing Scarlet had learned through the years it was how to bend the truth here and there to avoid the worst of her stepmother's wrath.

Her stepmother crooked a finger underneath Scarlet's

chin and forced her to look up. They locked eyes. Arwen's were as dark as pitch.

Maintaining eye contact, Scarlet said, "I managed to wound him and escape. I don't want to imagine what he would have done to me if I hadn't slipped out of his grasp. I meant no disrespect to your warrior, my lady."

For a long moment the two women stared at each other, Scarlet praying that Arwen wouldn't discover her deception. Her stepmother seemed to be deciding if she was lying.

After what seemed like an eternity, the woman pinched Scarlet's cheek—it smarted horribly from where she'd been hit —and a slow, lovely smile spread across Arwen's face.

"Such a good girl," Arwen said. "You got away from him. I'm proud of you. You must know that no one can have you but me." A small frown pursed her full lips as she scanned Scarlet's face. "Do clean yourself up. You're a mess. You're a reflection of myself. I can't have you looking like we beat you, can I?"

"As you say, my lady."

"Excellent." Her stepmother glanced at the tilled ground. "Now finish your work here. You need to till the blood into the earth before it gets cold." Her smile became a wicked grin. "It makes the poisons that much sweeter."

Chapter Five

Brine

The middle of the afternoon found Brine once more negotiating with a group of bloody pirates in the bowels of their ship. His nostrils flared wide as he exhaled the stale salt air. The negotiation had gone on far too long. Plus, Chesh was playing a dangerous game of insulting the pirates to see how far he could push them. He was on Brine's last nerve.

They were there to trade goods and information. Nothing more. He hated wasting time.

"We've been going back and forth on this for an hour now," Brine growled impatiently, his ears twitching atop his head. "You wouldn't even be talking with us if you weren't willing to trade for the diamonds in your possession. I'm done. Stop wasting our time and tell us what you actually want."

"Very well, then," the captain said, a short man with a balding head. He licked his lips nervously. "I suppose there's no point now in dancing around the subject."

Brine cocked his head and studied the captain. The man was surprisingly well-spoken for a pirate. He eyed the man's finely tailored clothes. It was clear he had money and prestige. Once upon a time, only rogues, bandits, and criminals became pirates, but ever since King Destin had been overthrown and replaced with his gentle daughter, the king's previous, staunchest supporters, who benefited from his corruption and theft of the lower classes, had been subject to increasing scrutiny and punishment. Many had been exiled; more had been imprisoned, and others executed.

And so it was that many wealthy merchants and, in some cases, lords and dukes thrown off their estates, had turned to piracy in order to maintain their wealth and the life they were accustomed to living.

Men like the captain who left their families behind and fled to the seas as *merchants*. That's what they liked to call themselves—the highborn turncoats of Heimserya—but they were pirates through and through. None of their business dealings were legitimate or honest.

Which was why Brine and Chesh were dealing with the sleazy captain.

"We might be inclined to sell these to you," the captain continued, fixing Brine with a calculating eye. Around the captain, his men subtly folded into a position Brine knew well—shoulder to shoulder, hands inching toward their weapons. This wasn't a negotiation. It was a mutiny. They were spoiling for a fight. "For the right incentives."

Brine rolled his neck from side to side. Whatever the captain's terms were they would not be something either Chesh or Brine could accept. The gems they'd been assigned to procure were unique stones—diamonds from Betraz. They'd already agreed on a price and Brine wasn't paying a cent more. It was already highway robbery.

"What do you want, old friend?" Chesh asked with a feline grin. "We've given you all that we agreed upon."

"Not quite," the captain said with a smirk. "We don't want your gold. There is something else you can acquire for us. We want the female Hound." Brine's ears began to ring. "We know you have a connection to her, and there are many who'd pay a fortune to get their hands on the queen's little bitch. Give us Tempest Madrid and the diamonds are all yours."

Red descended over Brine's vision. He wasn't sure if he or Chesh attacked first.

Pandemonium broke out as Brine tossed a pirate against the wall. His body shook as he locked eyes on the captain, who'd paled to a pasty white. No one went after Brine's pack.

No one.

Vaguely, he noticed Chesh snatch up the bag of diamonds in question and tuck them away in the fray.

"Kill them!" the captain shouted as he scrambled for the stairs.

Oh no. He wasn't getting away that easy.

Brine cast a glance at Chesh, who smiled like a loon. They were outnumbered, but they were always outnumbered on these missions, always one step from death. They'd grown accustomed to it. Death was almost a friend these days.

"You want to play with the kitty?" Chesh crooned as three pirates barreled his way. "Then let's play. Just be warned, my claws are sharp." Chesh hardly ever shifted. Though his lithe, large, feline body was an asset, he enjoyed the challenge of fighting like a regular human.

Brine didn't have the same quirks. He didn't waste another moment and shifted, feeling his muscles and bones warm, expand, and shift.

Vicious delight filled him as the scent of fear grew stronger in the bowels of the ship. His shifted state could make a grown man pee himself. Pirates scrambled back and fled in all directions. His ears flattened as the captain ran up the stairs. Brine snarled and dodged to the right as a brave pirate took a swipe at him. He darted forward and bit the man on the arm. The pirate screamed and dropped his sword.

One down. Many to go.

Between Brine's teeth, claws, and sheer size, supplemented with some deft swordwork from Chesh defending his flank, it wasn't hard to clear the room. They hacked and snarled and jabbed and tore their way out of the belly of the ship leaving terrified, broken pirates in their wake.

Brine bound up the stairs and launched himself onto the open deck.

The air was filled with screams and the tang of iron.

His heart raced, his blood rushing through his veins in almost an intoxicating way. This was what he loved, moments when he was protecting his pack.

Fighting had always made Brine feel truly alive. But lately the thrill of the fight felt hollow, and he couldn't pinpoint why.

Chesh cackled as he lit the nearest sail on fire. He wiggled his brows at Brine as it lit up like a gigantic candle. "Time to go. I rigged some of their black powder to blow."

That was all he needed to hear.

He followed Chesh off the ship and onto the pier as the first explosion went off. His ears rang but he kept running, keeping pace at Chesh's side. The feline took too many risks with his own life. But while the cat made Brine want to wring his neck most days, Chesh was as loyal as they came. That wasn't very common.

They reached the end of the pier and ducked into a shanty, where they'd stashed some of their supplies. Brine calmed his mind and waited for the shift to take place. Once back in his human form, he stood and walked naked to the broken window to watch the pirate ship sink in full view.

"You have the diamonds?" he asked gruffly.

Chesh handed him a bundle of clothes and then opened his jacket, revealing the velvet bag carrying the diamonds. "I do indeed. How could you doubt me?"

Brine rolled his eyes and dressed quickly before taking stock of his body. He had taken several cuts to his forearms, though he wasn't sure when in the fight they'd occurred.

Not bad.

Chesh flashed a grin, his green feline eyes filled with excitement. He remained entirely unscathed, even in his expensive clothes. There wasn't one spot of blood or soot. Not even a snag from a blade.

"You're worse than Pyre," Brine muttered.

His friend grinned, flashing sharp canines. Chesh did a mock bow. "I live to serve."

Brine huffed out a breath and yanked on his boots, then tossed a cloak carelessly over his broad shoulders. "If only."

"Come on," Chesh urged with a smile. "We must be off before someone notices what we've done. Let's have an ale and celebrate and lie low for a little while." He pulled the diamonds from his jacket and deftly tossed the velvet bag to Brine.

Catching the gems, he stowed them away and arched a black brow. "A bit late for that, Chesh," he said dryly, indicating toward the flaming mess in the water.

"Always so grim." Chesh flipped his cloak so the brown side was out and the black inside – another way to keep their identity hidden. The feline pulled the hood up and brushed by Brine and opened the rickety door of the shanty. "I tire of this hovel. Let's be gone."

Brine cautiously followed his friend out into the lane. On silent feet, they snaked their way through Callmai, the pirate city, until they found their destination.

The Tipsy Kraken—a tavern and inn owned by a Talagan in Pyre's employ.

"I wonder who wants Tempest so badly," Chesh murmured, when they slipped into their regular corner table in the darkest part of the tavern. The feline sighed happily when the deer shifter—a very pretty young woman named Sarah—set down two tankards of their favorite pale ale.

"Why thank you, darling," Chesh purred. "Are you finally starting to warm to me?"

She narrowed her eyes. "You are a blight on the world." She turned tail and strode back to the bar.

Brine hid his smile. He liked the prickly Sarah. She didn't let Chesh get away with anything.

Chesh sighed, his gaze still on the deer shifter as Brine took a sip of his ale. It was cold and satisfying as it slid down his throat, though he found that he didn't really have the taste for alcohol tonight.

"So?" the feline asked, turning his attention back to Brine. "Who wants our lovely Lady Hound?"

"There are hundreds of people on that list," Brine replied

darkly, setting his ale down a little too roughly, causing some to slosh over the edge. "Most of these bloody lords still believe she's the evil voice in Ansette's ear telling her to imprison them. They believe she is their ruin. That she is controlling the queen."

"And they would be right. She was their doom." Chesh chuckled softly. "Funny that the only time they've ever put stock in the intelligence of a woman is to insult the abilities of a teenage girl."

"Hilarious."

They fell silent, both lost to their thoughts.

It bothered Brine that someone was after Tempest. Their line of work wasn't the safest, and they'd fielded assassination attempts, but this was different. Someone wanted Tempest alive. They wanted to own her. *Control* her.

"What's with you tonight?" the feline inquired, slinging his feet up onto the bench he was sitting on.

Brine looked up from his ale, frowning. "What do you mean?"

Chesh chucked his chin at Brine's half full tankard that Brine had subconsciously been trying to squeeze the life out of.

"Even back on the ship I could tell you weren't fighting with your usual gusto. What's bothering you, my lupine friend?"

If this had been the Brine who had put Tempest through her paces when she'd first intercepted the Dark Court—the one who helped bring down Destin and all the rotten, hideous things he had done to his kingdom—he would have told Chesh to shove it where the sun doesn't shine and carry on with his business. But the wolf had started to soften lately around his friends, and with every passing day he found that he didn't mind them asking him personal questions as much as he had. He was tired of being alone. So he decided to accept the pack around him that had already accepted him.

"In all honesty," he grumbled, avoiding Chesh's curious gaze, "I'm not sure. I think I might miss home."

"Home?"

"Whenever I get tired like this, it's usually because I miss home. I haven't been back in ... well, years."

For good reason.

"There's a story behind this, I'm sure."

Brine nodded. "A story for another day. Or never."

Chesh snickered. "Some things never change, my friend. Well, you know where I am if you ever decide to become a sentimental mess of a person and let it all spill out." Movement out of the corner of his eye by the bar caught the feline's attention. He sat up abruptly. "That's Ali. If you'll excuse me..."

Brine rolled his eyes. The cat was insatiable.

Brine couldn't blame him. It seemed everyone these days was either courting their mates or creating families of their own.

Pyre had Tempest.

Damien, of all creatures, had Robyn.

And Chesh was out here chasing anything with long hair, swinging hips, and a promising swell of breasts.

But Brine...

His fingers tightened around his ale once again.

Thoughts of blond hair, large blue eyes, and a playful smile invaded his mind. Brine wasn't surprised by this. After all, he had only just been telling Chesh that he missed home. But what he missed about home wasn't just the place; there was a person.

Be honest. You miss her.

After his father had been killed, Brine had been taken to the province of Betraz. He'd been young—so young that nowadays Brine held few memories of his father—but he had been old enough to understand the fluttering of his heart when he first spied her. A little girl, with long, wispy blond hair, like dandelion fluff upon the wind. Her hopeful blue eyes had urged Brine not to be scared, even though he was.

Every time he hid on the grounds, she found him. Even when he snarled for her to go away, to leave him alone, she resolutely did the opposite. She found him, every time, and without a word she handed him a chunk of bread and a peach. It was her kindness that he remembered, and the sweetness of the peach.

Perhaps it was true that the way to a man's heart was through his stomach, for after that Brine and the girl had become best friends. It still haunted him to this day that when he couldn't bear his life in Betraz any longer, he had left the girl behind.

Even now, as his eyes began to droop sleepily downward, Brine wondered what happened to her.

Chapter Six

Scarlet

"He's an incompetent imbecile!"

She kept her expression placid as her stepmother raged at her cronies. Scarlet scanned the room from beneath the rim of her blood-red hood. All of the loyal wolves bowed their heads in submission. Her stepmother paced beside her long rectangular table, her black crinoline dress rustling in the silence.

"Well, has everyone nothing to say?"

That was a trick question. Scarlet knew it and so did everyone else.

You did not speak unless directed to by the alpha. Or at least that was one of her titles.

Old Mother.

Alpha.

Arwen.

Duchess of Betraz.

Stepmother.

Monster.

The last one was usually spat out by the human victims

who Scarlet's stepmother preyed upon.

A shiver ran through her, and Scarlet dropped her gaze to the floor as her stepmother studied the room full of people. That was another of the rules: never meet her gaze unless you wanted to challenge her or suffer the consequences.

Scarlet had only done it once.

It was right after her father died and she'd helped her friend Will escape Betraz. Her stepmother had threatened to hang her for her part in his escape. Scarlet had met her gaze, smiled, and said, "Try it." It had earned her a shattered cheekbone and a nasty scar, but it was worth it to see the smug smile knocked off the wench's face.

That had been years ago when she was only twelve summers. Now she'd never try something like that. Too many lives depended upon Scarlet catering to the whim of her stepmother. Plus, years of public humiliation, beatings, and punishments had since left her with a very healthy fear of the alpha. The ageless woman had a malicious streak leagues deep, which was part of the reason she made Scarlet wear her cursed red cloak. It was to mark her as property of the alpha, as a slave.

Her stepmother grabbed a handful of raw diamonds from the table and shook her fist. "Someone is stealing my diamonds and my mimkia right out from under that pompous pup of a duke. Who is it? Who is the Hood?" Her attention homed in on her second-in-command, Bright, an onyx, middle-aged wolf with streaks of silver through his hair.

Bright dipped his head. "My lady, we know that the Hood's men are commoners. Most don't seem to have any military training, but our spies have revealed nothing about the

Hood's identity."

"Nothing?"

Her stepmother pelted Bright with the diamonds. Scarlet inwardly winced as one cut him just above the eyebrow. The evil woman grabbed the edge of the table, her long black nails digging into the wood.

"This has gone on long enough! I'm tired of some little common upstart ruining my plans." She dropped her head, her long silver hair falling over her shoulder to the table. "And the dragon?"

"He's not known to us."

She slapped her hand against the table. "Dragons do not involve themselves in human affairs. Why is he doing so now?" A pregnant pause. "Red."

Scarlet shoved down her fear and clenched her fingers into fists to keep from trembling. Any trace of weakness and she'd be punished in front of everyone. She stepped forward from the back wall, making sure to keep her head down as the small crowd parted for her.

"Yes, Alpha?" she answered softly, halting beside Bright.

She shivered as her stepmother reached over the table and ran a long nail down her left scarred cheek. "I need you to fix this."

"As you wish."

Her cheek flared with pain when her stepmother pinched the skin a tad too hard. "See that you do. Don't fail me."

"Never, Alpha."

"Be gone from my sight. Your human stench offends me."

Humiliation burned in her cheeks as she backed away from the table, making sure to keep her head down. It was an old insult but effective. Her stepmother was always quick to tear her down for not being Talagan. When she was a child, she'd never seen a difference between those who could shift and those who could not. People were people. But now, she *hated* the fact that she was so weak compared to the wolves around her. No matter how hard she fought back, the shifters always won. Scarlet had heard whispers that humans in other provinces weren't enslaved and deemed as lesser.

She turned on her heel and left the room, walking down the long, dark corridor lined with wolves on guard. She'd always hated how dark her stepmother kept the house. Scarlet wasn't a shifter and didn't have night vision like everyone else. It was a constant reminder that she didn't belong, nor was she welcome in her childhood home.

Squaring her shoulders, she turned her attention to her task. She needed to learn the identity of the Hood. If this person had evaded Bright, then they were good with covering their tracks. But she was better. Scarlet had spent years hiding in plain sight, gathering secrets and hunting down leads to appease her stepmother. All she needed was a trap, and she knew just what to use.

People were predictable. Everyone had a weak spot.

Scarlet's was her people.

And the Hood had someone they'd die for.

She just had to discover who it was.

Scarlet sat in the back of the duke's war room, fiddling with the dagger attached to her wrist. Lord Merjeri slammed his hands against the table, but she didn't bat an eye at his childish outburst. She'd seen much worse from her stepmother over the years.

"I want the Hood's head by the wedding!"

The sheriff nodded. "It will be done, my lord."

"See to it, Gustav, or I won't be accountable for my actions."

She watched the handsome duke storm from the room and pursed her lips. The man was beautiful. Too bad his soul was rotted and ugly. Scarlet turned her attention back to the sheriff.

Now the games began.

The sheriff rounded the war table and scanned the room filled with wolves and guards. While the duke was dangerous in his own right, it was the sheriff she was wary of. He was like a serpent waiting to strike.

"We have the Hood's men and yet we've gained no more information on who he is." The sheriff's gaze landed on her and she repressed a shiver. "What say you, o' famed daughter of Old Mother? Have your interrogations yielded no results?" He gave her a nasty smile. "Or do you need a man to do your job?"

She pushed away from the wall and glided forward, her mask firmly in place. The sheriff thought he was something special by insulting her, but she'd heard it a thousand times. His barbs wouldn't penetrate her tough skin.

Scarlet pulled the dagger from the belt at her waist and tossed it onto the table.

"What is this?"

She nodded at it. "Pick it up."

The sheriff lifted it from the table and eyed the knife. "What of it?"

Scarlet arched a brow. "Can you not see it?"

He glared at her. "Out with it."

"It's a woman's weapon."

The sheriff scoffed. "It looks like any other blade."

"Except for the size of the handle. It's smaller than what you use. It's meant for someone with petite hands."

"You think the Hood is employing women?" The sheriff laughed. His guards snickered but the wolves were silent. They knew better than to insult the female sex. Their alpha was more powerful than most men in the kingdom.

Scarlet smiled coldly. "It's possible, but I have a theory of who the Hood is."

"Do share."

"Do you know much about dragons?"

"Enough."

"Good." She cocked her head. "Then you know that dragons are fiercely protective of those under their care and of their mates. When we set our trap, that dragon had ample opportunity to lay waste to you and your men. Yet he scooped the Hood up and disappeared." It shamed her but there was something satisfying about being a touch cruel and putting these men in their place.

"He?" the sheriff asked softly. "How do you know it was male?"

"The size and horns." Scarlet blinked slowly. "But I think you know this already. You recognized the beast. It's why you drew back."

His face turned red. "It was a tactical retreat."

"If you say so," she murmured softly. He was a bloody liar and they both knew it. The dragon had been coming for him. Somehow the sheriff knew the dragon and yet he was hiding the knowledge from everyone. Why?

"Do you have a point?" he sneered.

"That your Hood, the thief, is a *woman*."

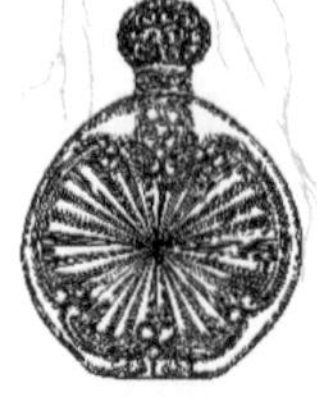

Chapter Seven

Scarlet

She'd made a mistake.

Scarlet gazed down the stairs that led to the dungeon.

You can't pretend this didn't happen.

Forcing herself down the curved staircase, she made it to the dungeon, her feet moving silently across the stone floor, down the long-curved corridor that held cells on each side. She might not have had shifter skills, but Scarlet had learned a few things over the years.

Stealth was one of them. She could even sneak up on some of the wolves despite their heightened hearing.

Mourne, one of her stepmother's wolves, spotted her from the end of the hallway.

Scarlet cocked her head and arched a brow. "Just you?"

"Do you really think they pose any threat now that they are in chains?" Mourne replied, his tone gruff like most wolves.

Scarlet flicked a glance to the left, eyeing three of the Hood's men they captured—one with a very familiar face. She kept all recognition from her expression and sighed. "No doubt you're right. I do need you to take a break."

Mourne's amber eyes zeroed in on her. "Interrogation so soon?"

"No time like the present," Scarlet answered. "Please station yourself at the top of the stairs."

The wolf's eyes narrowed. He knew the pecking order, and she was at the bottom except for times like these.

Scarlet touched her red cloak. "Do you know why the alpha has gifted me these colors?" she asked softly.

"Because you are her property."

She smiled. "Also to hide the blood." Scarlet pinned him with an intense stare. "Unless you want to interfere with what the alpha has assigned me to do, I suggest you *leave.*"

That got him moving. Mourne nodded and strode toward the exit.

"Make sure no one interrupts me," Scarlet murmured. "That duke and his sheriff are awfully nosy."

The wolf huffed and then disappeared up the spiral staircase.

Scarlet held completely still and listened for a few minutes to make sure Mourne wasn't listening. Most wolves wouldn't dare mess with orders from her stepmother, but every once in a while one would start getting a little too independent. Those didn't survive very long.

"Are you here to torture us?" a deep masculine voice asked.

She turned her attention to the large man who sported a red beard. "I'm not here for you." Scarlet focused on the man in the middle, who gazed at the ceiling with no expression, blood dripping from his black curly hair.

Will.

How many years had it been since she'd seen her friend? Six or seven? He had been a gangly young man the last time Scarlet had laid eyes on him and helped him escape. Now he was a man in his prime. And from the vacant look on his face, he hadn't lost his training. Will knew what her stepmother did with prisoners and deserters.

Scarlet reached for her hood and slowly lowered it, revealing her golden hair. She pressed closer to the bars and held on to them.

"Will," she called, managing to keep the wobble from her voice. He didn't stir. "Will, it's me, Scarlet."

The third man, tall and thin with dark-brown hair, frowned. "How does she know his name?"

"Quiet," the redhead admonished.

The brunette snapped his mouth shut and studied his hands.

That told Scarlet many things.

First, that either the redhead or Will was in charge. Second, they trusted each other. And third, they had prepared for this eventuality.

Smart men.

Scarlet pulled a sheathed dagger from the belt at her hip and tossed it through the bars onto Will's lap. "A gift for an old friend. Please look at me, Will." She swallowed. "It's Scarlet. Come back from your vault."

All the wolves were trained to find a vault in their mind where they could hide during interrogations.

Her old friend blinked slowly and dropped his gaze to the dagger on his lap. Slowly, he lifted his head and met her gaze. It was a shock. He'd lost all traces of the boy he'd used to be. A soldier stared back at her. His brows furrowed, and recognition dawned.

"Scarlet? What in the blazes are you doing here?" Will rumbled, his voice deeper than before.

"She's here to interrogate us," the redhead growled.

Will finally looked away from her face and scanned her from head to toe, lingering on her red cloak. His lips thinned and she knew what he saw. A tool of the alpha.

"I heard stories about Old Mother's red cloak," Will said, his tone hard. "Tell me those weren't about you."

Dread pooled in her gut. She'd been forced into situations over the years that would haunt her for the rest of her life. "I never got away," she said softly.

Will spat on the ground. "So you helped her?"

Scarlet held her chin high. "I do it to spare others."

Will laughed. "What are the odds that the same little girl who helped me escape that vile woman would be the one to send me right back to her?"

"I didn't know," Scarlet whispered. "I didn't know you were with the Hood."

"How could you not?" Will snapped. "Do you think I'd let the alpha invade Merjeri and enslave others?"

"Lower your voice," she hissed, glancing at the stairwell. "We are surrounded by wolves."

"I know. One is standing right in front of me wearing a red cloak."

That cut deep.

"Don't you dare judge me," she growled, gesturing to her scarred cheek and then to the cloak. "This was my punishment for helping you. Do you think I want this?"

Will's expression shuttered, and he picked up the dagger. "Why are you here, Scarlet?"

Her heart clenched and heat pressed against the back of her eyes. "Because you were once my friend and my father's friend. You protected me through the first of my stepmother's purges. You held my hand and sang to me while screams cut through the night. Do you think I would ever betray that?"

His expression softened just a touch. "You shouldn't be here."

"No, I shouldn't." It put everything at risk. "Friends never leave friends behind. You told me that, and I don't plan to now." She pulled several vials from her belt and knelt. Scarlet rolled them to Will. "Those should help healing and pain. There is some for all three of you."

"What then?" the redhead asked, running a chained hand over his beard.

"You survive," she whispered. "I'll be sent down every few days for interrogation until the execution. That will give me enough time to figure out a plan to get you out."

"The Hood will get us out," the brunette replied.

Scarlet smiled. "That may be so, but it's always better to have a backup plan, no?"

Will straightened, his eyes narrowing. "Someone is coming."

She pulled her hood over her hair. "Make sure to look appropriately drugged."

All three men slumped as the sound of footsteps moved swiftly down the stairs.

The sheriff.

Stars, Scarlet disliked the man. There was something off about him. Mourne followed on his heels, his amber gaze looking at anything but her. She brushed her hands off and met the sheriff head on. He eyed her cloak and glanced over her shoulder at Will and the other two men.

“I take it went well?” he asked lightly.

“My methods are effective, but they take time.”

“They don’t look too bad. I may take a crack at them.” The sheriff smiled and went to move around her. “Never send a woman to do a man’s work.”

She yanked a dagger from her wrist and had it pointed to his jugular. The sheriff froze and glared down at her. “I’ll ignore your last comment,” Scarlet said softly. “But I warn you that if you touch *my* prisoners, it will be Old Mother you’ll be dealing with, not me. I’d think very carefully about going against her wishes.”

The sheriff held his hands up. “I beg your forgiveness, my lady,” he muttered between clenched teeth.

“It’s not me you’ll be begging next time,” she warned.

He backed away and then turned on his heel, storming out of the dungeon.

“He’s going to be a problem,” Mourne commented, crossing his arms.

“He’s your problem.” Scarlet stashed her weapon and made sure to keep her eyes forward as she left the dungeon.

How the devil was she going to get Will out?

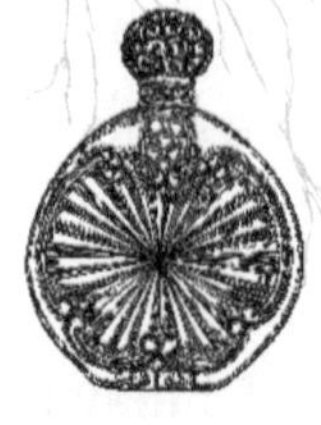

Chapter Eight

Brine

Pyre was nothing if not prompt.

Chesh and Brine had been in Callmai for a single day before the kitsune contacted them via his ever-reliable network of spies with orders to travel down the tributaries of the Fiergone River to the small freshwater port town of Samiliere. It was smaller than the seaport of Callmai but was just as popular with *merchants* and pirates alike to smuggle their stolen goods out of Heimserya to the open sea. Though Brine didn't especially want to deal with more lawless buccaneers, he nevertheless complied, as it was more trouble than it was worth *not* to heed Pyre's mysterious requests. The bloody kitsune was a nuisance to say the least when he didn't get his way. Brine still didn't know how Tempest tolerated the temperamental diva. Although, she was a force to be reckoned with. Pyre was no doubt on a short leash with her.

"What are you so happy about?" Chesh asked, arching a brow. He leaned against the side of the brothel, lantern light dancing in his eyes.

Brine frowned. "Nothing." He lifted the coded note from his pocket and held it to the flame of the lantern and watched as the hungry flames licked up the thick paper.

"You were smiling."

"I was not." He tossed the charred remains onto the ground before the fire could sear his fingertips, and stomped the small blaze out in the mud.

"Fine, keep your secrets." Chesh stretched lazily and grinned when one of the nightwalkers whistled and batted her lashes at the feline.

Brine's lip curled in disgust—not at the woman, but the way Chesh preened at her attention.

"It's time to go," he said gruffly.

"You're no fun." The feline pouted and pushed away from the brothel wall with a huff, pulling his furred coat closer to his body. "I refuse to go on another death march with you."

"Stop being such a pup," Brine grunted. "It's only a day's walk."

Chesh's eyes narrowed. "You and I both know its *two* days' walk. I am not hiking day and night."

"Princess."

The feline sniffed. "That's queen to you."

Brine's lips twitched in humor, and he almost smiled, but managed to smother it before Chesh began teasing him again. "It'll be a three days' walk at this rate."

"Don't test me, wolf."

"Yeah, yeah," Brine grumbled, leading the way out of the city. While he would have loved to run through the night in his wolf form, it wasn't worth inciting the feline's ire. Chesh held on to a grudge for a *long* time. At least Brine had a secret weapon.

He pulled a hunk of wrapped cheese from his pocket and tossed it over his shoulder without looking.

A gasp. "A present? For me?" Chesh asked with glee.

Hook, line, and sinker. The cat was a glutton for cheese.

"A gift for our journey."

"More like an incentive for me to hurry up."

"Perhaps." Brine did smile then. While Chesh loved cheese, he was loathe to eat it without a fine wine and bread.

They'd arrive in Samiliere in no time.

"You're a horrible bully and slavedriver," Chesh grumbled as they reached the pub the next night. "My feet are going to hurt for ages."

Brine rolled his eyes at his dramatic friend. "You'll live."

He pushed into the huge tavern and wrinkled his nose. The place was hot and damp beneath the sway of a hundred bodies. It seemed like every pirate who had docked in the port came to this one pub. More than one was in clear need of a bath. Brine scanned the area around them. No sign of Pyre yet, but that didn't mean anything. The sly fox was probably watching them right now.

"What I wouldn't give for a bath, a pint, a woman, and a bed," Chesh muttered in Brine's ear as they made their way through the throng. Brine glanced at the cat from the corner of his eye as Chesh cast a roguish smile his way. "Not necessarily in that order."

"Have you ever considered *not* vocalizing all the filthy thoughts in your head?"

Chesh shrugged. "Considered it, yes. Followed through on

it? No."

"Clearly." Brine's gaze snagged on a familiar pair of red kitsune ears, poking out of a floppy hat. "There's Pyre," he replied in a low voice, surreptitiously pointing toward the edge of the long bar that took up much of the space in the room. The wood was pockmarked with the scratchings of daggers, and was in need of a varnish, but it still fulfilled its job of acting as a surface to hold the drinks of twenty people well. A genuine smile tipped up Brine's lips as he spotted another familiar friend.

A bear of a man who was indeed a bear shifter. Briggs.

Brine's heart lightened when he saw his friend, who looked awkward as he tried to balance on the tiny barstool clearly made for a child. Brine hid his snicker as they approached.

Chesh snuck passed him and snatched Pyre's hat clean off his head. The kitsune smiled lazily as he turned to face them. The feline spun Pyre's hat around and around on his hand before handing it back to the fox with a chuckle.

"Didn't hear me coming, did you?" Chesh crowed.

"No, but I could smell the cheese you ate for breakfast," Briggs cut in, touching the tip of his nose before whacking Chesh on the back of the head.

"Hey! What was that for?" Chesh protested, as he and Brine sat down beside their friends and ordered some watered-down wine. "And I smell like roses, I'll have you know."

Briggs snorted. "If you want to lie to yourself." The bear glanced at Pyre and the laugh slid off his face. "In all seriousness, this isn't the time or place for your tomfoolery."

Brine blinked slowly at his friend and turned his attention

to the fox. It was then that he caught the tense set of Pyre's shoulders. Which was saying something, because the leader of the Dark Court almost never displayed how he was feeling on the outside—and certainly not in public.

"What has happened?" Brine demanded, Chesh uncharacteristically quiet by his side.

The kitsune's sharp eyes cut to his and he nodded minutely. Brine noted with concern the deep shadows beneath Pyre's eyes. Anxiety knotted in his gut. Whatever news the spymaster needed to share, it wasn't good.

"It concerns your pack connections."

A chill ran down Brine's spine.

"We've had to stop sending spies into Betraz," Pyre said in an undertone. "The last one just showed up dead. We sent him out a month ago."

All at once a wave of nausea overcame Brine. That was twelve in three months. *Twelve*. Too many good spies lost for one province. *His* province. His grandmother's greed and bloodthirsty viciousness truly was never-ending. Brine knew—and in fact had known most of his life—that this would come back to bite him. That he'd have to deal with his grandmother at some point.

Now it seemed that time had come.

"Lady Betraz and her wolves now have complete control over not just Betraz but over Fiergone," Pyre continued. He took a long swig of fire whiskey, downing his glass before indicating toward the barmaid that he wanted another. That meant things were very, very bad, indeed.

"Don't call her that," Brine growled. "She isn't the lady of anything. Call her what she is. A monster. Old Mother. A harpy deserving of death."

Pyre nodded once.

"And now she's teaming up with the duke of Merjeri to expand her enterprises farther into the country," Briggs finished for Pyre.

Chesh frowned. "I thought we had a plan to dispatch the duke?"

"I fear that may be too little, too late," Pyre said, frustrated. "Unless a miracle occurs and he's taken care of in the next few days, Old Mother will have enough time to utilize his resources before we can stop her."

Brine sucked on the curse that was dying to be let loose from his lips. He wanted to say that Pyre was wrong—that it wasn't too late, that a miracle *would* occur, that they'd be able to murder the duke of Merjeri and take his province as their own. But he knew such things were naïve to think. Certainly too naïve for Brine to believe, and the rest of his friends. And even if said miracle *did* occur and they took out the duke, the Old Mother still had his home province under her control.

Brine's grandmother had grown much too strong. It was therefore inevitable that a showdown with her had to happen.

"I hear tale of a woman in a red cloak in Merjeri," Chesh said, surprising all of them. Brine wondered what this had to do with the topic at hand.

"Where did you hear that?" Briggs asked.

The cat flashed a grin. "I wouldn't be a very good spy if I didn't have my own network, would I?"

Pyre let out a chuckle. "Remind me to never have you on my bad side. And yes, I've heard the same. A woman in a red cloak seems to be dealing in Merjeri on behalf of Old Mother."

"Has anyone managed to identify her?" Brine asked

hollowly. Stars, he hoped it was no one he knew. It was intriguing that his grandmother was using a woman. She usually saw them as competition and got rid of them almost immediately. What was so special about this hooded spy?

Pyre's shoulders fell. "No one has seen her face. Or, at least, no one who could live to tell the tale has seen it. Or will tell me what she looks like, if they've seen her. Or—"

"I get it," Brine cut in, impatient. "What has she been doing in Merjeri?"

"She's killed a few good men in the province." He sobered, then added, "But, on the other hand, some of the Hood's men have sworn that a woman in a red cloak has helped them disappear, right from under the clutches of Old Mother. And there are others who say she helped heal their grievous injuries, or healed the fevers set in from an infected wound. So Dotae only knows what's the truth. It could all be one of Old Mother's games."

"It could be two women," Brine suggested. "One of them taking advantage of the reputation of the other to get away with doing their work."

Pyre gave him an appraising look. "I was thinking the same. In any case, we need to investigate it, and fast."

"Then I—"

"No," Pyre interrupted, resolute. "Absolutely not. Damien and his mate are in Merjeri already. We have to let things play out a little longer so they can investigate before anyone else meddles."

"But—"

"After everyone we've lost so far in the province, do you seriously think I want to risk losing *you*, Brine?" It wasn't just Pyre giving Brine his undivided attention; both Chesh and

Briggs were too. They were looking at him as if he had a death wish.

Brine ground his teeth together. Of the three of them, only Pyre knew Brine's full history, though Briggs knew a little. But Chesh was clever enough to know that if Brine was willing to recklessly put himself at risk, then whatever he wanted to do was dangerous and likely foolish.

And it *was* dangerous. Foolish. Interfering with an agent of his grandmother's was perhaps one of the riskiest things Brine could do. But if he didn't do *something* soon, more blood would be shed.

Could he handle more lives on his conscience? *No*. It would break him.

He didn't like this at all. But with Pyre and Chesh and Briggs there to argue against him heading into Merjeri, Brine knew he would lose. He had never been one with words, not really, so he backed down. He'd patiently wait to strike.

"Good," Pyre said, relief plain as day on his face when Brine settled onto his chair and guzzled back his cup of wine. "If things change in a few days, we can discuss what to do next then."

Brine could do as he was told for a few days. He could remain in line without facing up to his past.

For now.

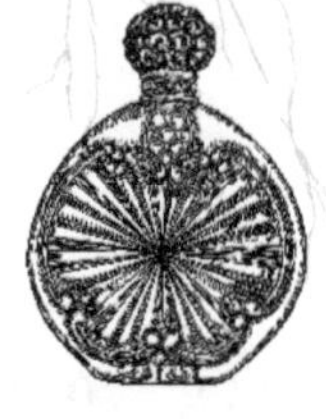

Chapter Nine

Scarlet

"There you go," Scarlet soothed, smoothing a hand over the small child's head. It was rare that she had a few solid hours free to help the sick and downtrodden, but Scarlet had *made* time to make this specific house call. It had involved calling in a few favors with the manor staff to cover for her should anyone look for her, but it was worth it.

For every life she'd taken in the past, she tried to save one. It didn't negate what she did for her stepmother, nor did it clear her conscience, but it was *something*. Her own silent rebellion against the monster that had taken over her life.

The child she was currently helping, Moses, had been unwell for weeks now. He had a chill despite the fact the weather was warm, and clearly his body was not up to the task of combating the disease on its own. Luckily, Scarlet had just the right potions and salves to help the boy.

The child's mother sighed with relief. "Just like that?" Riia asked, not daring to hope. "Just like that, he'll be all right?"

"Give him three drops of this every four hours," Scarlet instructed, turning from Moses to hand Riia a jar full of a deep purple liquid. "Make sure he takes the whole bottle. And I mean it—the whole bottle. Even if it seems like he's fully recovered, do not stop until the bottle is finished. Otherwise, the chill may come back. Then apply this to his forehead whenever he feels especially hot." Scarlet procured a pale green salve from her bag and handed this over to the boy's mother.

Riia nodded in understanding. She dared to smile at her husband. Abel was sitting in the corner, the better to hide his worried face from his son. His wolf ears perked up when he heard Scarlet's assurances though, and his expression brightened.

In Betraz, unions between Talagans and humans were forbidden. Prejudice still ran very high here. After all, the province had been one of the most staunchly loyal to King Destin, who had hated shifters. Even though Arwen and her pack of wolves were shifters themselves, they ruled the Talagans and their ill-fated human paramours with an iron fist. To that end, it wasn't safe for Riia to take her child to a normal healer. Hence why she'd begged for Scarlet's help.

With a small smile, Scarlet procured one final potion from her bag. Green again—this time the color of the forest. She knew from firsthand experience that it smelled of grass and sunshine and other pleasant things—she'd made sure of it. Scarlet got to her feet to stand in front of Abel, who rose from his seat to meet her gaze.

"So long as you can keep your true form from showing"—she pointed at his ears—"and take three drops of this potion three times a day, then your shifter scent will be hidden. Moses', too. At least then you should have more recourse to go about your daily lives."

Abel could only stare at her, bug-eyed with disbelief. "We cannot afford such a thing. And it is illegal."

"So is having a mixed child," she said, not unkindly. She held out the potion again. "As for the price, it's on the house. Trust me, if my helping you can ease your lives by even a small fraction, it will be worth it."

Abel fell to his knees and placed his forehead on the tops of her feet. "You are too kind, my lady."

Scarlet grimaced. She didn't deserve the family's thanks; helping them was just a small penance against the blood on her hands because of her stepmother. It truly was the least she could do. Not enough, but it was something.

She patted Abel on the shoulder and backed away, giving Riia and Moses one last glance before leaving.

As she snuck home through the dusty streets, the cool spring breeze causing her to shiver, she left food and supplies at several more houses—people she knew desperately needed it, other forbidden shifter-human couples; the very young and the very old, whose parents and carers had been ravaged by the mimkia epidemic and were now left to look after each other; maidens desperately trying to carve out an independent life so as to avoid being married off to much older men who everyone knew would treat them poorly; Talagan men who were in hiding, terrified of being driven once more into a war they did not choose and did not want.

In truth, the province of Betraz was filled with more desperate, broken people who needed Scarlet's help than those who did not. It was very much a region where the very few benefitted hugely from the many, and Scarlet hated it.

What she hated even more was that she helped reinforce the system that kept everyone oppressed. But no matter how long or hard she agonized over going against her stepmother once and for all, Scarlet found that she could not do it. She didn't have enough faith in herself to win against Arwen. She would only achieve her own death. And then what sort of change could she effect?

Nothing. None at all.

By the time Scarlet arrived back at the estate, tiptoeing into the kitchen, it was fully dark outside and her mood was ever darker.

"You best get upstairs quickly," Dris urged in hushed tones the moment she spied Scarlet. Her eyes were wide and panicked. "Your stepmother is in a rage."

When is Arwen not in a rage?

"What is it this time?" Scarlet asked, rubbing her fingers against her temple to ward off an incoming headache. This was the last thing she wanted to deal with tonight.

Dris glanced at the door leading out of the kitchen, ensuring that they were alone, before saying, "Apparently the duke of Merjeri died the night before last. And the sheriff has disappeared too."

Scarlet dropped her hands, and the blood drained from her face.

Oh no.

That changed things.

"Where is my stepmother now?" Scarlet questioned, barely able to ask the question as her brain chased after a thousand different questions. Who had killed the duke of Merjeri? Whose side were they on? Did they work for the Hood, whose men Scarlet had sometimes helped get out of tricky situations in Merjeri when she should have killed them? Or did they work for something more sinister? The

Dark Court? Did her stepmother know of her involvement?

"She will be home soon," Dris said. "The messenger she sent out first was terribly out of breath when he arrived. So I would get upstairs and tend to her fire before then."

"Thanks for letting me know, Dris," Scarlet said, placing a quick kiss on her surrogate mother's cheek before swiftly exiting the kitchen, rushing through the manor and up the grandest tower to her stepmother's rooms. They were expansive—half of the entire east wing of the house—and had once belonged to Scarlet's father. Once they had been a place Scarlet loved. They had been welcoming.

Now they were cold.

And empty.

Much like your soul.

Scarlet shivered and brushed away the dark thoughts. They wouldn't help her.

She wasted no time in attending to the hearth, creating a fire second nature to her now. Half an hour later, the fire was merrily crackling inside the hearth, and the heat from the flames was seeping into the room.

No sooner had Scarlet stood up to vacate the rooms than the voice of her stepmother met her ears.

Yelling. Screaming.

Getting closer.

Scarlet braced herself as Arwen stormed into her rooms, the door slamming against the wall. She didn't flinch at the stony expression on her stepmother's face as Arwen argued with Bright.

Scarlet could do nothing but watch as the woman slammed the door in Bright's face, locking it to prevent him following her. Abruptly, Scarlet turned her head down as her stepmother flew across the room, a tigress in billowing black silk. When she threw an expensive vase—a gift from the Giants—against the wall, Scarlet didn't even twitch. Her stepmother's violent outbursts were nothing new to her. Plus, emotional outbursts were always punished harshly. Which was somewhat ironic.

Without a word, Scarlet moved over to the broken pieces of the vase and began picking them up. It was better to anticipate her stepmother's needs before the monster had to ask.

"Ah!" she bit out involuntarily, when one of the smaller pieces cut into her hand. Her palm seeped blood.

"What have you done now?" Arwen demanded, no longer shouting but clearly irritated as she finally acknowledged Scarlet's presence. She swept over to her and elegantly knelt down beside her. Scarlet obediently gave the women her hand so that she could inspect the wound. For a moment Arwen's face softened, and Scarlet almost thought her stepmother was going to ask if she was all right.

Then Arwen inhaled deeply near the wound and her face contorted into a look of abject distaste. "You stink. Get out."

Scarlet pushed herself to her feet and made for the door.

"Wait."

She froze as her stepmother followed her. Arwen grabbed Scarlet by the cheeks and held her painfully in place. Arwen's black polished nails dug into Scarlet's face, threatening to break through the skin and give her a fresh set of wounds. Yet Scarlet remained calm. Showing emotions in the face of her stepmother's abuse only ever made things worse.

"Human women ruin everything," Arwen snarled. There was hardly anything Scarlet could do about the fact she smelled like a human, given that she was one, or that the blood pooling in her hand smelled the way it did. But there was something about the scowl in Arwen's comment that told Scarlet it had nothing to do with Scarlet herself and everything to do with what was causing Arwen's terrible mood. "If only we could do something about that damn Hood..." she muttered, more to herself than to Scarlet, though it confirmed Scarlet's suspicions.

Scarlet kept her eyes on her stepmother. She hardly had anything appropriate to say in response. Equally it was obvious the older woman was not finished with her. So she waited, and waited, and waited, until eventually Arwen brushed her hand across Scarlet's cheek and sighed.

"What makes men go so crazy toward weak little humans?" Arwen mused.

Again Scarlet said nothing, so her stepmother let go of her face and tossed her away.

Believed to have been dismissed, Scarlet moved away toward the door again as quickly as she dared. In truth, all she wanted was to run away. But Scarlet had barely touched the door when Arwen said coolly, "I didn't say you could leave. I have a job for you to do soon. Sit down so I can tell you the details."

All at once, Scarlet's stomach threatened to heave. She knew exactly what a job meant.

A job was code for an assassination.

Chapter Ten

Brine

(Four Weeks Later)

After spending weeks on Chesh's ship, the last thing Brine wanted was to haul his exhausted body through the slow, dawn-dark streets of Dotae in order to meet Pyre.

"Couldn't have met at the bloody docks," Brine grumbled, his eyes and feet heavy as he plodded along the cobblestones toward the fox's far more inconvenient meeting place: his favorite bakery. Brine was running on barely three hours of sleep, none of those restful given the uneasy sea he'd been sailing on.

He hated sailing.

Something about being on the water made him feel trapped.

Pyre had loved this bakery for years now; he especially loved it after he started using it to meet with Tempest long before she knew she was his mate. A small smile curled up his lips. Somehow that felt like years ago but he'd always known Tempest was going to be Pyre's. Brine's mood lifted somewhat as he reminisced about the past. He hadn't trusted

Tempest back then—not for a long time—even though Pyre insisted she would end up on their side. Even when she was being held against her will in the forest whilst her injuries healed. But Brine had come around eventually, and now Tempest was his favorite sparring partner, as well as someone Brine knew he could always trust to speak the truth to him. She was like a sister to him in the same way Pyre was his brother.

Chosen family.

His chosen pack.

Not cursed to be related to him by blood. Not like he was cursed to be the grandson of Old Mother.

His mood darkened.

He'd not stopped thinking about what was going on in his home province and how he might put an end to it. For he *had* to put an end to it, Pyre's orders be damned. In all honesty, meeting Pyre today was more out of courtesy and curiosity than obedience. The time had come for Brine to kill his grandmother. And if Pyre gave Brine more orders that were contrary to him upending his familial wolf pack—such as sending him away for weeks on end at sea—then Brine fully intended to ignore him.

It was with some relief that he reached his destination. The cozy bakery had a tower built above it, where Brine knew Pyre would be waiting for him. Hoping the kitsune had the foresight to have food ready for Brine, given that he'd eaten nothing but ship rations for almost four weeks, his stomach growled loudly as he tromped up the stairs toward the top of the tower, fatigue and hunger riding him.

Brine pushed open the door that led to the attic and stepped inside the spacious room.

Pyre lounged on the window seat to the east; as usual one of his legs languorously swung over the windowsill to catch the morning sun slowly rising over the horizon. A small spark of amusement lit in Brine's chest. The kitsune liked to pretend he was spontaneous, but deep down he was a creature of habit. The same meeting place, the same favorite spot to sit, the same black silk top hat upon his head. It was a wonder Pyre had never truly been caught by the crown, back when he'd been wanted dead by King Destin; it was easy to track his patterns once you knew him.

It was getting to know him that was the difficult part.

Brine tossed the thought to the side as he growled, "You know, it wouldn't kill you to meet in a more convenient location when your right-hand man has been traveling via his least favorite mode of transportation for almost a month."

Brine prowled over to a wooden crate and sat down, somewhat gratified to see that Pyre had at least procured a twisted loaf of sourdough bread and a large helping of generously salted butter from the bakery. His stomach growled again and Brine eagerly ripped into the still-warm bread. He almost sighed at how good it tasted. Baked bread was the food of the gods. Maybe it was a good idea that they met here.

Not that he'd tell the kitsune that.

Pyre had the audacity to laugh, his amber eyes twinkling. "Old habits die hard, I guess." He chuckled. He lifted a closed container from the window seat and held it out to Brine. His fingers curled around the warm package and he held it to his nose.

Bacon. His favorite.

Brine tore into the container and popped a crunchy strip

into his mouth. Embarrassingly, he did sigh like a contented pup.

"That good, huh?" Pyre teased. "Give me some."

Brine narrowed his eyes; his wolf ears flattened against his head. "Get your own. I've been living on bland rations for weeks."

Pyre held his hands up and grinned. "Touchy, touchy. I'll leave you to the bacon and I'm glad you didn't dally on your way over from the docks. Things have grown more complicated here." The grin faded from Pyre's face, making him look more like the Jester than his usual happy self. "Hopefully, that helps apologize somewhat for me picking such an out-of-the-way meeting place. But I needed to ensure I was talking to you on safe ground."

Safe ground?

Brine swallowed his bite and set the bacon aside. Whatever Pyre was about to say, it wasn't anything good. Especially if he felt like he couldn't reveal his thoughts in the palace.

He straightened his back, pricked up his ears, and listened. "Tell me."

"A lot has transpired since I sent you back to the sea," Pyre began, taking off his hat to twirl it in his hands. His hair was overgrown around his ears, curling wildly and untidily.

Another sign this was serious. Pyre was vain to a fault.

"You mean since you sent me off on a decoy mission so I wouldn't focus on Betraz," Brine corrected, as he took another slow bite of bread.

"Correct." At least Pyre never lied to him. "Not that it was a decoy mission. You gave me some useful intel by tracking some of the pirates into the Giants' territory."

The kitsune was stalling.

"Just tell me what you need to tell me and be done with it," Brine pressed. He smacked his lips when he sadly finished his breakfast all too soon, savoring the salt on his tongue before wiping his hands on his trousers like a brute.

The Jester fixed him with a level, liquid amber stare. "Long story short: the duke of Merjeri has been murdered."

Brine blinked slowly. "Murdered?"

"Well, actually, two dukes were murdered." Pyre laughed humorlessly. "The old duke—the one you knew—appeared to have died of natural causes, though a new informant has revealed that his son had him killed. And then said son took his place, and our very own lovely Robyn, the former Lady Lochslee, may have dispatched with him on their wedding night."

Brine's eyebrows lifted in surprise. "That—that slip of a girl who Damien claimed was his mate," he spluttered, "murdered the duke of Merjeri?" How intriguing.

"When will you stop underestimating every 'slip of a girl' you come into contact with, Brine?" Pyre cried in mock display.

"Apparently never. Did she really murder him?"

"Not intentionally. A flight of stairs was involved. She was distraught, of course, but terrified that she would be tried for his intentional murder and hanged. So we took care of it."

Brine huffed. "You mean you covered it up."

"We helped the innocent victim of a horrible man. It was also to our advantage. Now we have a duchess of Merjeri—not a duke—who is sympathetic and supports our new queen. But this, of course, presents us with new problems."

It didn't take Brine long to fill in the blanks. "This is the same as when Ansette took the throne," he said slowly, lips pursing. "Merjeri is full of corrupt highborns loyal to the old duke, or to his son."

"Yes."

"And Robyn will need protection."

Pyre nodded. "As quick as ever, my friend. I'd expect nothing less from you. Yes, Robyn has been invited to the capital to present herself before the queen and explain her case. Of course, Ansette already knows what's going on, but we need to do all of this for the sake of the public. She's meeting with her now. Tempest and I protected her on the way to Dotae. But Tempest must stay here, and I have something else to take care of, so I need someone else to guard Robyn on her way home. Someone I can trust."

"So you want me to do it."

"Right again."

Brine crossed his arms. "And what of her mate? Damien is good with this?"

Pyre smiled, but it wasn't nice. "That is what I'm going to find out. The bloody dragon has disappeared and I intend to bring him back to his senses, even if it means I have to drag him back myself." He ran a hand over his face. "At least I know where to start and that Robyn will be safe."

A burst of pride filled Brine's chest; this was what he lived for—actually helping people, effecting change. It had been pointless of him to miss the version of him that lived in his past, the one who used to live purely for long summer days spent with the blond girl with big eyes. That version of Brine was long gone.

Pyre swung his legs from the ledge of the window to stand, so Brine followed suit. He was taller than the fox, which was saying something because Pyre was tall and rangy. But in any case, Pyre had to tilt his gaze upward to meet Brine's eyes as he set his hat on his head. "Yes. I wouldn't trust anyone else for that. But I should warn you..."

"Just spit it out." That was one of the things that drove Brine crazy. Pyre rarely ever said what he wanted outright. *What now?*

"We'll be pushing out some of the wolf shifters from Merjeri in the process," Pyre said carefully. "The ones still remaining from Old Mother's now-destroyed alliance with Merjeri. I don't want you entering your grandmother's territory while we do this."

Brine considered this, studying the kitsune. Pyre arched a brow in challenge almost as if to say, *I know you won't listen to me, but you should. Entering your old territory is dangerous.*

"Fine," Brine said, even though they both knew it was a lie.

Pyre didn't push back, but nodded slowly. "Don't be stupid."

"I never am."

The kitsune snorted. "That's the bloody truth. But there's something about family that makes one crazy."

Brine said nothing and clapped his good friend on the shoulder. "Thank you for breakfast."

"You're welcome. Come to the palace. Ansette is waiting for you."

They left the bakery, and Brine watched the sun rise in the sky as the city of Dotae began to wake. One more task before he would go home. Leading the duchess of Merjeri back to her home would get him one more step closer to his grandmother.

Brine knew what he needed to do the moment his duties

as bodyguard to Robyn were over. He couldn't let his grandmother hurt anyone else. Not anymore. Not after all this time.

Come tomorrow, he would return to the province that had made him who he was and integrate himself into the pack of Betraz as his final mission.

He'd take back what was his.

His right as alpha.

Chapter Eleven

Scarlet

Scarlet worked in the storeroom near the edge of the estate, surrounded by all manner of bottles, round flasks, tall cylinders, and old, cube-shaped frosted glass. Every bottle was familiar to her, every tincture, every salve, every poison. This was where she did her most important and deadly work.

She placed a poison that made a person vomit themselves to death on a shelf above her working station and frowned at the vast array of poisons she'd brewed over the last few weeks.

What would Mother think of you? What would she think of you using your healing skills to harm?

She closed her eyes and sucked in a deep breath to keep the shame from drowning her. That question had haunted Scarlet for years. In fact, it flittered through her head at the start of just about every day she was working in the storeroom. Her mother had been a healer, using her aptitude for medicine to save people rather than to kill them. If she knew how Scarlet had used her own talents...

She'd disown you.

Scarlet shook her head. It would not do her well to think about it now. Both of her parents were long gone. There was only survival now.

She lifted a wooden spoon and stirred the poison she was brewing for the day. It was a vibrant, punchy red. This was due to the spicy powdered peppers added into the tincture to hide the taste of the deadly nerve agent hidden within. It was brutal stuff—not a peaceful death by anyone's measure. It was by far and away one of Scarlet's least favorite poisons to produce and made her eyes water for days, yet she had no choice but to follow her stepmother's orders and make it.

She pitied the soul of whoever this poison was being made for.

She jumped when the storeroom door slammed open, rattling the tinctures above her workbench. Scarlet stilled as the door closed. It wasn't Arwen or Bright. That wasn't their style of entry. The pit of her stomach quivered as she set the wooden spoon down. Slowly tucking her hair behind her ears, Scarlet turned around.

Her breath caught, but she managed to keep her expression bland.

Tarros, pale-faced, covered in bruises, leaned against the door, panting. Scarlet glanced down to his mangled legs and fought a wince. They looked horrible, but deep down she knew he deserved it, and more. He truly was a predator.

And she was alone with him.

Scarlet sidled around the large worktable in the center of the room to put distance between them. A move that Tarros unsurprisingly did not miss. He took a lazy step farther away from the door, using his cane to support his weight. Even severely wounded, he still moved better than Scarlet. Shifter genetics gave them such an unfair advantage over humans.

"Tarros," Scarlet said carefully. Her voice was infuriatingly small in the storeroom, for its walls were insulated to keep the room at a constant temperature.

The red wolf grinned at her, twisted by the wounds on his face that were well on their way to becoming wicked scars. "It's been a long time, Red," Tarros said. "Far too long since we've been able to talk." He took another step toward the table and her heart raced.

Keeping her eyes on Tarros, Scarlet nimbly grabbed the bag of powdered peppers she had been adding to the poison and slipped it up her sleeve.

"I can make you something for your pain," she said, casting a gaze up and down Tarros's frame as he stalked purposefully toward her. Though he was moving well, the flash of pain that filled his eyes every time his mangled legs hit the floor was not something he could hide. "But you'll have to come back for it later. I'm busy right now."

She rounded the table and reached for the door, only to find it locked. *What the devil?* The key hook next to the exit was empty. The hair at the base of her neck rose.

"Looking for these?"

Her heart battered against her ribcage, her mind racing as she panicked over how trapped she was. Surely if she would scream someone would hear her? Her eyes darted to the oven. She could burn the whole place down if she had to.

She tried again: "I'm not sure what you need, but if you tell me I'll make sure to brew you something special."

Tarros's ears twitched; his face broke into a horrible smile that made her pulse thunder in her ears. He could hear her fear. He yearned for it.

"I'm not here for medication. You know that."

"...so what are you here for?"

"I come for what's mine," he snarled, and then without warning he darted around the table.

Scarlet screamed and threw a stone bowl at him, knocking the keys from his hand. He growled, swiping at her hair with a clawed hand. She scrambled away from him, attention focused on the keys. There would be no escape without them. Scarlet managed to scratch the keys from the floor and bolted to the door.

Tarros snarled and launched himself toward her. With shaking hands, she managed to shove the key into the lock. The key had only just turned in place when Tarros slammed into her.

"No!" Scarlet yelled and yanked at the door.

"You're not getting away this time," he growled into her ear. His breath was sour and disgusting, with just a hint of fire whiskey upon it. She gagged and raked her nails down his arms, to no avail. Struggling against the superior strength of the red wolf would solve nothing. She had to best him with her mind.

Despite her terror, Scarlet changed tactics, elbowing him first in the ribs before swiftly kicking his wounded legs.

Twice.

Tarros howled, his grip loosening.

Scarlet used that precise moment to wriggle free just enough to turn around. She yanked the powdered peppers from her sleeve, ripped the bag open, and blew the contents into Tarros's face, mashing her palm against his nose, effectually breaking it.

He yowled, letting her go and scratching at his face. "It's burning me! What did you do, you stupid little witch?"

Scarlet edged away from him, her own eyes and nose stinging. He took a blind swipe at Scarlet but she dodged the blow just as the door swung inward, almost knocking Tarros from his feet.

Bringing in a fresh breath of air was the most welcome sight Scarlet could have been met with within the Betraz residence—Bright, perhaps the only wolf in the pack that Scarlet thought she almost liked. His midnight hair peppered with silver streaks reminded Scarlet of a memory long since passed, of a boy who'd once accepted a peach and her friendship.

But the boy was gone, and that version of Scarlet was dead.

She shook against the wall as Bright's eyes took in the scene in mere moments before locking on Scarlet, a flash of concern crossing his face.

"Are you quite all right?" he asked her. She appreciated his concern more than she could ever say; it was the gentlest thing she'd experienced in a long, long time.

She nodded. "I'm fine," she said, even though she wasn't, and she was shaking.

Bright turned his hard gaze on Tarros. "What are you doing here?"

"I came for some medicine. My arrival surprised Red and there was an accident," Tarros rasped, rubbing his eyes. "My legs make me clumsy, you know?"

"Is that so?" Bright replied calmly. He looked to Scarlet, who didn't say a bloody word to contradict the monster who'd come to claim her.

"It is. I'll be going." Tarros coughed, stumbling out of the storeroom, leaving Scarlet and Bright alone.

Scarlet trembled, and sagged against the wall, the back of her eyes burning for a whole other reason.

A few seconds of heavy silence fell between them.

Scarlet knew fine and well that the midnight wolf knew the truth of what had gone on in the storeroom, but she also knew he would never bring it up to Arwen. Just as Scarlet would never either. Bright might be a man who showed Scarlet compassion where he could, but he was still Old Mother's second-in-command, and followed her orders with stoic calm. To tell Arwen about what had happened here would only make Scarlet look weak, which they both knew she could not afford.

Instead, Bright held out a hand. It was a lifeline.

She seized his hand and he pulled her in for a hug, gently squeezing her shoulders, which finally quelled the shaking in her body. "Did he touch you?"

"No." *But he wanted to.*

"Where were your weapons?"

"Still strapped to my leg." She hadn't even thought about them. When dealing with wolves, weapons almost always got turned back on you.

"The peppers were a smart idea." Bright released her. "What will you do next time? He's not going away anytime soon."

"I don't know." Scarlet rubbed her red-stained hands on her brown apron. "I'll figure it out."

Bright's lips thinned and then he nodded. "I was sent to fetch you. Lady Betraz has summoned you for a mission," he said softly.

A chill that had nothing to do with what Tarros had done washed over Scarlet. She had only just returned from the last one that could have cost her everything.

Numbly, she followed Bright out of the storeroom and into the warm sunshine of the garden. Nestled in a perfect copse of trees was her stepmother, sitting inside a pretty mahogany gazebo covered with carefully cultivated, blood-red roses. It was in this way that Scarlet could not see who else was with Arwen until she was literally right in front of them.

Two people, on their hands and knees on either side of her stepmother, acting as side tables.

She jolted and quickly masked her expression as she recognized the couple.

Abel and Riia. The human-shifter couple whose child she had helped.

Nausea slammed into her and she almost wavered on her feet.

"You called for me?" Scarlet asked politely.

Her stepmother smiled broadly. With a click of her fingers, Riia on her left-hand side raised her head. Arwen squished the woman's cheeks together, forcing her mouth open. There was an angry, dark, bloody gash where the woman's tongue had been removed. Bile burned the back of Scarlet's throat and she blinked back tears.

"I have a job for you, Red," Arwen said, "and this time I have no need for that softness of yours interfering with my plans."

Scarlet wanted nothing more than to rush forward, to knock her stepmother to the side and help Riia, who had been rendered speechless. Instead, she stood stock-still, as still as Bright standing behind her, and allowed Arwen to continue talking.

Like a coward.

"There are consequences for your actions, child," Arwen crooned into the terrified face of Riia. "You must know by now that you are not the one who's punished when you hide and abet criminals like those in Merjeri. So I will only tell you this once: do not fail my next mission, or the child will suffer next."

Her blood turned icy.

She'd never fooled Arwen. Her stepmother had eyes and ears everywhere.

Feeling just as incapable of speech as the woman without her tongue, Scarlet mutely nodded her obedience.

"Leave my sight."

Woodenly, Scarlet stumbled from the gazebo before her stepmother could see a single tear shed from her eyes.

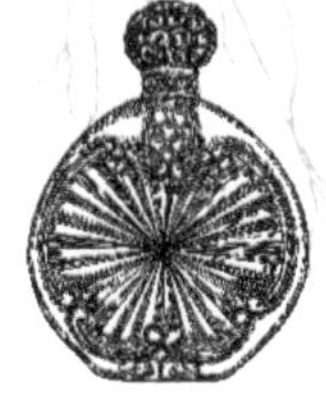

Chapter Twelve

Brine

Ensuring the new duchess of Merjeri, Robyn, returned home safely was not an easy task.

Even when they reached the manor—which Brine had learned on the road was not even Robyn's intended residence now that she had become duchess—he couldn't relax. The manor had been attacked no fewer than three times in as many days, and now Brine was panting and sweating through his fourth dispatch of intruders.

His grandmother's agents were relentless.

He didn't give himself long enough to notice if he recognized any of the wolves attacking the place, though he could do nothing to prevent his nose recognizing the scent of familiar wolves, men and women he'd trained with as a child and young man, wolves who might have been his friends once. Now they were just more foes to vanquish by teeth or by sword.

Brine had lost two men to the attacks on the manor, which could have been worse. Yet even so, there was a lingering sadness for losing any men at all. Brine had admittedly also thought—going against the creatures who had once been his pack—that he would feel sorry for *their* deaths, but all he felt was disgust and disappointment. Had a single one of them ever possessed a backbone? An ounce of integrity? They all easily fell under the heel of his grandmother. Of Old Mother. They knew what she was doing but instead of rising up against it they were facilitating her. Could they really be so ignorant to what Old Mother, along with deplorable men like the late duke of Merjeri, had wrought over the country? Brine could not believe they were so in the dark. But if they weren't in the dark, that meant they were complicit, and Brine knew his disgust was well placed.

The sound of a horn blasted through the air as Brine cut down his last opponent. The other wolves retreated into the woods.

He wiped the sweat from his brow and stared hard at the forest as he signaled for his men to turn back. It was no use to chase after them. They'd be long gone after they shifted. Brine scanned his soldiers and frowned at one of the younger men, who looked to be no older than fifteen.

"Go see a healer about that arm," Brine commanded, nodding at the young recruit, a promising cat shifter who had been recommended by Chesh, no less. It always surprised Brine when the cat had a good idea, or a good recommendation, even though almost all of them were great. There was something about him that suggested Chesh was constantly trying to make a fool of Brine just for the sake of it.

He smiled at the thought of his friend and realized he missed him. And Pyre, and Briggs, and Tempest. After weeks at sea and even now, commanding a small group of loyal men,

Brine felt alone. Once more he thought of how he'd been missing home, and wondered if the two were connected.

His band of men tromped back to the manor and Brine followed them. He watched as one of the older men greeted his wife at the entrance of the manor, then scooped up his young child into his arms.

Brine stared at them, a flicker of emotion in his chest.

At one time, he'd despised anyone settling down, but now...

I want that. Brine wanted a mate and children. A place to put down roots and put down his sword.

It was an unsettling realization.

Hope and dreams could break a person.

Brine wandered down the hallways with no destination in mind, and turned a corner. The previous, lingering smell of blood and battle that had been in his nose was replaced by something far more pleasant.

He stopped in his tracks, sniffing the air questioningly.

Ginger, fresh-tilled earth ... and something sweet.

It teased his nose, a memory lingering in his brain telling him that he had smelled this before, but couldn't place it.

Looking left and right, he tried to figure out where the smell was coming from. People were bustling down the hallway, servants, children and visitors alike—Robyn was transforming the manor into an orphanage, something Brine wholeheartedly approved of, and had caused him to immediately take a liking to the young woman while he performed his duties as her bodyguard.

His brows furrowed as he inhaled deeply, trying to catch the enticing scent once again. But the elusive scent came off none of them, nor did it come from the kitchen when Brine headed in that direction. Yet the smell got stronger. More pronounced. He could almost taste it on the air.

It was only once Brine traveled through the kitchen, past the servants' quarters and down the hallway that led to the expansive Merjeri estate gardens, that Brine came upon the source of the smell.

A young, curvy, blond woman dressed in a nondescript brown dress and a darker brown cloak scurried past him on her way out to the gardens. The smell from before overwhelmed Brine, coming off the woman in waves. He inhaled deeply, endorphins rushing his brain as her scent filled every pore in his body.

The hair along his arms rose and a growl rumbled in his chest.

Instinctually, he knew what it was.

The woman smelled like a *mate*.

Without thinking, Brine quickened his step until he was walking pace-to-pace with the woman. Everything inside him screamed to chase her down—to pin her to the wall, to bury his nose against the delicate skin between her neck and shoulder and mark her.

He exhaled raggedly.

You are not a savage.

But he wanted to be one. The woman's close proximity had set him on edge.

She turned her head, and her eyes met his.

A shock went through his system.

Blue eyes. Deep blue, beautiful eyes, but wide and wary.

She darted her gaze away quickly, hunching her shoulders forward before speeding down the hallway and out into the gardens. In that moment Brine realized he couldn't smell any fear coming off the woman, nothing to mingle with the intoxicating ginger, earthy scent emanating off her skin.

Calm down. You're making her uncomfortable.

Not sure what else to do, Brine turned around and headed back toward the kitchen. Each step he took away from the woman, his pulse slowed. One didn't have to act on someone's scent. He wasn't a complete brute.

"Brine."

He blinked slowly, noticing Robyn for the first time. Though she was the duchess of Merjeri, Brine had grown accustomed to finding her in the servants' quarters, talking to the maids and chefs and caretakers to ensure the place was fully transformed into the orphanage she dreamt of. Now, for example, she was tasting a roiling pot of soup being cooked over an obnoxiously warm fire. She nodded in approval to the chef, then turned her attention back to Brine.

"I hear I have you to thank for keeping us safe. Once again."

He inclined his head politely, despite the fact that he felt like crawling out of his own skin. "That's my job."

Robyn laughed lightly. Softly. She was a delicate woman on the surface, but Brine now knew it was all a ruse. Or, rather, only part of what made the duchess so special. Knowing that she was the Hood made Brine respect her in the same way he respected Tempest.

But she wasn't the woman who had just run into the garden. She wasn't *his*.

When was the last time he'd come across anyone who smelled remotely compatible? Years?

"Are you okay?"

He opened his mouth to speak but only grunted. It wasn't the right time for a wife or family, but he wasn't stupid enough to look a gift horse in the mouth. This could be his chance.

Brine turned on his heel and sprinted back the way he'd come, determined to catch up with the woman who smelled like hope.

He had no idea what to do if he caught her.

Chapter Thirteen

Scarlet

Moses was doomed.

Scarlet knew his life depended on her success in this mission, and yet she had failed. Here was an opportune moment to dispatch the new duchess of Merjeri—she was right in her grasp—yet Scarlet had done nothing.

Again.

"*You're a weak fool,*" her stepmother's voice rang in her head.

It made her sick to think she had to choose one life over another.

It took everything in Scarlet to not flat-out flee from Merjeri Manor, choosing instead to blend into the hustle and bustle of the estate in order to leave unnoticed. One of the new duchess' bodyguards—Scarlet suspected the leader of the pack by his size, though she'd been so scared of getting caught that she hadn't taken in a single detail of his appearance—had spotted her, but when Scarlet rushed out into the gardens, he had not followed.

She breathed a sigh of relief when she reached the edge of

a beautifully maintained pond covered in red-tinged lily pads and delicate white blossoms. Her pulse rushed at the base of her skull. She ran her hand over her long braid and tried to calm down. Just because she chose not to take out the duchess of Merjeri didn't mean Moses would die. If Scarlet moved quickly, she could save the child.

She glanced at the exit to the garden. She needed to move now.

That shifter knew something wasn't right about you.

Scarlet closed her eyes while her heartrate slowly returned to normal. It wouldn't do for her to smell like fear. She needed to look like she belonged.

Which was difficult when she *didn't* belong, and fifty different shapeshifters were mulling around the hallways and exits.

Surprisingly though, it had been unnervingly easy to get inside the Merjeri grounds. Arwen had informed Scarlet that the manor was a military base of sorts, but when Scarlet had entered it had been the exact opposite. Whoever had given the intel to Lady Betraz had clearly not known what they were talking about. Which had been good for Scarlet, except she hadn't expected all the Talagans. It was supposed to be a human compound.

Scarlet ran her fingers through her pale hair when a blustery wind blew it over her shoulder. It was a beautiful day, all white, puffy clouds, blue sky, and the warmth of the high-noon spring sun. She would have enjoyed it if not for what her stepmother had tasked her to do.

It was only in coming to Merjeri that Scarlet learned the full truth of the new duchess' background. She had been betrothed to the previous duke, then married to him, but upon their wedding night he had tragically fallen down the stairs. They had consummated the marriage, which made her the true heir to his duchy.

But Scarlet possessed the same sharp instincts of her stepmother, if not her malevolent nature. There was more to the story she was hearing, and she knew it.

When Scarlet had arrived in the province, she had been convinced that she was going to be met with a ladder-climbing, bloodthirsty woman whom she would have had no qualms with dispatching. Instead, Scarlet had found herself within the beginnings of an orphanage and a duchess attempting to make her province a safe place for all.

The series of attacks on the estate over the last few days from the wolves of Betraz had all been a cover to get Scarlet in to do her one job. Yet she hadn't actually needed the ruse; all she did was walk through the front door with a group of volunteers who wished to help transform the manor into an orphanage and place of solace for refugees. The wolves continued their attacks even once Scarlet was inside the estate of course, no doubt heeding Arwen's orders to cause as much damage as possible.

Scarlet had watched as they all fell, one by one, to the small but fearsome group of shifters Lady Marianne had protecting the people. Not that Scarlet had *actually* watched, but house gossip was almost as good as the real thing. There were celebrations each night over their victories.

Scarlet would have done the same, if she wasn't actually working with the wolves of Betraz.

She blew out another breath and ran her hands along the front of her simple dress.

It had taken her full three days to get close enough to the

duchess to actually speak with her. By that point Scarlet had learned enough—and witnessed enough from afar—to know that her job was going to be impossible. For what she found was a woman making scones, of all things, in the servants' kitchen with the cook and several rowdy children. Or cleaning the floors with the maids, laughing when a mud-caked dog was chased down the newly cleaned floor followed by three cackling little girls. Or telling stories to a snake shifter boy, and his smaller, sickly sister, until the sister's coughing subsided and she fell into an easy sleep.

The duchess had created a safe haven. The first ever Scarlet had witnessed firsthand.

Shifters and human children alike were welcomed into the manor, intermingling and screaming and playing as if they didn't have a care in the world. As if they hadn't been left on this Earth without parents, like Scarlet.

It was shockingly domestic. Disgustingly wholesome.

It was all Scarlet had ever hoped for as child, and it broke her heart.

The duchess of Merjeri was a good person. Robyn would achieve great things and help an even greater number of people than Scarlet could likely ever fathom.

She couldn't hurt the duchess.

Scarlet watched several brightly colored fish swim through the clear waters of the pond as she slipped her hand into her right pocket. The poison she had brewed—the horribly unpleasant one, full of the vicious peppers she'd attacked Tarros with—almost seemed to burn her palm.

Shame curdled her stomach. What had she turned into?

She had taken her stepmother's mission without a single question and had come here fully intending to cut an innocent woman's life short, a woman who only did what was best for people— for anyone who looked for help. Not a single person on her journey to and through Merjeri had anything bad to say about the gracious Lady Lochslee.

Think of Moses.

Scarlet gazed at her reflection in the pond between the lily pads and the golden shimmer of the fish. Pale, freckled, expressionless. There was the scar on her face from where she had helped Will escape Betraz—Will Scarlet, inextricably linked to her forever. They even shared a name. But there was no scarlet cloak to be seen in her reflection. Of course she couldn't wear it into Merjeri without being noticed. It was bad enough that Arwen had realized she was the one helping the outlaws on her previous mission because of that cloak. But it had been a very long time since she hadn't worn red.

Scarlet shivered, feeling vulnerable without the protection of that bloody color covering her shoulders. The women staring back at her seemed like an apparition. A ghost.

A child from another time, wearing Scarlet's face like a mask.

Who are you? When did you give up?

The space between her shoulder blades prickled and Scarlet froze.

Someone was watching her.

She slowly lifted her head from the pond and casually surveyed the garden, making it appear as if she was admiring the blossoms fluttering on the breeze.

Her gaze snagged on silver eyes.

It was the shifter who had noticed her earlier.

Scarlet stopped breathing.

Not possible.

At the time, she had not taken into account what the man looked like, aside from his size. Even with the distance between them, it was plain as day.

The man was the spitting image of Bright.

Dressed all in black.

Loose, black hair hung gracefully around his head and shoulders. He was tall with wide shoulders and arms that looked like they could crush a man's skull.

Run.

Scarlet took a step back, then remembered the pond was behind her, so she took a step to her left instead, then another and another. His black wolf ears twitched atop his head.

The wolf shifter mirrored her movements—each step calculated.

Her jaw clenched. This was what she hated about wolves.

They liked to hunt. And make no mistake, he was hunting her now.

You can't outrun him.

His strides were longer than hers and he was closing the distance slowly as she debated what his next move was.

Distract him. If he wanted you dead, you would be already.

Scarlet held up one hand as she slipped the other back into her pocket to grab hold of the sleeping powder she always carried on her person. It was one of her best defenses.

The moment he closed the distance between them, she would throw it in his face and run.

The wolf took a step toward her. Two. Three.

Her breath hitched when he was barely an arm's length

away. She trembled inside, her instincts begging her to run, but she knew that would trigger the wolf. He'd only give chase and win. This was her only option.

Scarlet readied her resolve, steeled her nerves, and dipped her fingers into the powder—while there was no aggression on the wolf's face. No anger. No suspicion, even. She wouldn't be taking any chances.

He inhaled deeply and she shivered as something deepened in his silver gaze as he peered down at her.

She knew that look. One Scarlet had only ever seen from Tarros.

Lust. Possessiveness.

Run.

But she couldn't move. It was like her feet were rooted to the ground. Partly from fear but something else entirely that she'd never felt before.

The wolf inhaled deeply, causing gooseflesh to pebble along her arms.

A smile bloomed across his face that completely transformed him from darkly handsome to boyishly attractive.

"*Mate.*" A growl rumbled in his chest as he smiled down at her. "*Mine.*"

Her stomach bottomed out.

Terror shot throughout her veins and burned away any sense of reason.

She turned and fled the big, bad wolf.

Chapter Fourteen

Brine

Logically, Brine knew he should let the young woman go.

Instinctively, he couldn't.

A low growl rumbled in his chest as he sprinted after her, her soft scent urging him to capture her.

Mine.

His prey darted into a copse of trees that lined the lefthand side of the manor grounds, and the hair along the nape of his neck rose. Brine was struck by the sense that something wasn't quite right. The woman fled from him but he couldn't smell her fear.

In fact ... he couldn't detect any of her emotions.

That was bloody odd.

His attention zeroed in on her as he decreased the distance between the two of them with lightning precision. His brows slashed together and he inhaled deeply. Why was her scent muted so much? And why the devil couldn't he scent her emotions?

She darted left and right, but he never lost track of her.

Claim her.

His eyes narrowed when she lobbed a rock over her shoulder at him yet never broke her stride. He dodged it easily and closed the space between them right as they passed the broad trunk of a mature oak tree. Just as he wrapped his arms around her waist, she stumbled, catapulting them into the tree. Brine pulled her back flush against his chest and tried to right them, to no avail.

A curse burst from his lips as they slammed against the bark, his forearms taking the brunt of the impact. Her head bashed his shoulder and Brine found himself not caring as he pressed his face into the crook of her neck. The female froze in his embrace, and disgust and self-loathing roiled in his stomach.

What the devil was he doing?

He was better than this.

You're better than your father.

"I'm sorry," he whispered into the woman's ear, even as he inhaled again. That delicate, ginger scent on her skin was bloody delicious. Enticing. It was all he wanted.

His primal side begged him to pull her farther into his embrace and ... his mouth watered at the thought of biting her. Of claiming his mate. How long had he been waiting for this?

She's not yours. You've no right to a mate.

"Give me a moment," he uttered. Brine squeezed his eyes shut and attempted to get control of his body. He took a shallow breath through his mouth to try to filter out her pheromones, but his eyes snapped open and he scowled down at her pale smooth neck even as he drew in a deeper breath. Something was muting her scent. He sniffed again and his mate stiffened further in his arms.

His nose wrinkled. Did she have perfume on? He couldn't detect any but—

A small pinch on the inside of his wrist dragged Brine out of his stupor and he cursed again as his arms refused to unwrap from the silent maiden in his embrace. He needed to think with his head, not his body. This was nothing more than a chemical reaction.

If only Pyre could see you now.

"I'm sorry," Brine mumbled again, inhaling a final time to try to get a sense of the woman's emotions. He couldn't get anything. Other than pinching his wrist, the woman wasn't shaking or screaming or fighting back. "I won't hurt you," he said, his voice low and gravelly. His jaw clenched as Brine eased away from her an inch or two. "I swear it."

A long moment of silence stretched out between them.

Brine focused on his breathing and fought to match his to the woman. Which was difficult even with her turned around. The way her hair draped over her shoulder, exposing the nape of her neck, was more than Brine could bear.

It was utterly disgraceful. It wasn't like he was a pup who'd just come into maturity. He'd even come across other potential mates in the last few years, but none of them had affected him this way.

The woman shifted slightly and whispered, "Can I turn around?"

He nodded and loosened his hold, dragging his hands along her sides before he took a small step back. Even that was painful. He could do this. It was only attraction. It was only—

Slowly she turned around, and all thought fled.

She. Was. Stunning.

Heat rushed through his body and he tried to take a step, but her hand on his chest stopped him from advancing. Brine placed his large hand over her pale, freckled one and focused on grounding himself. It was like silk.

He scanned her heart-shaped face and full lips.

"Are you alright?" she asked softly, blinking her big, deep blue eyes at him as she pushed a lock of wispy golden-blond hair from her face. There was something familiar about her.

"No."

She nodded and frowned slightly, causing him to notice a small scar on her left cheek. On another female it may have marred her looks, but on her—*his woman*—it only made her fiercer.

Another rush of attraction burned through him, urging him to crowd her against the tree once again so he could feel all her delightful curves pressed against his own body.

Get yourself together.

"Who ... are you?" Brine managed to ask, not moving an inch.

Her brows furrowed and she pursed her lips. Once again he was struck with the notion that he knew her from somewhere. Although if that were the case, he was sure he'd never forget such a sensual creature.

He blanched as he realized he'd leaned into her touch and had reached out to touch her face. Brine exhaled heavily and forced himself to drop his hand, embarrassment heating his cheeks.

"I'm so sorry," he muttered a third time. "I'm having a hard time breaking away."

"Such is the plight of being Talagan, or so I'm told," she said.

Her sweet voice washed over him and some of the tension in his shoulders ebbed away. She didn't seem angry or terrified.

He flinched and his lips parted when she inched closer to him and cupped his bristled cheek with her left hand. He sighed into the touch before he could stop it. So much for being a hardened warrior when a little slip of a woman could take him to his knees.

She smiled and he leaned toward her, wavering on his feet.

He frowned as the world blurred a little. Brine rocked back and lost his balance. A second later, he crashed to the ground, the taste of something bitter upon his tongue. He tried to speak but only garbled words came out.

What had she done to him?

The blond knelt by his side, rearranging his limbs into a more comfortable position before pushing a lock of hair from his eyes. He blinked as she gave him perhaps the saddest smile Brine had ever seen.

Who had put that look on her face?

"My name is Red," she said as the world went black.

Chapter Fifteen

Brine

"I knew I'd find you here."

Brine turned from his position on the ramparts of Merjeri Manor and spied Pyre, Tempest, and Damien—who was clothed for once—walking toward him. The moon was almost full above his head; Brine had been staring at it for Dotae only knew how long, thinking about the slip of a woman who had knocked him unconscious. Her scent, as muted as it was, haunted his every waking moment, and his sleeping moments too.

Who was she? She said her name was Red. Brine still couldn't believe she'd granted him one precious sliver of information before he closed his eyes and fell asleep for hours. When he'd come to, it had been dark, and Brine had shifted into his true form in order to follow Red's scent through the trees that lined the estate and into the forest they grew into. He'd loped through the undergrowth late into the night, and long after the woman's scent had disappeared from his nostrils. But he was desperate; how could he have found his mate and then so keenly lost her, mere moments later?

"Are you thinking of her?" Tempest asked knowingly, her tone teasing. When Brine had come to her to make a few inquiries about the woman, it had of course piqued the Hound's interest. But though she and Pyre and Damien all together had reached out for any information about a blond woman named Red who lived in the region, they had come up blank. It was as if the woman was a ghost, a figment of Brine's perverse, desperate imagination, a tantalizing apparition of something he longed for but could never have.

"There are more important things to think about than ghosts," Brine replied, pushing the thought of Red aside to focus on what truly was most important: infiltrating Betraz.

Damien and Pyre stood on either side of Brine, leaning against the ramparts to stare at the moon with him. "You're allowed to think about a woman and a job at the same time, you know," Pyre said, glancing at Tempest as she pulled an arrow from her quiver and checked its point to ensure it was still sharp. "Focusing on both often has far more appealing results." The grin he threw at Tempest was absolutely filthy. When an arrow whooshed through the air from her direction, the fox deftly caught it with a chuckle. "See what I mean? Completely worth it."

"Watch your tongue or you'll be sleeping alone tonight," Tempest fired back, though she was struggling to hide the laughter in her voice.

Pyre nudged Brine's shoulder. "I rest my case. You need someone challenging to be your mate. Otherwise, what's the point?"

Damien nodded his agreement. "The fox is right, Brine. And besides, the hunt is part of what makes finding a mate so interesting. So what if she's a ghost? It will make it all the more satisfying when you finally find her."

"I'd rather we focused on the job, all things considered," Brine said, running his hands through his hair to push it out of his face. He felt incredibly uncomfortable having everyone's undivided attention trained on him. "I've never been one for chasing women anyway."

Pyre rolled his eyes. "Don't we all know it. Every time you and Chesh come back from a mission, I hold out hope that he'd have just one salacious story centered around you, not him. But that hope is always in vain. It's time you loosened up, friend."

"*The job,*" Brine pressed, on the edge of losing his patience entirely.

"You know fine well why I'm stalling," Pyre said, drawing his mood back to serious as fast as the snap of a bowstring. He landed his topaz eyes on Brine's. "I don't want you to go back in there. We have other men who can infiltrate Betraz."

Tempest and Damien murmured their agreement, but Brine barked out a laugh at the thought. "You have other men, yes, but you'd be sending them to their deaths. You've sent too many already. If I weren't your friend, Pyre, you would have no problem using me for this. So use me. And besides," Brine muttered, staring up at the moon, "I don't have a choice. It's my kin who are causing problems. I can't run from them forever, even as I've been trying damn hard to do exactly that until now."

Damien rested his hand on Brine's shoulder, heavily enough for Brine's knees to buckle beneath him for the briefest of moments before the dragon shifter raised his hand again. "You have my respect," Damien said, "though I have to admit to being curious about how you plan to go about this. You can't just walk into Betraz and face your grandmother. She'll know something is up."

"I know. That's why I plan to attack her ship in Callmai."

"Interesting way to get in her good books," Tempest said, a frown coloring her brow. She crossed her arms over her chest as she tried to work out the logic behind Brine's plan. "Do you plan to—"

"Sweep in to save the day as if I wasn't the one who attacked the ship?" Brine finished for her, anticipating Tempest's keen strategic instincts. "Of course. Chesh has far superior connections among the sailors and pirates who go through that port. He has already agreed to help so I can mend fences with my grandmother."

Pyre chuckled appraisingly. "Of course the cat knew about this already and never told me. I have to say, it's as good a plan as any. But Old Mother's ship is due to leave port in two days. You don't have much time."

Brine offered him a feral grin. "I know. That's why I'm leaving now." He waved a hand down at the leather bag at his feet, packed and ready to go.

"Would you have told us about this had we not come up to meet you beforehand?"

Brine shrugged. "You're here now, aren't you? So all's well that ends well."

"Just so long as it *does* end well," Tempest cut in, her genuine concern warming Brine's soul with affection. He inclined his head when she nodded at him. "Be careful, Brine. Don't get yourself killed."

Brine said nothing. He knew he couldn't promise that, even though he wished he could—for his sake and for his friends.

But he had to do this. He had to settle things in Betraz, even if it cost him his life.

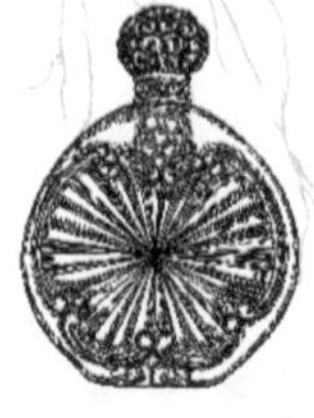

Chapter Sixteen

Scarlet

Scarlet was nearing the edge of the Betraz Manor. She'd spent the last few days returning from Merjeri, all the while mulling over the lies she would have to fabricate to cover up why she didn't assassinate Lady Merjeri. A shiver ran through her as she walked in the shadow of the immense pine trees. She glanced at the hem of her red cloak that hung out of her bag and clenched her jaw. It wasn't worth the risk for the warmth it would provide. It made it far too easy for anyone inside the estate to identify her, which was the last thing she needed.

Scarlet shoved the cloak deeper into her bag and pulled the flap over the top to hide it. She had to get back up to her room before anyone spotted her in order to get hold of everything she needed to perform one very important job before she had to face up to her stepmother.

Just in case the lie she told was seen for exactly what it was: a lie.

One always had to be prepared.

On silent feet, Scarlet passed a couple of wolves standing

sentry outside the manor's servants' entrance. Looking at them reminded her of the other thing that had been consuming her thoughts ever since she fled Merjeri.

The wolf who saw her.

The enemy who chased her down.

Who claimed she was his mate.

The wolf who looked like Bright.

Her stomach clenched.

Brine.

Her childhood crush and only friend at the time.

Bitterness seeped into her soul at the memory.

Logically, Scarlet knew he'd been several years older than she. Enough for him to think of her as a little sister and nothing more. Enough for him to run from the pack and leave her behind with the monsters, without ever looking back.

He never wrote.

He never came home.

That was when she'd stopped believing in heroes.

Swallowing down the past sorrow, she crept along the path in thought, making sure to keep out of the wolves' sight.

Why had Brine been prowling the corridors of Lady Marianne's estate in Merjeri? From the little information she'd gathered over the years from Arwen, he was part of the Dark Court. A group of thieves, murderers, and drug suppliers. It made no sense that he'd been in Merjeri. Was he on an assignment? Part of her had wanted to ask, but keeping her mouth shut had been the wisest course. Brine hadn't recognized her.

That was a blessing in of itself.

Knocking him out and running had been the best choice.

Reaching the kitchen, Scarlet crept into the bushes and

tossed a rock as hard as she could, distracting the guards standing outside the servants' entrance.

She snuck inside and closed the door firmly behind her.

"Gus," she gasped, breathless.

Gusal and his twin, Jaq, turned from the pantry, covered in flour, surprise plain as day on their faces at seeing Scarlet.

"We didn't expect you back so soon," Jaq said. His eyes narrowed. "Where is your cloak? You know Lady Betraz doesn't like it when you walk about without it."

"I need to do something first before I see her," Scarlet replied, pushing away from the door. She held a finger to her lips and lead them into the pantry so they could talk privately.

Gus leaned forward expectantly. "What is it?"

"Moses—the half Talagan boy," she whispered. "Where is he being held?"

Understanding dawned on the twin's faces simultaneously.

"You didn't assassinate the duchess of Merjeri? You never fail," Gus said in a hushed tone.

Scarlet exhaled heavily and shook her head. "I couldn't. If you had been there… if you'd seen… she's running an orphanage. How could I destroy someone who is that *good*?"

"The boy will pay for this." Jaq's mouth turned down in sadness. "And you're putting your life at risk for someone you don't even know. This is dangerous—even for you."

"I know, but I have a plan." Scarlet swallowed hard. "But I will need help."

Gus and Jaq exchanged looks then nodded. "You will have it."

She sighed in relief. They'd never refused her before but it pained Scarlet to ask them to risk their lives for her. "Thank you."

"We're family," Gus said softly. "It's what we do."

"Enough sentiment," Jaq cut in brusquely. "You need to get the boy out. *Now.* Give us five minutes and we'll find out where he is." He narrowed his eyes at her. "You can't stay here. We'll meet you at your rooms."

"Done." Scarlet tossed her arms around them, not caring about the flour and pressed kisses to their whiskered cheeks. "I can't thank you enough."

"Hug us when this is all over," Jaq said stiffly. "Then we will know you're safe." He untangled himself from her and grabbed a parcel of wrapped food from a back corner of the pantry and pressed it into her hands. "For your journey."

She nodded and tucked it into her bag. Next, Scarlet crept from the pantry through the manor using several dark hidden passageways. Every time she entered one, past memories threatened to overwhelm her. But she managed to anchor herself by running her fingers along the stone walls.

Once she reached her room, Scarlet tossed the food onto her small bed and took a moment to strip out of her clothing, making sure to sprinkle the soiled garments with a powder of her own creation that removed scents from the cloth. Now, no one would ever know she'd had contact with Brine.

Quickly, she redressed in a simple brown dress and cloak, then tucked her hair down the back. Next, she pulled out her red cloak from her bag and laid it across her bed. Her skin prickled as time tracked on and she packed. A few small knives, vials of poison, a sleeping powder, foodstuffs, and a perfume that diluted her scent. Scarlet rolled the cloak up with her supplies and she stuffed it back into her bag.

That had to be good enough.

If her stepmother did not believe her lies about why she'd failed to murder Lady Marianne, Scarlet would have mere seconds to escape with her life.

Providing she returned safely after saving Moses.

Three short knocks and two long raps on the door had her flinching.

It cracked open and the twins snuck into her room, closing the door silently behind them.

"Did anyone see you?" she asked.

"No. We were careful," Gus replied. His lips pursed and he crossed his arms.

That wasn't a good sign. "What is it?"

"Moses in being held in the lower dungeons." Jaq's voice was grave.

Hell.

Scarlet suppressed a shudder, bile burning in the back of her throat. That was where they kept the worst of the worst, not innocent sick children.

"It's too risky for you to go," Jaq added.

"I have no other choice." She gave the twins a weak smile. "It's my fault he's there in the first place. I meddled in his life and Arwen is punishing him for it. I can't stand by." She slung her bag over her shoulder. "Be careful while I'm gone and keep your heads down. Old Mother will be looking to take heads when she discovers Moses gone."

"Keep safe," the twins murmured.

She spared them one last glance before entering the secret hallway hidden beside her fireplace. Darkness closed in around her as the door swung shut and she took a moment to calm herself before she began running for the dungeons.

Over the years she'd memorized all the hidden corridors. The ones Arwen knew about, she avoided.

With no time to waste, she moved down two flight of stairs that connected with the lower dungeon. She paused at the door and strained her ears.

No sign of movement on the other side.

With care, Scarlet pressed the keyhole and the door swung inward. She stepped into the weapons room and fought to keep from gagging. Calling it a weapons room was generous.

It was the torture room.

Weapons covered in dried blood hung from the walls and chains dangled from the ceiling. She latched the door behind her, the fake stone blending seamlessly into the wall. Scarlet crossed over to the wooden door on silent feet and listened once again. No one was usually down here at this time of day but one could never be too cautious.

Luckily, there was no lock on this door.

Sure she could pick a lock but it would waste precious time.

Scarlet opened the door just a crack and scanned the left side of the dungeon.

No wolves.

She opened it farther and peeked right.

No guards.

Time to move.

She fled down the center aisle way of the dingy dark place.

Most of the cells were vacant. Her stepmother didn't like to keep prisoners for very long. She enjoyed killing them too much.

Scarlet's heart picked up as she spotted Moses in one cell

and his parents in the next one over. None of them looked alright. How the devil was she supposed to get them out? Abel's left leg looked mangled and Riia was one giant bruise.

Her heart sank. They would need to be carried out and so would Moses. Heat pressed at the back of her eyes. She couldn't save them all.

"Take him," a soft, almost inaudible voice begged her. Abel. He dragged himself to the iron bars and held up a shaking, almost skeletal hand in the direction of Moses' cell. "Please. Take him."

Riia rolled onto her side, eyes glassy and whimpered, pointing to Moses.

They knew they wouldn't survive.

"I'm sorry," Scarlet whispered before rushing to Moses' cell. She used her lockpicks that always hung from her garters and opened the iron door. It groaned and she flinched. Not much time now.

"Time to go, sweet one," she murmured as she scooped the child up. He was delirious, on the edge of unconsciousness. Scarlet laid him over her shoulder before running for the weapons room without sparing Abel and Riia a second glance.

This was their last request and she'd honor that. She'd mourn later.

Her breathing sped up as she closed the wooden door behind her and swiftly moved to the hidden stone door. She pressed a small divot in the grout and the door swung into the dark, narrow corridor.

Moses whimpered.

Scarlet closed the door behind them with her foot and ran a hand over his back. "I know it's dark but I have you. We need to keep quiet to hide from the big, bad wolves."

All too soon, Scarlet reached the outside of the manor. This was where it got tricky.

She hardly dared to breathe as she crept through the gardens and toward the edge of the estate. She thanked her lucky stars that she had Jaq and Gus on her side to help her escape unseen, otherwise she was bound to have been noticed.

Her skin prickled when the line of trees on the edge of the estate were within touching distance—the sound of a twig snapping on her left caught Scarlet's attention and she hid herself and the small boy into the shadow of a nearby tree.

They had been noticed. Scarlet had to hope she had not been identified.

With shaking hands, she gently hid the child in the undergrowth at the tree's base, hoping against hope that, even if she were stopped, by some miracle she might save his life.

Scarlet released a pair of knives from her wrist sheaths and pulled up the dull brown hood of the cloak she had been wearing in place of her red one. Footsteps came once more from her left. She backed herself against the tree and got into a ready stance.

The second the wolf rounded the tree within arm's reach, Scarlet slashed at him with one knife coated in her odorless knockout powder, then violently hit the back of his head with the second. His eyes rolled back and he crashed to the ground at her feet, out cold. He hadn't even seen her.

Relief overcame Scarlet. One obstacle down. Several to go.

She tucked away her blades and retrieved Moses, tucking his shaking body underneath her cloak as she raced through the woods toward the Fiergone border.

"Hurts," he cried softly.

"I know, sweet boy. We're almost there. You're doing so great. You're so brave," she murmured as sweat dripped down her back. It was hard going, fleeing with Moses and her heavy bag toward the river city of Samiliere. For though the boy was underweight for his age—skin and bones—he was still a weight in her arms, and Scarlet was already tired from days of traveling. Her muscles burned and her lungs screamed, but she kept going.

Slowing for one second could mean death for them both.

By sundown she had finally reached the edge of her stepmother's territory, where the rivers intersected between Betraz and Fiergone and formed a tributary that led to the sea.

There was one horrifying moment, just before they left the border, when Scarlet spied one of Texel's groups of wolves prowling, looking for trouble, but Scarlet knew this land better than anyone. Some clever footwork, several hiding places and a small detour later, and she had made it to her destination: the Port of Samiliere.

Scarlet hated that place but today it was beautiful.

It was where Arwen ran her goods out through to the coast, but despite this Scarlet did have one loyal contact within the confines of the city. An escaped wolf who lived on a small ferry that moved between the fresh water port town of Samiliere and the city of Callmai that rested on the edge of the sea.

Dead on her feet, she skirted down a dilapidated dock to a dingy looking fishing boat. But it was all a ruse. Mills' ferry was one of the nicest ships Scarlet had ever had the pleasure of riding in on the inside.

She hesitated on the dock and whistled three low notes, praying Mills was home and not drinking in the city.

The old wolf lumbered onto the deck and squinted at her. "Awfully late, ain't it?"

"I need transport."

He cocked his head and she opened her cloak, revealing Moses. Mills frowned but he waved her on board. She stepped onto the boat, managing not to stumble as the older wolf pulled a scratchy looking blanket from a chest. He tossed it to her.

"Lay down on the deck and cover yourself. We'll be out of here soon enough."

Scarlet did as he said, arranging Moses comfortably and covered them both. Her nerves were on edge as Mills untied his boat, whistling the entire time. The ferry began to move and she hardly dared to breathe as they left the Samiliere port.

"You can come out now."

She pulled the rough blanket from her face and sat up slowly. Moses whined and she pulled him onto her lap and cocooned him in her cloak and the blanket. His eyelids fluttered but he fell asleep on her, mouth hanging open.

As she lifted her head, she noticed Mills watching her.

He pursed his lips. "Is this one yours?"

"No." She looked down at Moses' sweet flushed face. "But he's my responsibility now." Scarlet lifted her head and met Mills' gaze. "Transporting us is dangerous."

"Helping any refugees is dangerous, lass."

"I stole this one from Old Mother."

He scowled but shrugged. "Makes no difference. He's just

a pup. He deserves protection."

"That he does." Her eyes began to burn and she blinked hard to keep her eyes open.

Mills eyed her. "Get some rest, lass. It looks like you've been chased by the devil. You're safe here."

She chuckled. What a novel idea. Safety.

"Nowhere is safe," she murmured as her eyes closed.

"Old Mills will keep an eye on you both. I won't let anything happen to you."

"Thank you," she whispered, cuddling her charge closer.

Mills grunted. "Not a problem, lass. We should be at Callmai in no time. The wind is with us."

Mills shook her awake.

Scarlet was grabbing for her knifes without thinking.

The old wolf clasped her wrist and squatted down next to her. "No need for that, lass. It's just me."

Her heart raced but she exhaled heavily as he released her wrist and stood. Eyes gritty, she thanked Mills and gently set Moses on the ship's deck. A groan escaped her as a myriad of aches made themselves known. "Feels like I just fell asleep."

"It's been about four hours."

She rolled her neck and examined the Callmai port. Mills had docked his ship in the sleepier side of the harbor while the larger mercenary ships anchored on the other side. "I can't believe I didn't feel you dock."

"You were pretty exhausted." A pause. "The little one needs care."

"I know. That's why I'm here."

She slung her bag over her shoulder and hefted Moses into her arms. Mills helped her tuck the child beneath her cloak.

"Thank you so much for your help. I'll get him settled and then I'll need a ferry back if you're willing."

"Anything for you, lass. It will be slower going on our way back unless the winds change."

She nodded and stepped off the boat, onto the short, wooden dock. "I won't be long."

"I'll be waiting for you, my lady," Mills replied. "Take care of yourself and the pup. Callmai has been rougher than usual in the last few months. Be careful."

"Always am."

She quickly moved past sleepy shanties on the poor side of Callmai, taking pains not to draw any attention from the brothels and ale houses. As she neared the merchant side of the port, more wolves began to appear. This was the part of the city her stepmother owned. It was teeming with Arwen's agents.

Some of her anxiety washed away as she spotted the Siren's Song, a pub nestled right by the docks. It was a popular spot of high-class merchants and pirates. But it held a secret known only to a specific group of people.

People who stood against Arwen.

Scarlet rounded the lively pub, keeping to the shadows. She skirted the building and edged down a hidden pair of stairs cut into the rocks that led to the sea. Scarlet entered the small hidden cave at the base, her feet sinking into the knee-high seawater. It was a bloody miracle she'd arrived at low tide.

She plowed through the water, her boots slipping here

and there on the stones below until she reached an iron door. Scarlet pulled the key from her corset while juggling Moses and opened the bars. She closed it behind her and began slogging up the stairs.

The air heated and relief filled her as she arrived at the ornate wooden door inlaid with shells and abalone. Scarlet lifted her left arm and knocked the password, chest heaving with the effort to hold Moses and stay upright.

The door swung open, spilling light into the stairwell.

"Surprise," Scarlet muttered.

Ari's bright violet eyes widened as she pushed her dark wavy red hair from her light seafoam colored face. "By the gods, Scarlet! What the devil are you doing here?"

"Long story, but I need your help."

Her half-human, half-siren friend stepped aside and waved them in. "Come in, come in."

Scarlet stumbled inside, clinging to her charge.

The basement to the Siren's Song was a safe place for those fleeing Arwen. Ari had long since left her own country to build a life here in Callmai. For years now she had been helping to smuggle refugees out of Betraz—perhaps one of the only good reasons for the city to exist.

"What's happened?" Ari asked, concern painting face. "You weren't due for another trip for another two months."

"I know but something came up." She opened her cloak to reveal Moses. "It was an emergency."

Ari's expression darkened and she stepped closer, running her hand across the boy's forehead. "He's too hot. Tell me what's happened."

"He had a fever a few weeks ago but I treated him for it." Scarlet swallowed. "Arwen discovered what I had been doing and punished me by hurting the whole family. I barely managed to get the wee one out."

Ari nodded. "Is he half-Talagan?"

"Yes."

"And his parents?"

"Gone." *Because of me.* "I couldn't save them."

"This is not your fault. This is because of Old Mother, not you. You must remember that." Her friend's eyes narrowed. "You look weary to the bone. Are you staying the night?"

Scarlet shook her head, and gently handed Ari the boy. He'd feverishly slept through their entire escape, blind to all that had transpired. Scarlet was grateful for it, though she could not imagine what the boy would go through once he awoke and everything had to be explained to him.

"I must be on my way. My mission in Merjeri has already taken longer than my stepmother expected. I can't risk it."

A flash of disapproval crossed her friend's face before she leaned closer and pressed a kiss to Scarlet's cheek. "Stay longer next time. I have updates for you on the last batch of folk you brought me. They're thriving on the other side of the sea. Because of *you.* Focus on that when things get dark in Betraz."

Scarlet offered her a tired smile. She was practically falling asleep where she stood. "Of course. Until then."

She kissed the top of Moses' head. "Be strong, little one."

Forcing herself to leave the way she came, for some reason she felt heavier. It would be so easy to just stay here and never go home.

You can't leave your friends behind—nor your people. Don't be selfish.

Each step became stronger as she moved from the cloak

of darkness onto better lit streets of the dock proper. The stores in the area were all still open despite the time of night. No one slept on this side of town.

She intended to visit two apothecaries—both favorites of her stepmother—in order to procure certain desirable elements of her favorite poisons to appease her. Maybe her punishment wouldn't be so harsh.

When has that ever worked?

Arwen didn't know the meaning of mercy.

Providing nobody had spotted Scarlet's escape with the boy, she could safely return to the estate. The lie she had been building was ready—that she'd volunteered to help set up the orphanage but Lady Marianne had guards on her at all times, even when she slept.

It was a flimsy excuse, but Scarlet would have to sell it nonetheless.

Her gaze roamed the area and she paused on a new ship that had arrived during the time she had been inside the Siren's Song. Her brows slashed together.

One of her stepmother's.

Scarlet slammed her back against the stone wall, using the shadows to hide herself. The dock would soon be crawling with Arwen's men. Being spotted by one or two strangers seen visiting an apothecary was one thing, but being spotted by a dozen wolf shifters close to the dock, where refugees were known to be shipped out from, when she was supposed to be returning from Merjeri? That would seal her fate.

She had to escape. She had to leave.

But she couldn't walk away or expose Mills.

What the devil was she going to do?

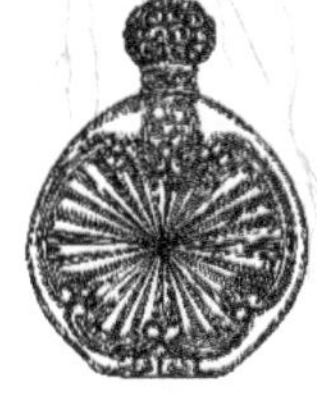

Chapter Seventeen

Scarlet

Move.

Despite the fact she knew she should leave, Scarlet's feet were frozen to the ground.

Rage she'd previously shoved down came bubbling to the surface.

Pain for Abel and Riia.

Regret for Moses.

Before she knew what she was doing, Scarlet had hidden her bag in the heavy vines that trailed across the stone wall she'd been hiding beside. Then she tied back her tangled, dirty, windswept hair, cringing when her fingers dragged through the many knots that had built up. With the hood of her brown cloak up, she walked like a confident but anonymous dockworker.

She should have cared about discovery, but Scarlet was blinded by her anger. This wasn't the sort of life she wanted. Hell, it wasn't even a life. It was prison.

She headed over to the docks with purposeful steps. Confidence was her friend right now. If she looked like she belonged, then everyone would believe she did. It was in this way that Scarlet headed along the jetty, her boots clipping against the wood in a satisfying manner as she followed three sailors onto Lady Betraz's ship, using their preoccupation in loading boxes onto the deck to slink around them and board the ship.

Her pulse leapt as a wolf passed her, not giving her a second glance.

What are you doing?

Instead of backing away and getting off the ship, she moved toward the captain's berth. There was hardly anyone around; everyone was focused on unloading and loading the ship of goods. The captain was long gone. None of Arwen's omega's stuck around to do hard labor. He was probably already off to the pub for a fire whiskey and a woman or two.

Fiddling with her garter for her lockpick, Scarlet closed her eyes, drew in a deep breath, then slipped the tools into the lock until she heard a click. Pleased with her quick work, Scarlet eased open the door and slipped inside. She returned her lockpicks to their hiding place and examined the room.

The captain's berth was in disarray, a clear sign that the man had been restless to return to shore for some time now. The ship had been gone for almost a month. Scarlet wondered what they had been smuggling into the country. She riffled through the paperwork on the desk until she spotted a cabinet full of scrolls, each parchment dating back across the last year.

Perfect.

Information was power.

Scanning through them, Scarlet found the routes for this month, and the next, and the next, a frown shadowing her brow as she looked over the contents.

"Explosives," she murmured, mouthing the word every time her finger ran over it on the page. But it was *only* explosives listed, from the north, from the west, and from the south. Enough to blow a bloody mountain apart. "Why in the name of Dotae does she need this many explosives?" It wasn't as if the mines in Betraz needed them. Humans did most of the work and they were much cheaper than procuring this much firepower.

A dark idea took root in her mind.

If someone was so inclined—they could make a lot of trouble for Old Mother with just one tiny spark. The whole ship would go up in flames.

Walk away.

She couldn't do it.

Scarlet could sink the ship right now.

It was a dangerous plan. Even more foolish than rescuing Moses in the dungeons.

It was because of Moses that she needed to do this. For Abel and Riia.

When would Scarlet have another opportunity to affect this much change? Cause as much damage to her stepmother's cruel reign on the province, and the country at large?

She didn't really know what she was doing, moving on well-honed, silent instinct as she wound her way through corridors and down tiny, steep staircases until she reached the bowels of the ship, where the main cargo hold was located. True to expectations, the hold was roughly half full of casks of explosive powder.

Scarlet made her way around the casks to find the best

one to set alight so she'd have enough time to escape out of the window in the process. She glanced behind the closed door. Many casks had been taken out already, if the clamor up on deck was anything to go by. Which meant there were more than these, so many more.

Scarlet had to get rid of as many of them as she could.

Finally satisfied with her choice of barrel, she pulled out a pack of matches from her cloak, getting ready to light one, when she heard two voices.

They were getting louder. Then the door swung open.

Scarlet didn't have time to think. She pocketed her matches, bent down low, and wound back through the room to try and escape through the door the moment the voices that had entered the belly of the ship were far enough away from her.

But the hold was dark, and Scarlet was only human. She did not see the full scope of the space and before she could make a move to leave, someone grabbed her. A hand covered her mouth, smothering the scream she had been about to emit, and she was yanked against a warm, firm body, taller and broader than hers. Stronger than hers.

She reached for her blades as she recognized the earthy, masculine scent of him. She even recognized the way his breath staggered against her ear, desperate with desire.

It was Brine.

Fate was bloody cruel.

Chapter Eighteen

Brine

"Red?"

Brine couldn't believe it. He had smelled her as soon as he entered the room, instinct forcing him to grab her and push her against him. Red was here. He was *holding* her. He could feel her against his chest.

What the hell is she doing here?

She wriggled against him, struggling furiously and putting up a hell of a fight given their difference in size. Chesh was getting ready to set up the remote detonators that Pyre had made for them using one of his many mysterious tricks. Brine had only entered the hold to doublecheck the fuses he'd placed on the ship minutes before. He and Red didn't have much time to vacate. One minute, maybe two.

Maybe less.

But Brine could hardly think of explosives or ships or mutiny when his nose was full of ginger and peaches, the smell of sunshine and the wind blowing through blond hair. Even though Red was currently soaked in days-old sweat, her hair scraped back against her head and full of grime.

What had she been doing?

"Red, stop struggling," he ordered in hushed tones, growing ever more frantic by the second. They had so little time. But when she bit his hand, Brine found himself barely able to suppress a smile. "If I pull my hand away, will you be quiet?" he asked quietly. There was an interminably long pause before she nodded. And so Brine took his hand away, his grip loosening just enough for Red to turn around and face him when it was clear she was keeping her word to remain quiet.

There was no light in the bowels of the ship, but Brine had wolf eyes. Through the darkness he could see Red, and he could see through the sweat and grime she was currently layered in too. He eagerly drank her in as if she were the most wondrous, beautiful woman he'd ever seen.

Because she was.

And that was a mistake. Brine had lowered his defenses around her once more, and once again the woman pulled something out of her cloak and blew it into Brine's face. This time, however, he did not breathe in deeply, and tilted his head to the side to try to avoid the worst of it. But some of the bitter powder nonetheless made it up his nose, spreading an overwhelming dizziness through his body.

Red made a run for it, making for a window even as Brine grabbed her wrist by instinct and bowled her up the stairs with him before his body could give out. Her struggles were much stronger now that the drugs were in his system, but Brine persisted. Regardless of what she'd been doing on the ship, Red surely could not know that the entire thing was rigged to blow. Under no uncertain circumstances was Brine going to allow her to die, even if she'd tried to flee and knock him unconscious twice now.

As he ascended the stairs, Brine thanked the stars that there were no other people around to witness their escape.

"Where are you—let me go," Red demanded through gritted teeth. Given that she was remaining quiet, Brine established that she was not, in fact, a welcome member of the ship's crew. She was a stowaway, or a spy. He resolved to get all the answers he sought from the mysterious woman the moment they were free from danger.

A loud explosion went off from down below, followed by a terrible tremor vibrating through the entire ship that almost knocked Brine and Red both off their feet.

"Bloody hell!" Red cried, no longer attempting to remain quiet over the sound of screams and shouts and, above all, more explosions. The air was thick with acrid, burning smoke, mixing with the drugs filling Brine's system until his brain and body felt too heavy to use.

Push through it.

"Hold your breath," he slurred out, knowing they had run out of time. Red twisted her head up to stare —blue eyes wide —at him.

"Hold my *what*?"

Brine rushed Red down the corridor and smashed through the nearest window before his senses left him entirely, wrapping his body around Red's to protect her before flinging them out into the bitter, cold water awaiting them at the bottom of their fall.

Then everything went dark.

Chapter Nineteen

Scarlet

Scarlet had always loved the sea. The raw power of it. The promise of escape—of another life beyond the waves that was as far away from her own as could be. This was why she sent refugees across the sea instead of over land, and kept finding herself returning to the pirate city even though she hated it.

But she didn't love the sea tonight.

Tonight, the icy hooks in her flesh promised death.

Everything was a mess. Scarlet's senses were going into overdrive, unable to comprehend what had transpired over the last five minutes. Brine had been there, in the bowels of the ship. He had stopped her dead in her tracks. He had clearly begun working for her stepmother again, if his presence on the ship was anything to go by.

Even though he had left Betraz because he vowed to never do so.

But even so, Brine had found Scarlet and he had grabbed her. Clearly he thought there was no point in her being dead and had intended to save her—even though Scarlet knew with certainty that he did not recognize her for who she really was. That one word he'd said before, the word that was wrong, bounced around inside Scarlet's head as the cold water of the sea pounded her brain.

Mate.

What had Brine meant?

But such thoughts drifted away as Scarlet kicked and thrashed beneath the water, desperately seeking *up* instead of *down* as Brine's arms, which had previously held her tight to protect her from the fall, loosened away to nothing.

Spots of light danced over Scarlet's eyes; her lungs were full of daggers. She needed air. She needed air or she would die.

It felt like forever had passed by the time Scarlet emerged above the crest of a wave and heaved in a breath. She swallowed a hefty mouthful of salty water, too, and coughed and spluttered until her lungs cleared out. Treading water by instinct, Scarlet looked left and right to get her bearings. Now that she was above the surface of the water, the heat from the fire overwhelming her stepmother's ship tickled Scarlet's skin. It was engulfed in flames. She doubted there would be anything left of the ship.

But she hadn't lit any of the casks. Someone else had clearly beaten her to the punch.

A glimmer of movement caught Scarlet's attention—a fin, slicing through the water in her direction. Scarlet had no more time to ponder who had set fire to the ship or why Brine was working for her stepmother again or what his intentions toward her were. She had escaped drowning, and now she had to escape the beast that intended to make her dinner.

Scarlet had never been afraid of animals—shifters and humans were plenty scary enough already—but now she was scared.

She channeled the fear and swam faster than she'd ever swum before, kicking onto the nearest sandy bay situated beside a blackened jetty just as the shape of the creature turned tail and headed back toward the ship for slower prey.

Scarlet hardly dared to breathe. She was alive, and relatively uninjured. Wiping excess water from her face, Scarlet forced herself into a sitting position and scanned the wreckage. Even the jetty that sat to her left had not escaped damage. The smoldering remains of several pieces of exploded wood had broken through its surface, splitting the wharf almost entirely in two. It was barely supporting its own weight.

So Scarlet crawled farther away from the dock, along the sand, until she spied a protective circle of large rocks just down below. She cringed when she jumped down onto them, the stones jarring the muscles of her legs straight through the soles of her boots. For though she was uninjured, her entire body felt broken, and beyond exhaustion. She needed to sleep for days—weeks, even—but knew she was still many hours from sleep, even now.

Only once she was safe from the tumbling jetty did Scarlet look out at the wreckage again. Everywhere there was carnage. Gunpowder in the air, intermingled with smoke and smog and screams and blood and iron. It was a nightmare.

Then Scarlet noticed a dark-haired figure floating in the water and her stomach bottomed out.

Brine.

How could she have forgotten about Brine already? He'd

wrenched her from the ship just in time to save her life. How could she have only thought about saving herself?

Despite the fear of the finned creature probably still lurking nearby, and her aching muscles, Scarlet forced herself back into the water, slid her arms around Brine's chest, and wrenched him out onto the shore. Once she could see him clearly, Scarlet saw that one of his legs was set at an odd angle.

Her stomach heaved but Scarlet knew what she had to do.

Steeling her nerves, she cracked it back into its rightful place, then, with Herculean strength that could only exist because of adrenaline, pulled off a piece of the damaged jetty. Ripping off part of her skirt, she built Brine a makeshift splint to help support his leg. This was all done on memory, skills that Scarlet had honed her entire life overwriting her fear of not knowing what to do. With trembling hands, Scarlet lowered her ear to Brine's lips and listened carefully.

A puff of breath ghosted over her jaw.

Brine was unconscious but still breathing.

Next, she ran her fingers along the back of his head. Relief filled her. There were no bumps or cuts or any other signs that he might have a concussion. So she pulled him farther up the beach, beneath the circle of protective rocks and out of sight.

Shivers wracked her body and she rubbed her hands along her arms.

What was she supposed to do now?

She stared down at the wolf and something in her stomach flipped. He'd been a cute boy when she was a child, but Brine had turned into a handsome man, Her eyes narrowed in disbelief and disgust. Even now, covered in soot and ash and smeared in blood, he was a striking figure. Brine possessed finer features than his uncle but raw masculinity radiated from him.

When Scarlet realized her hand was hovering inches away from stroking Brine's chin, she snapped it back to her chest and stood up.

She didn't have time for this.

Could *never* have time for this.

Brine had been Scarlet's one ray of sunshine when she was little girl.

He left you.

She forced herself to take a step away from her childhood crush. Scarlet couldn't afford to let herself be swayed by childish feelings. Brine was no one to her. Not anymore.

Scarlet limped away on jittery, leaden legs to jump back onto the dock proper to head back to the Siren's Song. She paused and looked over her shoulder at the unconscious wolf she left behind. He looked too vulnerable.

Send Ari to check on him, but leave now.

She turned her back on Brine and walked away.

He was nothing but heartache and trouble.

Scarlet had enough of that in her life already.

Then why was her heart squeezing painfully at the thought of leaving him behind?

Chapter Twenty

Brine

There was salt. There was cold. There was water. But there was also smoke and blood and fire. There were explosions in his ears but also the deafening noise of nothing at all. He was falling, falling, falling, but he wasn't alone. Because there was also the smell of ginger, and peaches, and the warmth of another body clinging to him, trusting him to stay safe.

Then that warmth was gone, along with the water and the salt and the explosions, but everything else remained.

And then there was light.

"Oh good, you're awake."

Brine sat up with a start and immediately fell onto his back. His entire body was in agony.

"Hey there," the familiar voice said. Brine fought through his sluggish brain to work out where he'd heard it. "You hurt your leg pretty bad, but it looks like someone's reset it for you. Might just be a fracture. If you get some mimkia on it, it'll heal in no time, but don't go running a marathon tonight."

It took him much too long to realize who had been speaking. His memory was so broken. But it was coming back in slivers, in tatters, and eventually the voice rang true in Brine's ears.

Chesh. Of course it was Chesh. Brine had been on board his grandmother's ship, rigging it to explode into a million tiny pieces. Everything had been going to plan, but then...

"Where—?" Brine coughed violently, curling onto his side to spit out deathly salty seawater intermingled with blood. He had never felt so rough, not even when he'd been helping Tempest escape Dotae with Briggs and what felt like a thousand city guards had been after them. As his vision grew clearer, he saw Chesh standing by the edge of the surf, tossing bits of torn-up fish into the water without a care in the world. The cat straightened when he felt Brine's gaze on him, picking up on Brine's anxiety when he realized that he was not the person the wolf had expected to be standing there.

"What's wrong?" Chesh asked, genuine concern on his sly face.

It took all of Brine's strength to mutter, "Red."

"...the girl you met before? The one you couldn't find?"

Brine nodded. "She was on—on the ship. I pulled her out before it was blown to smithereens."

Chesh's face lit up with a sudden understanding that escaped Brine. "I spied a figure running from you just as I spotted you. I could tell it was a woman, but she was soaking wet and I couldn't smell anything on her. But if Red was with you when you jumped ship, then it was probably her."

Brine dragged a hand over his face, beyond irritated. Red was alive, which was something, and she hadn't let Brine die, which was even more something, but then she left.

Again.

Just what was Brine supposed to do to get the woman to stay in one position long enough to talk to her?

Sweet poison, it was frustrating.

"How long was I out?" Brine moaned, as he finally managed to force himself into a sitting position. Chesh had spoken true; his leg hurt acutely, indicating that something was broken, but the break had indeed been reset and held together with a makeshift but very good splint. Brine would have to use a *very* generous dose of mimkia over the next three days, but he really would be healed in no time. He patted down his chest, stretched his shoulders and twisted his neck. Everything ached, yes, but nothing else was injured.

Except his pride.

Chesh chucked another dead fish into the water. A fin slid in and out of view just on the edge of Brine's vision, circling in on the tidbits. "About twenty minutes," the cat said. "I tried to wake you but you wouldn't budge. Did Red knock you out again?"

"Shut up," Brine grumbled, hating that in his desperation to find her he'd spilled every detail of his encounter to Chesh like an untried youth.

His friend snickered. "So she did... brut she didn't let you die, and even fixed up your leg. That's something. She's certainly an interesting woman, I'll grant you that. Dangerous, clearly, and potentially mad, but interesting. And you said she's beautiful?"

Brine glared at him and swayed dangerously when he managed to clamber onto his feet. "Stop feeding the damn sharks," he growled, ignoring Chesh's previous jibes. "We have work to do."

The feline complied, throwing the rest of the fish to the

shark or whatever other deadly creature was patiently waiting for the fires to go out on the burning ship before scavenging for fresh, roasted meat. He wordlessly slung an arm around Brine to help him hobble down the docks. There, Brine shrugged off his friend's help before any of his grandmother's men could see them. Needing help was a weakness for them. It wasn't something the wolves of Betraz needed to see.

A look of disapproval crossed Chesh's face. "If you say so," he muttered, rolling his eyes, before taking a respectful step to the left. The docks were a mess, teeming with Old Mother's cronies running in every which direction, unsure about what to do. Out on the sea, the ship was a smoldering ruin, no longer full of the sounds of screams and explosions but eerily quiet.

Brine didn't want to think about how many men he'd just killed.

Despite the chaos on the docks, it was easy for Brine to spot the shifter in charge. He was the only one standing in a singular place, barking orders instead of doing anything himself. Brine charged at him, as fast as his leg would allow, and only stopped when he was face-to-face with the man.

"What do you want?" the man demanded, bristling, before making to bodily shove Brine out of the way. But then he got a good look at him, and he frowned. "Do I know you?"

"Probably not, but you'll be glad to know me now."

"And why is that?"

"Because I would like to offer my services, men, and ship to the Lady of Betraz to help recover everything lost this evening. For a price, of course."

For a moment it looked like the shifter would punch Brine

in the face. But then his expression broke, and he laughed heartily. "Do you know who you're getting into bed with?" He chortled, the audacity of Brine's offer clearly sufficient to break the tension of the ship exploding.

A slow grin crossed Brine's face. "I guess that's something I'll find out in time, won't I? In any case, I'm not rescinding my deal if scaring me off is your intention."

"Then I guess we have a deal." The shifter held out his hand, his shake strong and sure when Brine grasped it. Going by the way the man's entire body relaxed, it was clear he was pleased by this turn of events.

I've no doubt made his job a whole lot easier, Brine mused, *and given him leverage against being punished. Of course he's pleased.*

The first step of his and Chesh's plan had been executed almost flawlessly.

Almost, because Red had been there, and now she was gone, and Brine had no idea if he would ever see her again.

For the sake of his duty, it was better for him if she disappeared entirely, like the ghost she was.

He knew that was the last thing he wanted.

Chapter Twenty-One

Arwen

She had always been attracted to flowers.

Arwen ran her fingers along the tops of the purple blossoms of the mimkia plants. Not because they looked beautiful and delicate, but because they held power and death. Everyone underestimated a flower just like they underestimated her.

A sigh escaped her as a moment of peace settled over her shoulders like a childhood blanket—warm and comforting. There were no schemes or betrayals here in her underground fields. Only a gardener and her garden.

She inhaled the sweet scent of the flowers. If she closed her eyes and pretended, it almost felt like home. A pang of homesickness struck her chest and she gasped at the unexpected pain. Arwen growled, claws elongating from her fingertips as the pain turned to rage. She tore at the flowers at her side and threw them through the air, dirt spraying around her. She tipped her head back and howled, the pained sound echoing around the cavern.

Even here in her place of solace, the past haunted her. She

gritted her teeth and stomped over to the uprooted flowers. Gently, she plucked them from the path, got to her hands and knees, then used her claws to dig a small hole in the earth.

It enraged Arwen that the elves could still affect her after so many years. Carefully, she set the mimkia roots and plant into the hole, filling it with dirt. Patting the ground around the plant, she leaned back on her knees and stared blankly at the wilting flower. Maybe the elvish elders had been right about her—her emotions ran too deep.

Don't let them get into your head. You're not that young half-breed anymore. You're a queen. Act like it.

Bowing her head, Arwen slowly calmed, watching as her claws retracted until only the black tips were visible. How many times had she tried to rip them from her body as a young girl? Trying to eradicate any evidence that she was both elf and shifter? They had been her greatest shame.

A sharp smile curled her lips.

Now, they were one of her greatest weapons.

The elders had been right about her. Not because she'd been born of two peoples but because of their own cruelty. They'd created their own monster and then condemned her for it.

The elves should have killed her instead of sending her into exile.

That was their mistake.

Arwen had a very long lifespan thanks to her elvish mother—stars rest her soul—and Arwen had been planning for years to make the elders suffer for their crimes.

Her head snapped up as she heard someone enter the cavern. There was only one person brave enough to invade her haven without express permission.

Bright—her second—her youngest son.

She slowly rose to her feet and brushed off her black dress, dirt still staining her fingers. She watched him stride down the winding path through the mimkia. The alpha never went running to anyone. They came to her.

Bright bowed low and waited.

A smile lifted her lips. He was such an obedient male—always had been. Too bad he hadn't been the eldest. He would have made a perfect alpha. Thoughts for another time.

"What is it?" she asked, still not giving him permission to rise. "I assume you have dire news if you seek to ruin my time of reflection?"

"I am sorry, my lady. It was not my intention to ruin your solitude, but I must speak with you."

"Rise," she said, irritated at his sincerity. "What is it?"

Bright rose slowly, his silver gaze hovering near her cheek, not looking Arwen directly in the eyes out of respect. "There has been an attack."

She pursed her lips and arched a brow. "There are attacks all the time. You must be more specific, darling."

He nodded once. "One of the cargo ships carrying goods bound for the hinterlands was hit."

Now that was a piece of interesting news. No one had been bold enough to touch any of her cargo in a *long* time. No one stupid enough, anyway.

"And the cargo?" she drawled.

"At the bottom of the sea."

The empress would not be pleased at the delay, but Arwen could handle the viper-like woman. She was only human after all. Practically an insect. "Who?"

Bright's expression didn't waver, a trick she'd taught him herself. "There are no leads."

"Not a single person has laid claim to this act?" Usually, men loved to brag about their deeds.

"No. There's not a bloody whisper about who orchestrated it all."

It was an inconvenience that would surely end in bloodshed, but it intrigued Arwen. She loved a game of cat and mouse. And it had been a long time since someone had tried to match their wits against hers.

"I do have a bit of good news."

"Oh?" she said, eyeing Bright.

He lifted his chin and met her gaze for the first time. "We managed to procure another ship to replace the one we lost."

"Pirates, I presume?"

"No." Bright shifted his feet, the first sign of any feeling on the matter. "Someone we know."

"Out with it," she barked, hating how long this conversation was taking.

"It's Brine's."

Arwen blinked slowly. Brine. What a surprise. She'd anticipated dragging him back into the fold by his tail. "And what does he want for such an offer?" Everything had strings attached.

"It is an act of goodwill so that he may come home."

She grinned. No one left the pack for good. They always came home. It had only been a matter of time before her wayward grandson came back where he belonged. He'd dallied with the Dark Court for long enough. While she appreciated his endeavors of building something on his own, he belonged here among his own kind.

"Well then, we should welcome him home with open arms, should we not?"

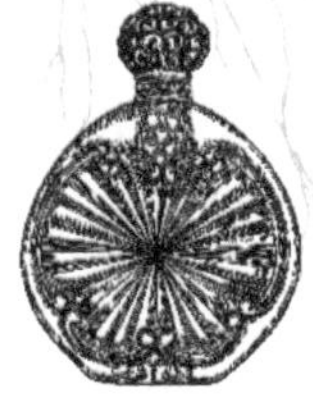

Chapter Twenty-Two

Scarlet

The beating had been worth it.

It had been the worst beating Scarlet had ever experienced. The longest. The bloodiest. The most public. But she had gotten away with saving the half-shifter boy, and had even witnessed her stepmother's ship being blown to smithereens.

A smile pulled at her split bottom lip.

That was something she'd never forget.

At least, no one had figured out she'd been in Callmai or that she'd been the one to free Moses.

The beating she had been given as punishment for failing to dispatch Lady Marianne was something Scarlet could definitely take.

She sighed, her knuckles cracking as she scrubbed the floors of the manor. That was only a nuisance. With each movement, pain radiated from her hands and knees so that it was all Scarlet could do to inch, millimeter by millimeter, across the varnished wooden surface to perform her daily chores.

Her gaze flicked around the room once. No guards were watching her. That was something.

She was working at a snail's pace; by the time she finished work today—if she managed to finish at all—it would be time to start cleaning the floors all over again come morning.

With a sigh, Scarlet pulled herself up into a sitting position, though the sigh turned into a gasp of agony as the fresh wounds on her back from the whipping cracked open, aching and bleeding anew. She grimaced as the linen of her dress stuck to her back.

The back of her neck prickled and she wiped all expression from her face. A group of wolves were travelling by on their way to the grand reception hall. Scarlet forced herself to hold their gazes and not cower away from them, though they leered and laughed at her in obvious delight.

This was also part of her stepmother's plan to punish her, to humiliate her: to ensure she knew her place. Yes, they all knew she performed each and every one of Old Mother's dark and dirty jobs, but she was not infallible. She could fail just like the rest of them and, just like the rest of them, Scarlet was also punished.

Worse than everyone else.

It kept everyone in line, knowing there was someone on the ladder lower than them.

Her punishment had begun by stripping off her clothes, because what was punishment if it wasn't naked? Then the lashing of her back had begun, the narrow leather whipping into her skin again and again and again. At this point Scarlet had firmly believed she could no longer feel any pain, but she'd been wrong. For then all the wolves present had tossed ash on her, the dark, dusty mess stinging her fresh wounds with an indescribable new wave of agony. The ash filled her lungs too, stealing her breath and making her unable to hold back her coughing and spluttering.

But even then the humiliation had not been over.

Arwen ordered Scarlet to clean the floors, which of course never stayed clean because the ash clinging to her body, congealing in her blood, would fall to the wooden floor as she moved. Then Scarlet had to start all over again.

This was Scarlet's third day in a row of cleaning the floors. At least this time she was clothed. Come tomorrow she was finally allowed to apply mimkia to the wounds. Scarlet was, quite literally, counting down the minutes until she would finally experience some sweet, cool relief.

The only other relief she'd had for three days was thinking about escaping… and Brine.. Scarlet knew she shouldn't. It would get her nowhere—only hurt her further—to think of him. But his amazement and delight at seeing Scarlet once more, despite the circumstances, was impossible for her to forget. Not to mention the way he'd so earnestly protected her from the burning ship, protecting her body with his own as they crashed through the glass and fell into the sea.

In return she'd drugged him, and almost caused his death.

You're poison.

Guilt wracked Scarlet. She'd asked Ari to look after him, but she'd found out that morning by way of secret messenger that Brine hadn't been lying on the beach when the siren went out looking for him. Scarlet could only hope this meant someone else had helped him.

He left you and he's working for them. Don't spare a second thought.

Don't think about it, don't think about it, don't think about it, Scarlet thought over and over again, like a mantra. But, as if on cue, Arwen's voice then filled the corridor, and Scarlet realized she had paused in her duties for several long minutes. She began scrubbing again.

Lady Betraz glided down the hallway as if walking on air, resplendent in ornate black silks and transparent, gauzy material enveloping her arms. Her silver hair was elaborately woven and braided back with heavy black diamonds worth half a kingdom. Blithely, Scarlet wondered who the imminent guest was. All the wolves were congregating in the reception hall and her stepmother was dressed so richly.

When Arwen made her way over to Scarlet, she dismissed Bright—who had been watching over Scarlet's chores to ensure she did not try to escape them—with a wave of her hand. He had been silent as he observed, as usual, but Scarlet had been glad for his company nonetheless. At the very least, it had stopped Tarros from bothering her, which was infinitely worse than the punishment she had been made to suffer in front of him. The jeering, twisted, filthy curses that he threw at her as she was flogged had perhaps been the worst part of the entire ordeal.

Once they were alone, Arwen circled Scarlet in slow, deliberate steps. "It pains me to see you like this," she complained. Scarlet did not look up from her soapy brush as she scrubbed, though her back ached with the strain. "How disappointed I am in you, daughter! You must know this. But alas, you must also know that this is your fault."

She waited for Scarlet to respond, but Scarlet did not think she had it in her to speak a single word. Instead Scarlet nodded.

"I suppose we must all make mistakes sometimes," she said, stopping her circling to stand directly in front of Scarlet, right where she had just cleaned. With a twitch of anger, Scarlet noticed Arwen's heeled shoes had trailed dark muck in from outside. Scarlet would have to clean the entrance hall.

Again.

"It is a shame that you failed such an important mission. But a good leader always has a backup plan. So do not worry, daughter of mine, for Merjeri and Heimserya at large shall soon be mine." Silence followed then, soft and threatening, which was why Scarlet knew to tense up just as Arwen bent down and roughly grabbed Scarlet by her hair, dragging her to her feet.

Scarlet bit back a cry of pain, her spine tingling as blood began dripping down her back, beneath the fabric of her dress. She had never been so grateful for the red cloak around her shoulders, enshrouding her from others having to see her so weak.

Arwen's eyes were humorless as they locked on Scarlet's, dark as pitch and just as sparkly as the diamonds in her hair. "You may have gotten away with your insolence," she hissed, all previous gaiety lost in an instant, "but know that it will not be tolerated. Just as you have been punished for failing in Merjeri, so you have been punished for helping that filthy mongrel boy. I can't prove it was you—you're far too clever for that, you are *my* daughter after all—but know that his parents have been executed. Their deaths were not pretty. I imagine you would have hated it. *You* are responsible for them. Remember that, daughter dearest."

Scarlet wanted to scream. She wanted to pull at her

stepmother's hand and bite down into the meat of it. She wanted to drive a dagger slowly but surely into the snake's heart. She wanted to find out how Moses parents died and inflict *that* upon her stepmother.

For a moment, she thought of how alive and dangerous Brine had felt, when he was pressed against Scarlet, and how easily he would have been able to take down a woman such as Arwen. He'd possessed the strength and speed and smarts for it. He *could* do it, even though he wouldn't, because he was working for her again.

She hated everything. Brine, her stepmother, and especially herself, for despite her anger Scarlet still found herself frozen in her inability to do a bloody thing.

But that knowledge helped immeasurably in maintaining Scarlet's blank face, for which she was grateful. It would not do to show her stepmother how upset she was.

Arwen traced a long nail down the scar on Scarlet's face, the smallest of smiles curling her lips. "Good," she whispered. "Keep it all inside. I trained you well."

"Lady Betraz," a servant said when he approached from a side door. He bowed politely. "Your guest is almost here."

Arwen dropped Scarlet to the floor as if she were nothing of importance, ignoring her splutters of pain and the blood she leaked onto the varnished wood, then turned on her heel and left.

Scarlet wanted to curl up and cry. She wanted to scream. She wanted to hurt her stepmother. She wanted to hurt herself.

She kept on scrubbing.

Kept pretending that everything was okay.

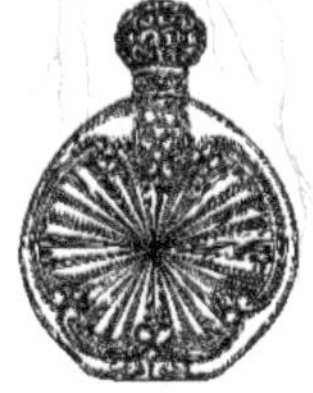

Chapter Twenty-Three

Brine

Brine stood in the reception hall of the Betraz Manor awaiting his grandmother. She had made him wait two full days before accepting an audience with him. In truth, he had expected her to test his patience much longer. He'd known she would make him wait; it was her style. But considering the unstable state of affairs within the country, Brine reasoned Lady Betraz couldn't afford to wait long.

So here Brine was, alone, having left Chesh behind in the pirate city with instructions to keep working with his grandmother's captain and the other ships trading in the area, gathering as much information as was possible. They needed every snippet of gossip to use to their advantage. This, at least, Brine knew he could entrust to Chesh. No one was better at coaxing out gossip than the feline—not even Pyre.

Which was saying something.

His uncle had accompanied Brine to the manor, having shown up Salmiere a day's ride from the province of Betraz, along the Fiergone River.

The man hadn't spoken a word to him throughout their entire journey back to the place he had once called home. His uncle was as tired and stoic-looking as ever, but now there was more gray in his hair than Brine had remembered seeing on him as a child. He decided the silver hair looked good on him. Made him look more refined. Regal. Even the ropey scars that littered his skin added to the look, though Brine knew far better than to place much stock in appearances.

His uncle was still working for Old Mother after all. He could have left when Brine's father died, taking Brine with him, or he could have left with Brine when he decided he could no longer stand to live in Betraz. But the older wolf had done neither of these things. He remained where he was, for whatever reason Brine had never fully understood. It wasn't as if Bright was close with Arwen. Brine was sure his uncle didn't even like her. But still, here Bright was, doing her bidding in bringing Brine along to the province of Betraz.

A loyal dog.

It made Brine sick.

A nameless crew of young wolves that Brine did not recognize had met them when they entered the estate, taking over Bright's duties so his could race on ahead to the manor proper to respond to some order or other. He was *escorted* to a log cabin along the edge of town and locked in. Two uncomfortable nights later, Brine found himself now in the reception hall with dread creeping down his spine.

A hundred horrible memories assaulted him as he remembered everything that had gone on here. The blood, the beatings, the pain... He exhaled slowly, keeping his mask in place. While this place held mostly bad memories, he had a few precious good ones. All of them involving a blond-haired, peach-carrying little girl.

Every time he found her she was in a garden or amongst the old book in the library.

Both places of peace.

His mood soured. The reception hall was not one of them. It was where Arwen made her victims wait their punishments.

You are not one of her victims. She is your *prey.*

His attention snapped to the entrance as Bright stepped into the hall. The older wolf didn't even nod at Brine, let alone speak. It had always been safer not to speak back in the day. Words could so easily be used against you, especially when others were taught to always listen and report back to Old Mother. Brine could appreciate this far more now than when he was a child—he'd learned so much from within the safety of the Dark Court—but it still put him on edge. What was his uncle playing at? Was it all a game? Or something more heartbreaking? Had Bright completely lost his soul and will to Arwen?

Bright kept his attention focused on the figure behind him and opened the door wider to let someone in. Brine braced himself.

Here we go.

His brows furrowed slightly as he spotted two figures just outside. He inhaled deeply and stiffened. A faint, familiar scent. Something wasn't right. A spy perhaps?

Brine stared hard as his grandmother garbed in fanciful black silk sauntered inside. He brushed off his curiosity and forced himself to focus. Bowing low, he allowed his grandmother to walk past, her onyx dress whispering over the stone floor. He kept his eyes pinned to the ground despite how the hair at the back of his neck prickled. His grandmother may have been *ignoring* him but make no mistake, she was sizing him up.

"Rise."

He straightened as she turned her back on him and wasted no time in moving toward a second set of doors that lead to her reception hall.

"Follow," she called over her shoulder as Bright opened the doors for them, the second figure staying far back behind them.

Brine moved to stand in the center of the room, silent shifters standing along the walls of the room. His grandmother moved to pour herself a drink, a smile teasing the corners of her lips. Seeing her once again was shocking. With her half-elven blood she looked much younger than her age, flawless and beautiful in a terrifying way. There was a predatory, hawk-like look to her dark eyes as she trained them on Brine. Her long, midnight black nails tapped a calculating rhythm against her arm goblet as she took a healthy sip. She raised a black eyebrow, as almost in a challenge.

He knew the score.

Brine knelt in the middle of the room and waited.

His grandmother placed her cup on the gold tray and approached him. He held completely still and allowed her to circle him like a shark. Silence followed, punctuated only by the clack-clack-clack of Arwen's heels upon the floor. Not a single shifter in the hall dared speak. It felt as if nobody was even breathing, including Brine.

She circled him for so long Brine became certain that his grandmother was going to cut along his exposed neck, lopping off his head, and for a horrible second he realized he'd walked into a trap. But it was too late now to save his life if the purpose of him being here was to die, so Brine stayed still and steady.

"How you've grown," she murmured. "Rise."

Brine did as he was told, keeping his gaze on the floor. No need to challenge her.

Yet.

Arwen was shorter than him, but she was wearing high-heeled boots that brought her almost up to his eyeline. Gently, so gently, she cupped his cheek, his sharp black nails whispering across his cheekbone.

Brine braced himself. He also knew what came after such tenderness.

Pain. Always pain.

When the slap came, it hit hard and fast, the woman's talons just barely slicing into the surface of his cheek. He rocked back, stunned by the strength in Arwen's hand, but didn't stumble. He held his ground and simply stared down at his grandmother in silence, knowing he had to wait for her to speak first.

Very slowly, her smile transformed into a full-on wolfish grin—though she hated the wolf side of her ancestry—and spread her arms wide. "Welcome home, grandson. It is good to have you back in our midst."

Brine breathed an internal sigh of relief.

The second hurdle of his suicidal plan had been successfully cleared.

He'd been accepted back into the pack by the Alpha.

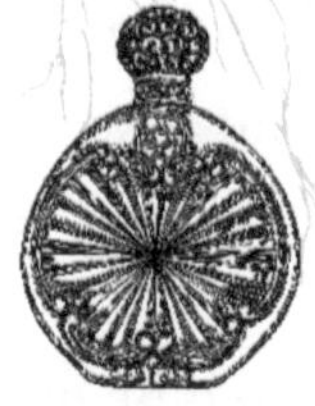

Chapter Twenty-Four

Scarlet

"Did you hear? Lady Arwen's grandson has returned!"

Scarlet froze with a spoon halfway to her mouth. The contents spilled back into a wooden bowl. "What do you—what do you mean?" she asked the servant who had come to change the linens.

"He arrived three days ago. You really didn't know? That was who Lady Arwen was entertaining in the reception hall! Scarlet, are you ... all right?" The servant frowned in concern. Scarlet couldn't even force a smile to her pale face. She got to her feet, abandoning her breakfast, and wordlessly bowled past the servant and out of her room.

No.

That's who had been in the grand entrance earlier this morning. She hadn't even dared to look up from the floor when they'd entered the house. Arwen had been in a foul mood that Scarlet didn't want to test.

Stupid, stupid, stupid.

She gasped, her breathing labored as she skidded downstairs and along hallways until she reached the kitchen.

Never had she been so glad for mimkia. The wounds on her back barely even smarted now, even at her breakneck pace through the manor.

He can't be here. If he's here, then...

Scarlet was buggered.

"Jaq! Gus!" Scarlet cried the moment she burst into the kitchen, then, "Dris!" when she saw that she was thankfully also there. They turned to her in surprise, which rapidly evolved into fear when they saw how panicked she was.

"Whatever is the matter?" Dris asked, dropping the rolling pin in her hands to rush over to Scarlet. Her sons were quick to do the same, though the rest kitchen staff did not stopped what they were doing. None of them would get to eat if the people responsible for cooking breakfast for the residents of the manor stopped working. They had long since learned not to get themselves involved with any and all drama involving Scarlet.

Her hands shook as she ushered all three of her friends into the pantry.

"What is wrong dearest? You look like you've seen a ghost," Dris said, eyes crinkled in concern.

"I've made a horrible mistake," Scarlet whispered. "I'm going to get everyone killed."

Jaq's eyes narrowed. "Explain."

So she did.

About meeting and helping biracial couples and children. Meeting Brine in Merjeri, about how she couldn't dispatch the Lady Marianne, about the Callmai. About a haphazard, stupid plan to blow up her stepmother's ship, and how she had run into Brine there once again. How he had caught her red-handed, ready to light up the casks of explosives, and how he had saved her life. She had done the same in return, even though it was clear Brine was working for his grandmother once again.

"He's back," she said, voice trembling.

Wordlessly, Dris yanked a rough-spun bag from beneath the floorboards in the pantry and shoved it into Scarlet's arms. The bag had been placed there years ago, constantly restocked so she could leave at a moment's notice, should she need to. Such as right now.

"You must go, Scarlet," Gus urged, his brother nodding in agreement.

"But..." Scarlet didn't know what else to say. What about the three of them? She didn't want to leave everyone here. Her friends. Her people. Her home. She couldn't run away and leave them to Arwen and the wolves. She had sworn to free the humans from the diamond mines, but she could do nothing of the sort if she ran away. "I can't leave you."

"You cannot stay either," Jaq replied.

Dris pushed Scarlet out of the pantry and through the kitchen, the twins following closely behind. "We're not taking no for an answer," the older woman urged, quickly kissing Scarlet on the cheek goodbye before shoving her through the door, the twins in tow to help her through the gardens. That has always been Dris's way. Quick, efficient, and a spine of steel. No nonsense. A kiss on the cheek was perhaps the most open gesture of affection she had ever shown Scarlet despite how much they deeply loved each other.

Tears filled her eyes at the prospect of never seeing her surrogate mother again, but Scarlet forced them back. She couldn't cry now.

Just as the three of them reached the gate, Texel stopped his perimeter sweep with Tarros by his side. Her blood ran cold and a shiver of fear ran up her spine. On instinct, she dropped the bag at her feet and stood over it, obscuring the pack beneath her cloak. Her heart raced as the pair caught sight of her, Tarros's gaze turning molten as it always did when it lingered on her for too long.

Her breath caught and time seemed to suspend itself.

Tarros smiled and then glanced away, the moment broken as they continued on, his limp still pronounced.

Scarlet stared at the twins in dismay, so weak in the knees she almost collapsed onto the damp morning grass. She could not leave now.

"Too many eyes have seen us," she rasped, feeling sick. "If I go now, they'll kill you both. There's no way I can leave now."

"You must," Gus said, picking up the pack. "Don't worry about us."

"No." Scarlet shook her head. "Your mother will be punished as well. You know that. I could never do that."

For a moment, the twins looked like they were going to argue with her, but ultimately, they knew better. They both knew that Arwen would slaughter her way through the staff in punishment.

She curled her fingers into fists and swallowed down her fear. Arwen had been threatening to kill her for years. It shouldn't scare her. She'd finally have peace for the living hell that inhabited her life. Heat pressed at the back of her eyes.

Stay strong. Don't cry.

"Lady Scarlet," a soft but authoritative voice said from behind them. "I have been looking everywhere for you."

Scarlet blinked hard and turned. The voice belonged to Mourne, one of her stepmother's enforcers. He was of a lighter complexion than most of the other wolves, with pale amber eyes and light sandy coloring to his cropped hair. Scarlet sparred with him sometimes, because he was one of the only wolves who didn't go out of his way to inflict as much pain on her as possible.

But that didn't mean he was a friend either.

He was as much of a spy as she was.

Scarlet inclined her head politely. It was the only thing she was capable of accomplishing. "What is it?" she managed.

"Lady Arwen has summoned you. If you would follow me to the reception hall, I'd be much obliged."

A polite command.

Scarlet fought her shaking hands and unease that filled her. Her veins thrummed with adrenaline, her fight-or-flight response ready and raring to go even though she could do neither.

Arwen knew.

This was it. This was how she died.

Still healing from a flogging, her body aching, unable to fight back.

Surrounded by wolves that would revel in seeing her break in two.

All at the hands of her oldest—and once only—friend.

Chapter Twenty-Five

Brine

Brine was standing before what he used to call "the throne" as a child. Of course it wasn't a throne, because sat upon it was not the ruling monarch of Heimserya. But to his small eyes the large, ornately carved mahogany chair with gold trim seemed plenty extravagant enough to be a throne.

As was the woman who now sat upon it, flanked on either side by his uncle and several other high-standing wolves, including a red wolf who rankled Brine to no end. His name was Texel, Brine was fairly certain. And in the small crowd of wolves milling around in the room waiting to hear what news Brine had for the group, was another grizzled, maimed, mangled wolf Brine was fairly certain was Texel's son.

Not only that: the son fit the description of the shifter Damien had so thoroughly dismembered in the forest several weeks before. He had done so to save a maiden, though considering it was Damien, Brine was almost positive he always used a maiden as an excuse for his bloodshed. Regardless, Brine did not like the father or the son upon immediate observation.

In truth, he didn't like the look of most of the wolves in the pack. They looked weak, and cruel, and too eager to follow instructions without thinking about what those instructions really meant.

The entire pack needed gutting from the inside out. Which was exactly why he was here.

"So what have you been up to all these many years since you left home?" Arwen said from her throne, almost lazily. She said it as if Brine had gone on a trip, rather than to flee as far as he could from her, as if she had the plague. She tapped her nails impatiently upon the shiny surface of the desk in front of her chair, though it was bereft of documents or adornments and so seemed to Brine functionally useless aside from a surface upon which she could tap her nails.

The act irritated him, but Brine made sure that his irritation did not show in his countenance. He had to appear principled, disciplined, and strong, not short-tempered or emotional. If he showed his emotions he was as good as dead.

He took a breath and plunged headfirst into the story Pyre had helped Brine concoct; the fox's imagination was far superior to his own. "I was young and hungry to make my mark," he said. "I wanted to try and strike out on my own. So I helped to create the Dark Court. This I am proud of. But when the Jester decided to side with the weak young queen, I knew my time with them was up. So I left. And here I am."

Arwen's dark eyes fixed on him. "So what of Merjeri?" she asked. "I know you've been causing issues there. Issues that directly affect me. So why should I trust you?"

Pyre told him to expect his grandmother to know of him causing problems in Merjeri. So for this he had yet another lie. "It was the last job I chose to do for the Dark Court in order to get close to the dragon and his mate," Brine said, ignoring an insatiable urge to scratch his nose. It was vitally important he remained stock-still while he lied, keeping his heart as steady as possible. "Given what they've been up to the last few months, I believed you would want to take vengeance against them for destroying your links with the head of Merjeri. Not only that..." Brine stopped for effect. "...the Dragon King has access to travel through the mountains to the elven lands. That vengeance is personal for you, I know. But if there was a way to capture his mate and use her as leverage against him, I have no doubt you could find a way to best use the Dragon King's travel routes to your advantage."

This piqued Arwen's interest in the precise way Pyre, Damien, and Brine all knew it would. She sat up straighter on her throne, unable to hide the fact that Brine's news was both unexpected and very, very welcome. Then, out of the corner of his eye, Brine spied a red-cloaked figure step through a doorway, followed by an unfamiliar shifter with sandy hair.

The scent that wafted through the door was familiar, and Brine stiffened.

Sweet poison, *no*.

The cloaked figure was Red.

His Red.

His *mate*.

A shudder ran through his body as he forced himself not to move in her direction. He watched her from the corner of his eye as she approached the throne, crimson cloak brushing the floor.

A chord of familiarity struck him.

The red cloak…

He'd heard gossip in Merjeri of a crimson cloaked assassin who worked for Old Mother. Though it was said she had saved several members of the Hood's men and allowed them to escape Arwen's clutches…

It can't be.

Yet there she was beside his grandmother. Arwen grinned at him as Red knelt next to the throne. She pulled back Red's hood and stroked his mate's long, wispy, blond hair.

Everything in Brine rebelled at the action.

Rage ignited in his gut as he spied the bruises across her face. Someone had struck her several times. His gaze latched onto his grandmother's hand petting Red and it made him want to tear the appendage from her body.

How dare Arwen touch what was his? It was outrageous.

Calm down. She's playing with you.

Brine managed to keep his emotions in check. It was only a show of power. Arwen didn't know what Red could mean to him. She was just showing her dominance over the young woman and yet… she was watching Brine with anticipation. What was her game?

"My dear grandson, I thought to introduce you to my blade."

"Your blade?" he said, voice bland.

"Yes. You see Red is my personal helper in all things."

"How fortuitous for you."

Arwen chuckled. "You have been gone for a long time. I'm surprised you don't recognize her."

Waring bells rang in his head. "Whatever do you mean?"

"It seems you forgot your closest childhood friend."

His blood ran cold and then hot as Red lifted her head and met his gaze square on, her blue eyes burning into his.

"Let me introduce you to Lady Scarlet of Betraz."

The room wavered around him. It all made perfect sense.

Why he was drawn to her. Why she seemed familiar.

Red was Scarlet, his young childhood friend.

Arwen had known they were close when he was young—had known she was one of the only bright spots in his life before he ran away.

The sweet little girl he remembered was nowhere to be found in Red's expressionless face.

His gut churned. Had Arwen been grooming Scarlet this whole time as Red just to use her against Brine in the eventuality—the inevitability—that he would return? Was she truly that coldly calculating?

Brine could not doubt it, but he couldn't face it being true either.

"Your information is more than interesting," Arwen said, still patting Red's—Scarlet's—hair. Scarlet remained expressionless and silent, even though Brine couldn't tear his eyes from her. He couldn't help it. "But you must know we cannot just welcome you back. You need to complete a trial to be accepted into the pack."

Brine had expected this. With difficulty, he dragged his attention from Scarlet, which was difficult given how enticing she smelled, and nodded his consent.

An ugly grin spread across Arwen's face, and he knew he would not like what she said next.

"If you are successful," she said, emphasizing the *if*, "then at the end of the celebrations you must choose a bride. Then and there. This is not for discussion. As my grandson, you are thereby my only remaining blood relative from my firstborn capable of fathering a child. I will not be without an heir to my enterprise again."

This Brine hadn't expected. Every hair on his body stood on end. The woman had an agenda.

Well, she always has an agenda, but what's her play this time?

He couldn't work it out.

He locked eyes with Scarlet, even though there was nothing in her gaze for him, and he nodded again. "Of course. I accept."

"Begone then. The preparations will be made."

Summarily dismissed, Brine turned tail and stalked through the reception hall. As he reached the edge of the room he found cause to glance back over his shoulder, and caught the mangled red wolf in the crowd staring covetously—dangerously—at Scarlet. The shifter was scratching at his hands in his effort to keep them to himself.

Brine's hackled rose and he smothered a growl.

Was Scarlet the maiden Damien helped? How long has this pathetic wretch of a wolf been bothering Scarlet? What has he managed to do to her so far?

A horrible shudder rattled Brine's body as he forced himself to leave the hall. He had no idea who Scarlet really was, and whose side she was on, but regardless of her uncertain character, Brine still felt an overwhelming possessiveness, and protectiveness, over her. The mere thought of another wolf digging his claws into her was too much bear.

Calm down. You're letting yourself be sucked in again.

He pushed the thought from his head to focus on what the

next few days would have in store for him. Before his trial, he was determined to work out who the devil Red, or Scarlet, truly was.

Now there wasn't much time.

Was she the soft-hearted girl who saved his life when they were children ... or the coldhearted double-crosser who both committed evil assassinations for his stepmother whilst at the same time saving members of the Hood's Merry Men—who'd saved Brine's life even as she drugged him?

Brine doubted he would get any answers unless he asked Scarlet directly.

This time, he'd make sure she had no pockets of sleeping powder.

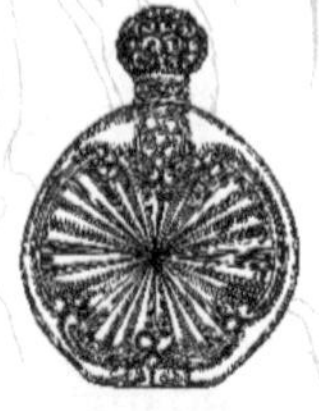

Chapter Twenty-Six

Scarlet

It had been two days since Brine recognized her and stayed silent.

Through the combination of her hidden supply of mimkia and sheer determination, her wounds had healed and she hadn't slept. Every time the sun went down, she sat next to the door with her weapons and waited for the inevitable.

But Arwen's wolves never came.

Neither did Brine.

She rolled her neck and tossed her cloak onto the fence surrounding the sparring yard. Mourne eyed her from the far side of the ring.

"You ready?"

"As I'll ever be," she muttered, bracing herself. "Go!"

The wolf launched himself at Scarlet and she entered fight mode as he swung at her. She ducked out of the way and danced out of his range. Mourne never let her down when it came to sparring. He always made time for her. And today, all she wanted to do was let off some steam.

She was filled with anger and fear.

Every time she spotted Brine around the estate, Scarlet had managed to avoid him. That couldn't last forever. Arwen wouldn't allow her to skulk around. She liked to watch Scarlet squirm too much.

Scarlet landed a punch on Moune's ribs and rolled out of the way as he sent a jab her way. She danced out of the way, mind full of too many questions.

Why had he been on her stepmother's ship? Why did he want to know why she was there? Why did he say silent?

Because he thinks you're his mate.

Which was really laughable. As if a wolf and a human could make a life together in Betraz.

Plus, a mate wasn't something special. It was a physical reaction of the pheromones of another. It wasn't preordained. It was coincidence. Nothing more.

Her mind wandered back to the night in Callmai. It was one of the stupidest things she'd ever done. It rankled that she didn't know why Brine was there. Something just didn't add up. Who would target Old Mother's ship? Sure, there were those disgruntled with her, but none crazy enough to try anything.

What bothered her the most was the fact that Brine seemed to *anticipate* the explosion. Could he have been the cause?

"Pay attention!" Mourne chastised, kicking the back of her knees, sending her sprawling to the ground. "It isn't like you to be in your own head when you're fighting."

"I know," she grumbled, allowing Mourne to give her a hand to help her back to her feet. She groaned and rubbed her bum. Her tailbone smarted. "The trial was on my mind though. There hasn't been one in years."

Mourne nodded. “Indeed. What do you think about it? I’ve heard rumors that Lady Arwen’s grandson is not allowed to shift during the trial.”

Scarlet held a hand to her mouth, uncharacteristically unable to keep her emotions from her face. “But that’s ... he’ll surely die!” The idea bothered her more than she liked.

“One has to wonder if that’s the point.”

Scarlet considered this carefully. Was that what she wanted? For Brine to die? Truly, Scarlet had no idea how loyal he was to her stepmother. She supposed it made sense that, even if he wasn’t all that loyal to her, there was no point in openly displaying this. But if he submitted to this trial then he was dead.

She sighed.

What was the point of it? Scarlet was tired of the games. Regardless, she knew constantly troubling herself with Brine’s fate would ultimately lead to nowhere but misery.

She rubbed her temples and winced. While she was able to heal her hidden wounds, Arwen had expressly forbidden her from healing the ones on her cheeks. Her face looked like an overripe fruit.

“Are you ready to go again?” Mourne asked as he picked up two wooden practice swords.

She nodded and took the sword from the wolf.

They got in position.

“En garde!” Mourne shouted.

Mourne and Scarlet twirled and danced around each other, neither one of them letting up an inch. Mourne was only three inches taller than Scarlet, and lean rather than broad, so they were well-matched in the fight. Scarlet was faster than him, but Mourne was a killer with a sword. All

Scarlet needed was an entrance through which she could dart out with her dagger to beat him, but it was tough going when she hadn't sparred since before her ill-fated trip to Merjeri.

But then, when she was wiping sweat from her brow to stop it from stinging her eyes, she noticed that Mourne seemed to lean ever so slightly on his left heel whenever he was about to make a full strike on his right. Testing this knowledge, Scarlet went through the motions of believing the parry to be real, even though this meant Mourne got in a hit on her left shoulder that sent her teeth chattering.

Two minutes later, Scarlet saw him lean on his heel again, so she let him strike—this time on her waist—just to confirm her suspicions. Satisfied that she'd learned one of Mourne's tells, she let out a shuddering breath in surrender, and clutched at her winded chest.

"You win. Until next time?"

Mourne grinned, flashing long fangs in victory, completely oblivious to the fact that Scarlet had now worked out how to best him in the future.

Next time, my friend.

She wondered how long it would take him to work out she'd figured out his tell.

Just then, as if Scarlet were attuned to his movements, she saw Brine approaching.

Run.

He had not yet noticed her, so she chucked the wooden sword at Mourne, ducked under the fence, tossed her red cloak over her shoulders and scurried away, not even saying goodbye to Mourne when he bit out a noise of confusion.

If she held out for a little while longer, the trial would

happen tonight and either Brine would end up dead or he'd be the heir to Arwen's enterprise. He'd forget all about her.

Hopefully.

Is that really what you want?

She squashed the thought immediately. They had nothing in common.

And make no mistake, Brine is the enemy.

Her stomach knotted as she entered the manor. She was terrified, there was no point in denying it. He held dangerous information about her. And the trials were always bloody affairs, but set up this way...

She didn't want to imagine it.

Scarlet stopped by her room to wash and clean up, then dutifully headed to her workroom to experiment with a couple of concoctions she'd been trying to perfect over the last few months. One of them was a poison that made its victim blissfully numb and immobile and sent them into a deep sleep. The other one was a potion made to bring them back out of this state. She had mastered the first, but not the second, and was intent on completing the project tonight.

She opened the door and halted.

A dark-haired, handsome, achingly familiar wolf stood in front of her worktable, waiting for her.

The big, bad wolf has come for me.

Brine must have seen her at the sparring ring and had used the misdirect in order to capture her alone here. She glanced over her shoulder and back to Brine.

"You wouldn't make it far," he remarked softly.

And there it was. The first threat.

She instinctively knew there was no point in trying to leave. He was stronger and faster than her—she had learned that over their last encounters. Normally, she'd avoid being in a closed space with any of the pack, but she couldn't risk anyone hearing anything Brine might say. Scarlet closed the door behind her, and leaned against the heavy wood.

"You lied about your name," Brine said, his voice practically agreeable. "Why?"

"I didn't lie," she replied, careful to keep close to the door, with the table between herself and Brine should she really have to escape. One could never be too careful. "Many in Betraz call me Red."

"Because of the cloak?"

She nodded. And because Arwen wanted to strip one more precious thing from Scarlet.

The name her parents bestowed upon her.

"I've heard of you," Brine said, carefully impassive. Scarlet reckoned that if she could hear his heartbeat, Brine would be keeping it at a steady pace, even though her own was racing. He crossed his arms over his chest as if sensing where Scarlet's thoughts had wandered, then said, "Or what seems like *several* women dressed in red cloaks, since their motives and actions are so different. So which one is the truth—is it only you, or are there others?"

"Why would I tell you?" Scarlet replied, though she was pleased by Brine's supposition. It had been what she was hoping most people would think when she began helping out the obviously poor and good people who aided the Hood in their attempts to aid the smallfolk of Merjeri province.

"We were friends before."

Lies.

"Friends don't leave friends," she retorted, before she could help herself. She snapped her mouth shut.

This was the most emotion she'd allowed herself to show in front of Brine so far—in front of anyone, in reality—and it was because he had left her? She'd never even *asked* Brine to bring her with him. She was just a little girl with a crush on an older boy.

Had her young heart been broken since then?

Brine took a step toward her and paused when she wrapped her fingers around the doorknob. He leaned back on his left leg, uncrossed his arms and placed his hands on his hips, as if the conversation they were having was casual and relaxed.

"So you do remember me," he murmured.

"What of it?"

"In the reception hall, you did your damnedest to look right through me."

"That meeting was about you not me."

"I'll give you that. So what is your agenda, then? Why did I find you surrounded by explosives on your stepmother's ship?"

He was baiting her. Two could play that game. "And you would believe I was there to do that because...?"

There was a ripple of something across Brine's expression then. Annoyance, perhaps. After all, he had only seen Scarlet hiding behind a barrel. She hadn't had a match or flame out. She hadn't even opened a barrel. So why would he have thought she was blowing up the ship?

Unless he had been there to do that. Unless that was on *his* mind.

Leverage. Maybe he wouldn't hold all the power over her now.

Time to rattle him.

"What are you really doing here?" Scarlet demanded, closing the distance between them. Surprise flashed across Brine's face. Toe-to-toe, she had to look up at him, but she knew her closeness was the easiest way to throw Brine off. For one thing, she'd learned over their last few interactions that there was something about her that the wolf was helpless against.

Her heart thundered in her chest, blood rushing in her ears as she placed a hand on his broad, muscular chest. "Why did you come back?"

He placed his hand over hers, skating his claws gently over her delicate skin. "Oh, what games are you playing, little red?"

An unfamiliar thrill raced through her blood and caused her stomach to flip. She leaned into him, pressing their hands between their bodies. "Any game you like, if you give me what I need."

Brine gulped. The curve of his throat bobbed, and his ears twitched in agitation, his eyes dropping to her lips. She took in every motion, hoping that just one more second close to him, then another, then another, would cause Brine to reveal the truth.

"Do we have a deal?" she whispered, fighting the urge to succumb to the incorrigible desire held within her to touch him. He was just so warm and big.

Yet the wolf said nothing.

He gnashed his teeth together so roughly he caught his bottom lip between them hard enough to draw blood. Brine cursed and then deftly jerked back, circled around Scarlet, thrust open the door, and left the room.

She stared at the entrance with wide eyes.

Brine had been so close to breaking.

So had you.

Surprise and shame mingled in her chest.

It would have been easy to let him wrap his arms around her.

Succumbing to him is too dangerous.

Scarlet touched her fingers to her lips.

Her interrogation didn't go the way she'd planned. And for some reason, it felt as if he'd won this round.

Chapter Twenty-Seven

Brine

The silver moon was a sickle in the sky. There was barely enough light to see by within the confines of the forest in which Brine's trial was taking place. The trees were full and dark and bushy, filling Brine's nose with the scent of pine needles, decomposing leaves, and moss. All around him was the kind of quiet only found in a forest in the dead of night.

Despite all of this, Brine had keen senses, even by wolf standards, in his human form. And especially against his useless kin of the Betraz wolf pack.

A minute noise to his left informed Brine that another opponent was upon him. All he had to do was remain where he was, motionless and apparently none-the-wiser to the wolf stalking him, for the foolish shifter to come out of the shadows and launch himself at his back.

Brine nimbly avoided the gray wolf, knocking them unconscious with a quiet snap of his hand to the back of their head, letting them fall gracelessly to the ground. It was the seventh wolf he'd knocked unconscious over the last hour, and he was growing impatient.

He hadn't been allowed to shift for his trial. Neither had he been given any weapons. The latter was usual for a trial in Betraz, but the former was not. Brine knew fine well it was his grandmother's twisted punishment for him leaving the pack, but Brine took it on the chin.

After all, he'd learned much in his time with Pyre in the Dark Court. He knew how to dispatch wolves and lions and bears alike with nothing but his human hands and legs as weapons. The trial was easier than anyone could have imagined it would be, though this gave Brine no comfort.

By trial law he was supposed to kill everyone who came across his path—ten opponents in total. Even as Brine looked over his shoulder, another two attacked him in tandem. *Eight and nine*, he thought, twirling out of reach and grabbing a short sword from the seventh fallen wolf. Everyone who attacked was in wolf form of course, but some of them had weapons attached to belts around their necks in case they found themselves having to attack as humans.

This worked in Brine's favor. Though he hadn't begun the trial with any knives or blades or bows, after taking out the first three wolves with rocks thrown with a deft eye straight at their heads, Brine had acquired two daggers and now a sword.

But Brine still chose a rock to the face to battle wolf number eight as it charged toward him. It hit the creature directly in its left eye, causing them to whine and growl in protest and veer wildly off course. Brine used this distraction to turn around and grapple with the ninth wolf, bowling straight at it and launching his full weight around the wolf's back legs, locking them in place.

The wolf snapped at him, bucking its hips to dislodge

Brine, but he hadn't spent many an afternoon sparring with Briggs for nothing. Brine held on fast, then lodged one of his daggers into the wolf's front right leg.

It tumbled to the ground just as Brine rolled away. Throwing a handful of dirt at the eighth wolf when it came for him once more, blinding the poor fool for the second time in a row, Brine returned to the injured wolf and wrapped his arms around the creature's thick ruff, squeezing tight.

The wolf tried its best to buck Brine off, but Brine's entire body was honed to a fine point for this kind of work; the corded muscles in his arms flexed with the effort it took to choke the wolf out, and eventually its head sagged to the side, and Brine let go.

He barely avoided an attack from the eighth wolf this time, some quick thinking and the cold steel of his sword the only things protecting his right arm from being ripped off entirely. The wolf snarled at Brine—a clear show of intimidation—but Brine didn't care. He rolled behind a tree, leaped for a branch, and then used the momentum from swinging off it to kick the wolf squarely in the face. Brine dropped on top of it, punching the creature in its stomach again and again and again until the wolf spat blood.

Brine punched it in the head for good measure, and it fell silent. Silent, but not dead. None of the three wolves were dead, and neither were the previous six Brine had knocked out. Instead, he had cut a fistful of hair from each and every wolf, then nicked them to draw enough blood to smear it upon his bare chest. From the ninth wolf, Brine didn't even *have* to nick its skin. It had coughed up more than enough blood for Brine to use.

He'd already sent word to Pyre and Damien about the

trial, and they were on hand to remove the wolves Brine took out and transport them to the Dark Court. A group of ten wolf shifters of Betraz as prisoners was a boon for the Dark Court, and of course removing them from the trial grounds served to make it look as if Brine had really killed them. A punishment for failure, those deceased were left to the carrion in the woods.

He turned on the spot, breathing hard, on the lookout for the tenth and final wolf. Now that he had a moment to himself, Brine's thoughts inevitably drifted back to Scarlet.

Of course they did.

He couldn't believe he hadn't recognized her until she was literally right in front of him, a pet of his grandmother. And then, when he confronted her, it had been Brine who had given away part of his intentions, not Scarlet. Just who was she now? Was she Red? Whose side was she on?

She held dangerous information. He shouldn't have been on Old Mother's ship. If anyone found out... he'd be dead within the hour.

For lack of anything better to do, Brine wandered for the next fifteen minutes in the direction of the entrance to the trial. Something told Brine that his final opponent would be near the edge of the estate hoping that he would be too injured and too exhausted to fight properly. True to instinct, as he crossed the threshold into a small clearing before he reached the exit proper from the forest, Brine heard a rumbling.

He didn't give the wolf any quarter. He had gone through rougher fights in less favorable conditions in order to defend Heimserya against its previous traitorous king. And he regularly fought a bear, of all things. A single wolf was nothing.

He avoided the wolf's attack as if he were dancing, elegantly dodging any and all charges from the shifter until the wolf snapped back around to hit him again. Brine leapt onto his attacker's back as if the shifter were a horse, roughly shoved his fingers into the wolf's eyes, then nimbly jumped away just before the wolf rammed into a tree and knocked itself unconscious.

With a grim smile, Brine wiped the wolf's blood across his chest. The previous smears of blood had dried and crusted over to form a second skin. Then he cut a wad of fur from behind the wolf's head, and kicked the creature into the undergrowth for Pyre and Damien to take away.

He headed to the entrance of the trial, victorious.

In truth, Brine felt the opposite of victorious. He hated these trials. These mirthless, pointless trials, where you had to whittle out the weakest members of the pack in order to be accepted. *All of these wolves could have been trained better,* he realized sadly, thinking of the training he had received at the hands of the Dark Court. *All of them could have been true warriors. Fighters worthy of my time. Instead they're all simpering pups.*

When Brine reached the edge of the woods, where the evergreen pines thinned into large, broad-leaved oaks and beech trees with large swathes of grass between them, and the paved courtyard where everyone waited for him was within sight, the mangled red wolf who Brine had immediately disliked suddenly appeared from behind a tree.

He wasn't part of the trial—he would have been no challenge considering his injuries—but he stood in Brine's way nonetheless.

Tarros, he thought, squaring his shoulders and holding himself at his full height when he realized there was no way he could get away with ignoring the despicable wolf. *The one who covets Scarlet.* Brine had learned this from the maids in the manor, who had been fearful about telling him. Clearly Scarlet wasn't the only human Tarros antagonized.

"Step aside," Brine said calmly, nostrils flaring under the heavy tang of blood and sweat clinging to his skin.

Tarros spit on him instead. "I know what you've done," he seethed quietly. "You won't get away with your tricks."

Brine's best defense was to ignore him. After all, who would believe him? He pushed the wolf aside. Tarros growled and snapped at him but otherwise did nothing. For Tarros *could* do nothing against Brine, even after he'd spent the last two hours fighting ten opponents without a break.

Then he left the trial grounds, walked across the threshold into the courtyard, and readied himself for the days-long celebrations that always followed a trial.

Brine had no idea how he would pretend he was happy about the whole thing. More than that, he dreaded what he had to do on the final day of celebrations: choose a bride.

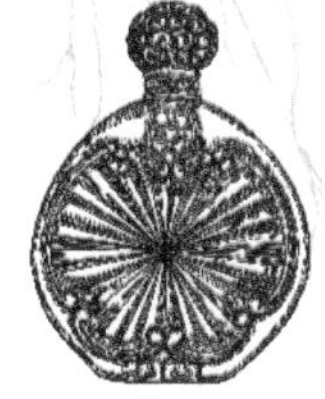

Chapter Twenty-Eight

Scarlet

Under normal circumstances, Scarlet loved helping bring babies into the world. It was one of the best uses of her talents after all, and was something she knew her mother would have been proud of. The look of relief on the father's face when the child was born safe and healthy, and his wife was still breathing—still alive—was a drug more intoxicating than any Scarlet had concocted on behalf of her stepmother.

But the birth of half humans within Betraz was terrifying. For any mother in the province, the birth of a mixed child was a delayed death sentence.

Scarlet was beyond exhausted. It was the night of Brine's trial, which of course she hadn't been invited to, but she *had* intended to watch it from the sidelines. But then Scarlet had been called out in the middle of the night—a call she could not ignore—to help with the difficult birth of the baby. Dimly, she felt guilty about how wrapped up in her own problems she was. They seemed so insignificant compared to what the family she'd just helped were about to go through. Giving birth to the child was only the beginning.

Now they had to find a way to live safely from prejudice, imprisonment, and death.

All Scarlet could do, if the family willed it, was securely place them on a ship with the help of Ari and send them off across the sea. It was the only way to guarantee their safety, though the babe had to be healthy and old enough to travel first.

It was two hours from dawn when Scarlet passed the courtyard, the broad-stoned area that led out to the entrance to Brine's trial. Her stomach lurched. Had he survived? The odds were drastically against him, but in her heart Scarlet knew he would be successful. There had been a glint in his eye, even as a boy, that told her Brine was a survivor. He would not be taken down so easily. But even so, Scarlet worried that he might have gotten hurt—perhaps irreparably so.

Then she listened to the din from the courtyard, still rowdy even this early in the morning, and Scarlet frowned. They certainly didn't sound like the violent, jubilant cheers she would have expected if Brine had come back damaged or dead. Rather, everyone sounded surprised. Surprised but delighted. Which could only mean one thing.

Brine had won.

He's now one of them.

Scarlet felt sick. No she hadn't wanted him to die, but for him to win? He had to commit murder over and over again to become blooded. She swallowed thickly at the thought and tried not to retch.

She hovered in the back of the courtyard to watch as Brine prowled through the crowd. His skin was shining with sweat, his chest covered in blood, his midnight hair wild around his head. A feral grin on his face made him look every inch the wolf he was even in his human form.

It disturbed Scarlet that she found Brine attractive even when he looked this savage. Perhaps that was *part* of the appeal, though Scarlet didn't like that idea one bit. Her heart was thumping regardless, blood rushing to her face as Brine scanned the crowd, hopefully looking for...

Her?

Stop it.

Scarlet's attention dropped to Brine's claws. He clutched clumps of hair in different shades and textures.

Trophies from his kills.

Once more her stomach lurched; Scarlet held a hand over her mouth to stop herself from retching and slipped into the woods. She couldn't watch anymore, but nor could she bear heading back to the manor where she would have to face all the servants who would be equally as happy that Brine had just killed ten wolves.

Ten of his kin.

It was too much death. Too much blood. She wanted out.

Scarlet ran.

She ran until she was exhausted, even though she'd started *out* exhausted, tired of the never-ending ache in her body from unending punishments from her stepmother, and from the pain of people dying on her watch, and from the reality of just plain existing. She ran until her lungs were filled with needles, her skin shiny with sweat just like Brine's had been.

Scarlet ran until she stumbled over the trunk of a felled tree, cursed, and fell flat on her face. She didn't get back up.

She didn't have the energy.

Her heavy cloak seemed to pin her in place. It held the weight of her sins.

She frowned as she heard the rumble of conversation.

"...never knew he was so efficient," a low voice grumbled, somewhere to Scarlet's right, behind the trunk she had tripped over. And even though she wished she could close her eyes, sink into the leafy underbrush and never get back up, Scarlet forced herself to listen.

Another voice replied, "I told you. Brine is one of the best. If you want to incapacitate someone without killing them, he's your man."

"He always struck me as the kind who went for *instant* death."

The other man chuckled. "He certainly gives that impression. But he's a softy, deep down. He'd kill you if you knew that, though, so keep it to yourself."

As quietly as she could muster, Scarlet dragged herself to her knees and peeked over the fallen trunk. It was clear even in their human forms that the two strangers conversing in the distance were shifters. One had a pair of red fox ears peeking out from beneath the brim of a top hat. He was handsome in a more elegant, refined way than Brine. The other shifter was handsome too, and absolutely gargantuan. For a moment Scarlet thought he might be a bear, but then she noticed the faintly green, iridescent sheen of his skin—she'd dismissed this as an effect of the trees around him at first—and realized with a barely suppressed gasp that he was a dragon.

A dragon shifter, in Betraz? Was it the same one as before?

If only she could see their faces.

The two shifters were dragging away the bodies of three wolves—both alive, groaning from wounds sustained to their faces but not dead.

What the devil?

Quickly, Scarlet pieced together this information with what she'd just heard the two shifters saying: Brine had not killed the wolves in his trial. He had merely knocked them unconscious. And the two men were ... hiding the evidence?

She leaned a little closer for a better look when a twig snapped beneath her knee. A whispered curse fell from her lips.

The fox's ears perked up and he turned to face Scarlet's direction. The dragon located her immediately. It took Scarlet a second to understand what was going on. This was the dragon who had saved her life, in his human skin. The dragon who had maimed Tarros beyond almost all recognition. His inhuman eyes locked on Scarlet's, and she found herself helpless to do anything but stand up, amble over the tree trunk, and join them.

There was no point in running.

Her best bet was to talk her way out of this mess.

She almost felt as if she were a puppet on strings and someone else was controlling her movements, though Scarlet knew she had been in charge of each and every one of them.

Perhaps that was simply the way she'd always felt.

"Well, if it isn't the little lady Red." The dragon smiled, pleased by her presence. "I think it's time I call on that debt you owe me."

She *did* owe him a debt.

He'd saved her life.

Memories of that day crashed over her and she almost fell to her knees, overwhelmed by her own horrific experiences. But she forced herself to hold herself together and nodded slowly. “What would you have me do?”

It was the fox who spoke, amber eyes keen but serious. “Keep quiet about what you’ve seen and heard tonight,” he said, voice soft and gentle. He watched Scarlet with interest, almost recognition. Did he know who she was? He made her feel as if he could pull all Scarlet’s secrets from her soul. “Can you do that?”

“I do not owe you a debt,” she replied frankly, her focus shifting to the dragon. “It is the dragon I’m indebted to.”

“This time it is one and the same,” the dragon rumbled, crossing his arms.

“My life debt canceled for my silence?”

“Yes.”

She looked between the two shifters and nodded. “I’ve been keeping silent all my life,” she said quietly, almost sadly. “What is another secret to pretend I do not know?”

The fox’s curiosity increased. “How I love a lady with secrets.”

“I’d like to be less intriguing.”

Understanding flitted across his face, and a small smile curled his lips. “I understand the sentiment. May you find some peace in your life.”

Scarlet blinked slowly at the stranger’s genuine words. Her chest warmed and she decided at that moment she liked him. He felt like a kindred spirit of sorts.

“I will leave you to your night’s activities,” she said and began backing away.

“Very well, then, Red,” the fox said. “I will trust that you’ll keep your word."

"And if you don't, I know where to find you," the dragon joked, though to Scarlet's ears he sounded entirely serious, despite the jovial look on his face. Not wishing to risk her good luck—if the fox was a *friend* of Brine's, then he was a member of the Dark Court after all—Scarlet retreated from the pair of shifters as quickly as she could.

Brine was rigging the trials.

If he was an unconscionable killer, he would have taken the wolves lives. Instead, he knocked them out. He'd come back to the pack for a reason and it wasn't to be a lacky for Arwen.

The Dark Court had no dealings with the Pack of Betraz.

Was Brine here on their behalf?

Either way, he was keeping secrets. Huge secrets.

Unease once again trembled in her chest.

Scarlet knew Arwen better than Brine did with all his years away from the pack. She was cleverer than anyone ever seemed to give her credit for. It was only a matter of time before Brine's secrets were discovered. By someone who would use them against him.

By someone who would want to see him killed for them.

And you as well. You're duplicitous.

Her heart sank. She was as culpable as Brine was now.

For some reason, the universe kept pushing them against each other despite the fact Scarlet wanted Brine as far away from her as possible. Deep down, she knew he'd be the death of her.

She had to do something.

To save them both.

Chapter Twenty-Nine

Scarlet

Scarlet hated how long the celebrations for successful trials in Betraz lasted. There had been the revel in the courtyard immediately after Brine completed the trial. There had been two days of secret meetings, which of course Scarlet had not been part of. Now it was a celebration dinner for the residents of the manor, and then at the end of the week there would be a ball held in Brine's honor. There he would choose a wife from the eligible women of the province.

After that, his position as heir to the pack would be secure.

Scarlet was serving food at the celebration dinner. Arwen did not waste a single moment in which to humiliate her stepdaughter, even though Scarlet herself was the *real* heir to all of Betraz. It was why she supposed that Arwen had kept Scarlet alive all these years. She was the source of her stepmother's power. Arwen had married Scarlet's father and gained the title of Duchess but without his child, the title would go to the next member of the family.

It was ironic really.

Scarlet should be duchess and yet she was a pauper

dressed in rags, cinder, and ash.

She glanced around the room, her gaze momentarily pausing on Brine. His attention shifted in her direction, and she glanced away immediately. He'd been in her thoughts more than she'd have liked.

Scarlet hadn't been able to stop thinking about her encounter with the dragon and the fox shifter in the woods and had sworn herself to secrecy on their and Brine's behalf's. For Brine wasn't on Old Mother's side, not by a long shot.

And neither was she.

But if they were both against Arwen, and Arwen was trying to control the two of them, couldn't they stop her … together? Didn't it make sense to join forces? They were, ultimately, powerless without each other. Scarlet didn't possess the influence to take down Arwen on her own, and Brine lacked the knowledge and scheming required to win against her without losing his life in the process.

Dangerous musings indeed.

She poured some wine into someone's cup and kept moving, hardly sparing them a thought as she drifted in her own mind. There was only one idea that she kept coming back to. It was crazy and Arwen wouldn't like it, but it might be their only choice.

Scarlet had to marry Brine.

It was plain and simple.

She'd find a measure of protection in his name and he'd have the wife his stepmother demanded of him. It wasn't perfect by a long shot but becoming his wife would protect them both.

All that remained was getting him to choose her.

The wolf in question was sitting up on the dais in the dining hall beside his grandmother, looking every inch a pagan prince. His ink-black hair was braided away from his face, accentuating the severe lines of his handsome face.

So far Scarlet had only seen Brine dressed to fight, his clothes covered in grime and mud and soot. But now he was dressed in midnight velvet and a white silk shirt. Scarlet knew her stepmother's influence when she saw it. She had no doubt Brine had not chosen his clothes—if the uncomfortable way he hooked a finger around the high collar of his shirt was anything to go by—but even so, the close-fitting clothes suited him well.

Stop staring.

This was what would bring the real trouble. Her inability to stop noticing how he'd changed over the years and how devastatingly attractive he'd become. Scarlet hated herself a little more as she peeked at him from beneath her lashes as she continued to serve the room. He was nothing like the young boy she remembered.

He laughed at something a wolf said, his silver eyes twinkling. Brine didn't fit with his company. It was nothing about the way he looked, more how he carried himself.

Brine held power.

Scarlet could sense it and so could Arwen if her smug expression was anything to go by.

Scarlet moved back toward the wall, near the end of the dais. Arwen never wanted Scarlet too far away.

Once again, Scarlet found herself wondering about his plans. What had Brine come here planning to do? Steal his grandmother's province? Spy for the Dark Court? Burn everything to the ground? As much as Scarlet loathed most of the wolves in the pack, she knew she couldn't allow that. Like it or not, some in this manor were family. She had to protect them.

She wished she'd asked the fox and the dragon what their intentions were for Betraz.

"I have top-of-the-range silk from the Giants," Lady Mistel of the Betraz court excitedly announced to her neighbor on her left-hand side. "You wouldn't know how talented they would be with silk, given their size, but it truly is the best in the land!"

"Well, they have to be good for something," Texel said, laughing gruffly. He held the same prejudice toward other species as Arwen. Scarlet had never understood it, not really. The Talagan shifters faced the worst kind of prejudice from the kingdom of Heimserya The Dark Court had been about rebelling against that prejudice for years. So why did the wolves look down their noses at other kingdoms, and other species? Why did they hate humans so much?

Likewise, why did Arwen hate the shifters so? Scarlet knew she was half elf and half wolf. She could shift at any point, but Scarlet had never seen her do so. Did she hate her own heritage so that she wished to stamp it out wherever she saw it?

It was hardly as if Arwen were kinder to humans either. All Scarlet had to do was look at how she was treated by her. But it wasn't the same as her hatred for shifters, though she surrounded herself with them. Not for the first time Scarlet wondered if she worked with the wolves simply because to her they were expendable.

"Top up my glass, Red," a jarringly familiar voice called out, taking Scarlet out of her head and beckoning for her to serve him. *Tarros*. She could do nothing but bow her head gracefully, emerge from her invisible position against the wall, avoid eye contact, and pour him more wine.

Be quick about it. Just get it over with.

Just as she finished replenishing the glass and set it down, Tarros not-so-subtly glided his hand up Scarlet's leg, below the hem of her dress, and squeezed roughly into her bare thigh.

Scarlet jerked away, disgusted, almost dropping her wine carafe.

He looped an arm around her waist and yanked Scarlet into his lap, much to the convulsive laughter of everyone at the table—save for Bright and Brine. This kind of behavior was not unheard of between the wolves and the servants who were there to satisfy their every whim, and it certainly wasn't new to the people in the room that Tarros would treat Scarlet this way.

Though she burned with humiliation, Scarlet remained calm the way she had been taught to, and daintily tried to get back up even as Texel laughed at her predicament. Tarros tightened his burly arm around her waist, his grip strong and unwavering.

He wasn't going to let her go.

She glanced toward Arwen who did not do anything but drink her wine and continue on with her conversation. There would be no help from her stepmother.

A prickle of dread ran down Scarlet's spine. She did not need to look at Tarros's eyes to know that they were trained on her, hungry and resentful in equal measure, though she stole a glance at his expression nonetheless. She immediately regretted it, for the look in his eyes was so much worse than it had been before the dragon shifter had mauled him on her behalf.

Tarros looked at her as if he were sure she was doomed to die by his hands.

Just try it.

"Won't you drop the servant girl?" a voice cut through the air—Brine, carefully casual as if Scarlet was merely a semi-interesting topic of conversation. She did not dare stare at him. "It's poor taste to do such things at the dining table. And it is, after all, a dinner in my honor, is it not?"

Tarros had the audacity to laugh, his breath heating Scarlet's neck. "Are you challenging me for her? She's human. Fair game to all of us in here."

Brine took a breath, ready to reply, but it was Arwen who spoke. "Is that true?" she purred. "Because last time I checked, dear Tarros, Red was *mine*."

That caused Tarros to drop Scarlet like molten rock. She retreated from the table quickly, flushed with shame and desperate to run from the room, but she knew she couldn't. Despite her anger, she kept on working.

All that would await her was some horrible punishment if she didn't.

It was a long, drawn-out night before Scarlet finally made her way back up to her room, beyond exhausted. She decided that enough was enough.

Perhaps her mother had been wrong. Kindness got you nowhere in Betraz. Maybe she'd been too tenderhearted all this time to people she should have fought with steel instead.

Tonight had made it abundantly clear she needed to fight fire with fire. If Brine was determined to fit in with the rest of the pack—and tonight's dinner only proved that—then

Scarlet wasn't going to be able to make Brine take her on as a wife through ordinary means. But if she was going to gain power and freedom over her whole life—over her own people—then the bride Brine chose *had* to be her.

It was the only way she could get out from underneath her stepmother's thumb.

If it was an insult for Brine to choose a human as his wife, as was typical of the rest of his kind, then Scarlet would have no choice but to blackmail him. What the dragon and the fox had been doing was dancing in her head, including the threat against her speaking the truth of what Brine had done. But Brine himself did not know that Scarlet would never out him to her stepmother. He didn't know her intentions, after all, and that would play to her advantage now.

Brine would think he didn't have a choice.

He would marry Scarlet or she would reveal his entire plot to Arwen.

She was done playing nice.

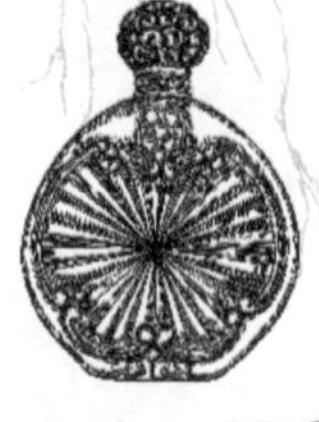

Chapter Thirty

Brine

Brine was thrown back into pack life but all he could think about was Scarlet. She was on the edge of his vision everywhere he went within the Betraz Estate. She cleaned the floors. She served meals. She tended to the gardens. She acted as the punching bag sparring partner for many of the wolves.

The mangled red wolf, Tarros, had his eyes on her everywhere she went.

Brine knew he had to forget about her. He had a job to do, and so far he had been doing it poorly, inasmuch as he had not learned anything that Pyre and the Dark Court had not already known.

Stop thinking about her. She'll be the death of you.

Arwen had shown him the fields of mimkia that she'd been cultivating in mountain caverns. She had been using a specially bred strain of the flower that fed off of darkness, not light, which was why it had evaded observation for so long. Brine witnessing it only served to confirm suspicions.

Still, now the Dark Court knew that no land was safe from

the spread of the drug. It could be grown almost anywhere, at any time of year, for anyone. That was a serious problem indeed. Brine sobered at the thought.

He dipped his hand into the warm bath and leaned his head back against the tub, listening to the wind whip the curtains back and forth.

With the exact locations of the fields of mimkia confirmed, at least the Court could move against them. But so far Lady Arwen had been tightlipped on the location of her diamond mines. These, of course, were her true treasure, so Brine understood why she wasn't keen to talk about them. Mimkia was her way of exerting control over the kingdom of Heimserya; the diamonds were her way of amassing wealth to become a force to be reckoned with farther afield—to overthrow the rule of Queen Ansette and become a mover and shaker on a global scale.

It was something the Dark Court had to stop, and quickly.

He sighed and sank deep into the tub. It was a wide, deep, steamy marble monstrosity, taking up half of the bathroom, and deep enough that Brine could kneel in the middle and submerge his head. It was nothing like the baths he'd taken within the Dark Court. It was almost sickeningly luxuriant, though Brine had to admit he enjoyed the smell of peppermint in the air to clear his senses. He had spent all day sparring with his new and old pack members, pleased that the old pack members, at least, were an especially tough bunch.

From the newer members there was Mourne, who was good enough to be impressive, though Brine had identified a tell of his after they fought twice. Tarros had apparently been an excellent fighter, though now he was of course functionally useless.

His uncle, Brine knew, was stronger than him, but they were yet to spar against each other. Was it that Bright was afraid to fight him—to discover that Brine might actually be stronger now? Or was there another reason?

The thought of his uncle dragged Brine's mind back to the topic at hand: his grandmother and the diamond mines. He doubted she would reveal anything to him until he had a bride and an heir on the way. Only then would she be secure in her hold over him, and the province at large. The thought alone made Brine want to vomit, even though the peppermint was clearing out his sinuses.

There was no bride Brine wanted to pick except Scarlet. And he couldn't pick Scarlet.

She was human.

And your true mate.

He couldn't endanger Scarlet that way, even if he knew for sure that she would actually *want* to marry him. Brine had a notion that she was at the very least attracted to him, if her physical reactions to him were anything to go by. But more important than that was the fact that Brine didn't trust the woman. Scarlet showed no hint that she was anything but loyal to Lady Betraz.

So what was she doing in the magazine of Arwen's ship?

With a growl, Brine remembered the celebration dinner from three nights ago. Tarros's hands had been all over Scarlet, feeling her up despite the audience. Brine had wanted to tear him apart from his head to his toes, leaving nothing but entrails across the floor. It wouldn't have mattered if Brine had been thrown in prison for such an act; any punishment would have been acceptable simply to see the reprehensible creature die.

He touched my mate. My mate.

Not yours. Yet.

It galled him how protective of her he was. He'd come across several potential mates over the years but none of them had affected him to this degree. Was it because he felt guilty for leaving her here in this hellhole?

He partly felt responsible for what she'd become and endured. And yet, he'd shamed her at the table. It was only on Arwen's demand that Tarros let Scarlet go, not Brine's, which caused Scarlet's torment to end, though his grandmother let Tarros degrade Scarlet in the first place. She degraded Scarlet every minute of every day. Who were they to each other? Master and slave? Or did Arwen really view Scarlet as her daughter, but also her pawn?

You're a lost cause.

He ran a wet hand over his face. It seemed he was doomed to think about Scarlet even though he knew he shouldn't. He closed his eyes, for once resigning himself to his fate, and allowed his mind to focus on her more positive aspects. Her sapphire eyes. Her gilded hair he'd like to see wrapped around his fist. Her pale, delicious skin that he wanted to taste. And the scent of ginger and peaches and green earth on the air, relaxing him down to his very core...

His body heated and he inhaled deeply.

Her scent was imprinted so clearly on his mind that he actually *could* smell these things through the peppermint oil he'd put in the bath. They were faint but definitely present in the air.

His eyes snapped open as the scratch of steel settled across his throat. He huffed. His little mate was good. Brine hadn't even heard her approach. She would have made an excellent member of the Dark Court, should she have been raised with them instead of Arwen.

"What do you want?" he asked lazily, careful not to react in any other visible way. Below the sudsy water, however, Brine's entire body was reacting to Scarlet's scent, and how close she was. It was impossible not to. His hands twitched to grab her—to pull her close.

He resisted.

Barely.

"We need to speak." The words were cold.

"That we do."

The blade wavered by his throat; all his resistance went out the window. With one smooth movement Brine reached over his shoulder and bodily pulled Scarlet into the massive bath.

The water rolled over the rim of the tub in a mass flood, giving Scarlet the distraction she needed to wrestle Brine away from the bath's edge and into the deeper middle section. He was only too eager to comply, grappling with the woman in a way that made his body come to life.

He growled as she kneed him in the gut.

Even the pain couldn't diminish what he felt for her.

She was wet and in his arms.

Brine wanted the moment to never end, even though he knew the reason for this interaction was not one of lust or longing on Scarlet's part but one of violence. He'd always like a woman with fight.

Brine focused on Scarlet's furious face as she scratched at his arms, trying to gain purchase on his wet skin, because if he didn't focus on her face then his eyes were sure to wander.

Her wide blue eyes were dark with purpose, but Brine could sense a little excitement there too.

His little peach liked him too. The thought just made him hotter.

He used his superior strength to pull himself and Scarlet back to the edge of the tub, where she ended up straddling him, her knee pressed to his chest with a dagger at his throat. Brine hissed as she grabbed a handful of his hair and yanked his head back. Her dress floated along the top of the water.

It would be easy to reverse their positions. True, he risked getting his throat cut, but Brine almost wondered it if would be worth it. Although, his mate straddling him in the bath, giving him her undivided attention wasn't such a hardship at all.

Scarlet's chest was dripping wet, pale and heaving. So close he could bite her. She yanked on his hair again, pulling his attention back to her face.

"I want a truce," she breathed, cheeks flushed.

"You have an odd way of showing it," he quipped, unable to stop the incredibly Chesh-like response from leaving his lips. The bloody feline was rubbing off on him.

The barest flash of irritation crossed Scarlet's face, but other than that she did not react. Brine wished to shake her, to force her to display some form of emotion. Where was the little girl he had known as a child? Gone? This woman was practically a husk.

"I have a way for both of us to get what we want," Scarlet said, her voice slightly husky.

Brine somehow doubted that. How could their interests line up that well, after everything that had happened so far? But Brine didn't want this moment to end, so he humored her.

"So tell me. How do we both get what we want?"

He couldn't have possibly been prepared for what Scarlet said next.

"Marry me."

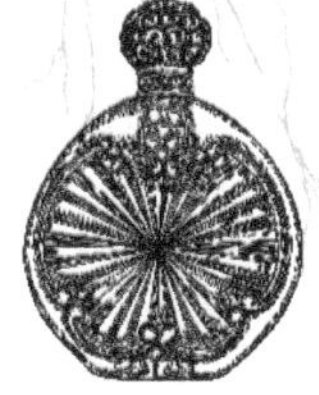

Chapter Thirty-One

Scarlet

"Marry me."

"...excuse me?"

"You heard me," Scarlet urged. "Marry me. Name me your bride at the celebration tomorrow."

A beat of silence passed between them. Two. Three. The scent of peppermint and something moody and masculine—Brine—filled Scarlet's nostrils. His hard body beneath her was distracting enough. If she hadn't been trying to keep up a careful act in front of him, she might have given into the man. It would be easy. She'd never been attracted to anyone like Brine. Everything about him made her feel tiny and... safe. Her body was a traitor as she leaned closer to him, droplets of water on his lips entrancing her.

But then he laughed.

And part of Scarlet shriveled up at the sound.

Don't let him get to you. Fight.

She couldn't be cowed. Just because her childhood friend had clearly disappeared to be replaced by a mean, calculating shell of a man who had no problem infiltrating his old pack in order to take it down, who hid behind secrets upon secrets, who worked for the Dark Court, didn't mean Scarlet should give up on her plan. His cruelty meant nothing. She had her own goals, and Brine was a pawn in that plan.

"You will not laugh if you hear me out," Scarlet retorted. She pressed the dagger closer against his skin. She was begrudgingly impressed when he didn't gulp, not even when she drew a single drop of blood. "I can give you what you want. I am the heir to Betraz. Everyone knows it. The only way my stepmother can get around this is if someone in her immediate bloodline produces an heir. But what if your heir is also mine? Not only will you then hold your grandmother's organization in your hands, you'll have a legitimate tie to the Betraz province as a whole. The manor will be yours. You'll be the duke. Not even Queen Ansette herself can take it from you. Isn't that what you want? Control?"

"No," Brine said simply.

That wasn't what Scarlet had expected to hear—not at all—but she was used to scheming, and compromise, and bribery. All she had to do was find out what Brine *really* wanted. If power was not what he was going for, then he had to be protecting something.

"I know about the dragon and the fox."

That caught Brine's attention. He snarled, bearing his fangs. Scarlet didn't blink. She'd seen worse. "I do," she insisted, when Brine stared at her in disbelief. "I saw them, in the forest, after your trial. Don't think that I won't expose you if you don't make me your wife."

By the new look on his face, Scarlet knew she had him. Brine was trapped in her hands. A lowly human who everyone had underestimated her entire life. A warmth that had nothing to do with the bathwater nor the damnably handsome wolf shifter beneath her reddened Scarlet's cheeks.

Pride. Satisfaction.

She hadn't felt them for a long time.

Brine chewed over her threat for a long moment. "It's brave of you to come to me like this. I could kill you now and get rid of the problem."

"But you won't," she whispered, "mate."

He glared up at her. "It won't be easy. You will be expected to carry my scent after we're married. Do you know what that means?"

"Of course I know what it means. I'm not a child."

It meant they would have to be constantly intimate to pull the ruse off. She would have to lie with him more than once to fool everyone into believing the relationship was wanted and genuine.

In truth, it had been one of the first parts of the plan Scarlet had accepted.

It was just bodies. Nothing more.

"I know what I'm getting into," she insisted. She pressed herself a little further against Brine's chest, ignoring the warming coil beneath her stomach when Brine let out the softest of groans in response. "I want this too."

"But … why?" Brine asked, though he had some difficulty getting the question out. "What do you get out of this deal?"

"That's my business and mine alone," Scarlet said, before swiftly trying to leave the bath lest things get even more dangerous for her. She let out a yelp when Brine yanked her back down, pressing her chest against his, so close that their noses were almost touching.

"If you betray me," he murmured, silver eyes probing into hers, intent and terrifying in an alarmingly enticing way, "I will ruin you."

It was meant as a threat. To put Scarlet in her place.

Scarlet laughed like she had never laughed before. It wasn't a humorous sound; it was unhinged and maniacal. It wiped the threat straight off Brine's face. She slapped his hands away and, this time, managed to successfully escape the tub, her clothes dripping violently onto the hardwood floor.

She glanced over her shoulder at the confused wolf. "I'm already ruined."

Chapter Thirty-Two

Brine

Brine still couldn't believe what he'd gotten himself into.

Well, not really.

He hadn't done anything. Scarlet had torn his plan to shreds.

Nearing the meeting spot, a growl escaped him and he kicked a rock across the ground.

What he couldn't comprehend was how his sweet childhood friend had turned into a blackmailing temptress. What was worse was how she'd neatly trapped him and then left him aching in the bathtub without a second glance.

"*I'm already ruined,*" she'd whispered.

Just what had his grandmother done to Scarlet?

"Brine."

He jerked. Pyre leaned against a nearby tree to the left of a small cabin just over the Merjeri border. The kitsune smiled and tilted his top hat in welcome. "A penny for your thoughts, my friend?"

Damien's wry voice came behind Brine: "Something weighs upon his mind. I've never been able to sneak up on him."

Brine cursed and spun, his nose wrinkling at Damien's nudity. While naked bodies didn't bother Brine in the least, the Dragon King had a way of flashing his shaft everywhere he went.

"Is that really necessary?" he commented dryly.

Damien grinned and shrugged a green scaled shoulder. "I hate clothes. Why should I wear them when I don't need them?"

The dragon had a point. Why was he being so sensitive?

Pyre cleared his throat, pulling Brine's attention back to his oldest friend. The kitsune's amber eyes studied him thoughtfully. "What's going on? I can almost feel your hackles from here. Has Old Mother done something?"

"No, but we have a complication." A complication that he didn't want anywhere near him and yet ... all he could think about was how perfectly he fit between her sweet thighs.

Get your head out of the gutter.

Damien inhaled deeply. "Well, that's potent stuff. What female has you panting over her? You smell of lust."

While being Talagan had its advantages, rarely was anything private. He gritted his teeth as Pyre rubbed his nose and tried to hide his smirk.

"I am not panting over anyone, but we *all* have a female problem."

"Do tell," Pyre drawled.

Brine stomped over to the small cabin and plopped down on the old porch, the wood groaning ominously. He clasped his hand between his knees and sighed. Time to come out with it.

"My grandmother's assassin—Red, as you know her—

cornered me yesterday. She knows of your involvement."

Damien cursed. "I presume she wants something?" the dragon surmised.

The tips of Brine's ears heated, and he said gruffly, "She wants to mate with me."

"As in…?"

"A bond. Not just sex," Brine replied, his voice rough.

Pyre whistled. "And the plot thickens. Do you believe Old Mother set her up to this?"

Anyone else would be offended at the idea but not Brine. His grandmother was a creature of darkness that bent anyone she wanted to her will.

"I thought about that, but I don't believe so. She hates humans. Shifter and human pairs are forbidden in Betraz. Anyone caught fraternizing with each other are punished severely. No, Scarlet wants this for herself."

"Do you think she will cause problems for you?" Damien asked. "It would be easy to make her disappear."

Brine snarled, surprising himself, and abruptly cut off the sound as two pairs of eyes narrowed on him. He cleared his throat. "She has been trapped in Betraz for a long time. I think she wants the same things as we do but is going about it a different way. I can't be completely sure what her motives are."

"Then we proceed with caution," Pyre replied, brushing off the front of his coat. He lifted his gaze and stared Brine down. "A bond is for life. We are not asking you to make that sacrifice for our cause. You do not need to take a mate because Old Mother demands it and you want to take back the pack."

"If this goes wrong, I won't live long enough to regret my

decision." Brine rolled his neck. "And if we do succeed, and Scarlet is on the wrong side ... well, she will be imprisoned, and I will live my life like I expected. Alone."

"Then it is settled," Damien commented. "I will return to my duties and my wife." He smiled once before sprinting away, the woods swallowing him up.

Brine turned his attention back to Pyre, who had been uncharacteristically quiet during the entire exchange. He glared at his friend. "Out with it. I know you have something to say."

Pyre pushed away from the tree he was leaning on and approached, sitting next to Brine. "We are pack."

"We are," Brine echoed, side-eyeing the kitsune.

"You're courting danger with your Scarlet. You need to tread carefully."

"You don't have to worry about me. I have it under control."

But do I really?

Pyre chuckled. "The one thing I've learned in my life about women is that they're uncontrollable. Be careful, my friend. I don't want to see you hurt."

Brine's lips flattened. He would have to acquire a heart to get hurt. His grandmother had beaten and whipped it out of him as a child. "I will."

"Protect yourself. If she steps over the line, show her the big, bad wolf."

Brine smiled, his fangs peeking out.

He liked the idea of unleashing his wolf on little Red all too much.

Yet not in the way Pyre was insinuating.

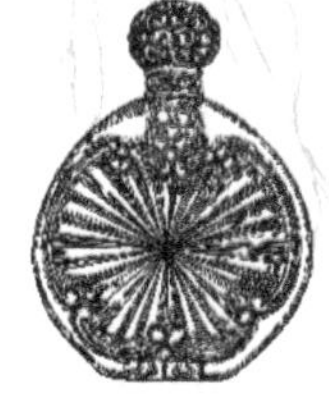

Chapter Thirty-Three

Scarlet

For what felt like the millionth time in several weeks, Scarlet thought she might be sick. Her own actions caused nausea to roil her stomach. She hadn't even eaten all day, she had felt that unwell.

Tonight was the ball, the final night of celebrations for Brine's trial, his introduction back into the pack, and the night he'd choose his bride.

Scarlet could not mess up.

Her dress for the event was old and tattered, a faded blue that was almost white with age. But it was still pretty on her, and she was fiercely proud of it. It had been her mother's, and was one of the only things she still possessed of her. Scarlet considered it a great honor to wear the dress for perhaps one of her greatest challenges.

Dris had ensured the garment was pressed and ready for what was to come next. Within the province of Betraz, among the wolves, picking a bride was not so simple as a man and a woman choosing each other and saying, "I do." Scarlet would have to fight off her competition, and win. There would be multiple simultaneous bouts, and then Brine would have to choose from the top three competitors. The female wolves were all faster than Scarlet, and stronger too—but none of them trained the way she did. None of them trained with the men. Or spent their days working as a spy and an assassin. She had strengths they did not possess, and Scarlet was determined to let them all be on show tonight.

Even though the dress was dated and in need of repair, a swift and harsh inspection of her reflection informed her that she still appeared pretty and presentable. Her hair was woven away from her face—the better for fighting with—in a style that imitated the way Brine braided his hair back.

But Scarlet's hair wasn't covered in the usual grime and sweat of her day-to-day life. For once it was clean and shiny and lustrous, and smelled strongly of ginger, earthy cinnamon, and pine— her favorite scents.

Her face was clear and largely unadorned, though at Dris's insistence Scarlet had added just a touch of dramatic black liner to her eyeline. *It gives you fox eyes*, the housekeeper said, *fox eyes to fight the wolves*. Scarlet thought of the fox shifter in the woods—a kindred spirit—and smiled.

Like a sly fox, she would best the female wolves, claim Brine as her husband, and overthrow her stepmother.

It was only right.

But as Scarlet made her way through the manor toward the prepared battle arenas, which were set up on the courtyard where Brine's initial celebrations had taken place, she ran into her stepmother doing the very same thing. The two women paused in their tracks as they took in the appearance of the other.

Arwen's viper face broke into a heavenly smile. "And

whatever do you think you're doing, Red?"

"...going to the ball," Scarlet said carefully, knowing every word counted now. "There is no law expressly forbidding me from doing so. As a lady of the manor, I have every right to be there."

There. She'd marked her stake. Arwen could do nothing against it—not legally.

The smile slipped from her stepmother's face to be replaced by a snarl. She closed the distance between the two of them, grabbed the upper hem of her blue skirt, and yanked down, ripping the dress in two. "It appears your dress is ruined, daughter," Arwen said, all humor lost from her voice.

The blatant act against her caused something to snap in Scarlet. Her plan would not be stopped because of a *ripped dress*.

So she did something stupid. Foolish. Dumb.

Scarlet struck her stepmother.

Arwen responded in kind. Of course she did.

Scarlet didn't even try to run from the blow. But Arwen's slap hit far harder than Scarlet's did, her elven blood giving her strength that nobody her size should ever have. Scarlet hit the floor hard, rubbing her hands along her jaw as it buzzed with pain.

With a dismissive wave, Arwen indicated for her two bodyguards to pick Scarlet up and drag her back to her bedroom. She yelled as they slammed the door shut and locked her inside. She pounded her fists against the door and fought back tears at the state of her dress.

Another thing of her mother's ruined.

What are you going to do?

She could pick the lock and just go. Scarlet had sneaked

out like this countless times to help the small folk of Betraz. All she had to do was wait a few more minutes to ensure her stepmother was truly gone from the manor and then she was free to do so.

But what the devil would she do about her dress?

And would her stepmother prevent her from the challenge once they were in full sight of everyone? She didn't think so. It wasn't Arwen's style to so flagrantly ignore the law. She much preferred to manipulate things from the shadows long before the *law* became a problem. So Scarlet could sneak out. But if she didn't leave soon, she would lose her chance to legally stake her claim. She had to move fast.

Without another moment to spare, Scarlet pulled out her lockpicks from a hidden pocket of her mother's dress—old habits truly did die hard, for it was nestled in there with a dagger—and she prepared to free herself.

She did not expect to be facing her friends, Jaq and Gusal, the moment she opened the door. But it wasn't just the twins on the other side.

A stranger was with them.

A woman, perhaps a little older than Scarlet, with long, periwinkle hair, leather armor, a tall bow strung over her back, and the walk of a queen.

"Oh, Scarlet," Gus said, sadly staring at her dress.

"What have you done?" Scarlet asked softly, trying to hold her torn dress together. "Who is she?" The question was harsher than she meant it to be.

"Your fairy godmother," the woman replied with a smile.

"We'll watch the door," Jaq said, when Scarlet did nothing but stare, mouth agape, at him. He and his brother allowed the stranger into Scarlet's bedroom—Scarlet numbly stepped to the side—before Jaq dutifully closed the door.

When they were alone, the mysterious woman cast her gaze from Scarlet's head to her feet, then back up, then held out a long bag for her.

"Go on," she said, her voice somehow both soft and sharp as a sword. "You will need it."

Scarlet hesitantly took the bag, placed it on her bed, and opened it. Inside was perhaps the most stunning dress she had ever seen. A figure-hugging bodice, inlaid with tiny rubies, with slits cut into the long, flowing skirt to allow for movement. For fighting. It was the color of wine—so dark it was almost black—and was perhaps the most *Scarlet* dress she'd ever seen.

Not that anyone else could have known that, but Scarlet did.

She turned from the dress to face the mysterious woman. "Who *are* you?"

The woman smiled warmly. "A friend, if you'll have me. I'm here to help."

"No one does something for nothing," she said reflexively.

"Maybe among Old Mother's ilk, but that is not the case for the rest of the world."

"I don't trust you."

The woman laughed. "I suppose you don't. That will come with time." She headed for the window. "We will be friends, just wait and see," she said in an assured manner Scarlet desperately wished she could claim for herself. She nodded toward the bag on her bed. "There are boots in there too. Until next time. And remember … it's almost midnight."

Then the woman leapt through the open casement. Scarlet ran across the room to hang out the window to see where she had fallen but found no trace that the woman had ever been there.

Sweet poison. Maybe she was her fairy godmother.

Scarlet stared out at the sky. The moon was barely visible, having been absent from the sky three days prior. She wished it was full. It had always comforted her.

She glanced back at the dress. Her mother's dress was now torn beyond repair. Scarlet couldn't repair it in time and had nothing else to wear. Except this one perfect dress, serendipitously gifted to Scarlet at the very moment when she needed it most.

Could she trust the woman? Probably not. But could she wear the dress?

There was no other choice.

"Stepmother be damned," she cursed, shaking out of her ruined clothes as quickly as she dared. Her hands were trembling. This was the riskiest thing Scarlet had ever done before. The most flagrant display of disobedience.

She knew she'd make a scene when she appeared at the celebration.

Scarlet steeled herself.

Have courage, her mother had always said.

"Please help me," Scarlet whispered to the empty room.

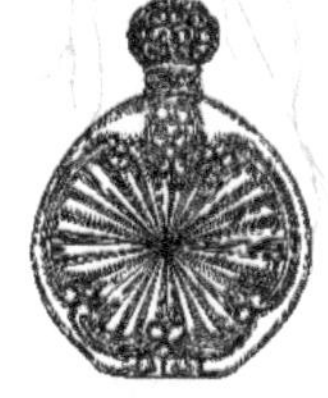

Chapter Thirty-Four

Brine

The waning moon was high in the sky. Everyone was dancing and singing and drinking, and midnight was just around the corner.

Scarlet was nowhere to be seen.

The courtyard was full to the brim with revelers. Upon a raised gazebo was a four-piece fiddle band, their jaunty music adding to the din of the party and driving the guests into a frenzy. Wolves were quick to anger, yes, but they were just as quick to party the night away.

Someone howled, then another and another.

It was the kind of party Pyre would love. Lots of alcohol, lots of laughter, hedonism in every dark corner. Ordinarily, even Brine would have enjoyed such a celebration, but the folk around him were strangers.

And his true pack wasn't there.

It had been years since Brine had been what he would consider *nervous*, but now? Now his nerves crept through his veins like a sinister poison, threatening to take him down before he could truly affect any kind of change in the world.

And Scarlet was the reason. She had made him like this, though she had spoken barely a handful of words to him.

But how could Brine not replay every interaction between them inside his head over and over and over again until he felt dizzy with it? In the bathtub, when she'd blackmailed him, there had been no denying the electricity between them. The way they'd pressed their bodies against each other in ways entirely unnecessary for fighting, he'd wanted her, and she'd wanted him. Scarlet's tamped-down emotions be damned, Brine now knew without a shadow of a doubt that she wanted him.

But if she merely wanted him in a purely physical sense and nothing more, then that was more than Brine could bear. He wanted Scarlet, body *and* soul. She wanted him to achieve her goals. The two of them were not the same.

And yet with every cell in his body Brine longed for Scarlet to appear and stake her claim as his bride. He didn't want to marry anyone else. He only wanted her, even if her intentions were impure.

At this point, Brine would take whatever of her he could get.

"It is time!" Lady Betraz called out. An immediate silence swept across the courtyard, save for the fiddle band still playing in the background. Every guest stood frozen, mid-sentence and mid-gesture, tense with anticipation. Arwen beamed at her captive audience. "All women wishing to be chosen as Brine's mate please step forward."

As expected, an unnervingly large number of women were quick to step forward. Marrying Brine and siring the heir to Arwen's empire was no small feat. There would be many people vying for his hand, but still … he didn't see Scarlet among them.

His heart sank.

However, as the female shifters moved into a line in front of Arwen, readying to get sorted into groups to fight each other, a hush somehow fell across the already quiet audience. Brine darted his head left and right, looking for the source of the distraction, only for a familiar figure dressed in the telltale red cloak to part straight through the crowd like a knife.

A bloody knife.

Obediently the red-cloaked woman joined the line of prospective brides, pushed back her hood and then unbuttoned her cloak, tossing it behind her to reveal a stunning dress so deeply red that it was almost black. It hugged every one of Scarlet's curves in a way that set Brine's mouth to watering. His eyes were dragged down to the double, thigh-high splits that allowed Scarlet full movement in the dress, the better to fight in.

Scarlet's pale blond hair shone in the light of the flickering lanterns all around her, twisted and woven into a number of braids that, Brine realized, copied the way he often wore his own hair, only more elaborate. His swallowed down a growl of pleasure.

He caught a whiff of ginger on the air, stronger than usual. *And … cinnamon? Pine?* His mouth watered at the mere thought of tasting it on his mate's skin.

Scarlet offered him a soft, lovely smile—the kind he had not witnessed since their shared childhood, and he froze. It was all he could do not to grab Scarlet and run off with her there and then.

Brine couldn't take his eyes off her. His nose. His tongue.

All that was missing was getting his *hands* on her.

This was what his bride looked like.

His mate. No one else's.

Brine forced his attention over to his grandmother. She was furious, Brine could tell, even though she remained serene on the outside. Her fist was weakly shaking at her side; her pupils were reduced to slits. Like this, it was easy to see that Arwen was part wolf, though she despised that aspect of her parentage.

It was clear his grandmother wanted to say no—that Scarlet throwing her ring in the game wasn't allowed, wasn't legal. But it *was,* and when Brine eagerly turned his attention back to Scarlet he knew that she knew this too. She might be a human, but she was a lady of the manor.

Around him, the crowd grew bloodthirsty and excited. They fully expected the female wolves to tear Scarlet to shreds, and couldn't wait to witness it. The other bride candidates tittered at the mere notion of "fighting" the lowly human.

But Brine knew better.

Brine knew she could beat them all.

"All combatants are ... valid," Arwen announced, as if the admission pained her. She closed her eyes for the briefest of moments, then held her hands up high. "Let the bouts begin!"

There were six bridal candidates in total, for three simultaneous bouts. Brine knew before the pairings were announced that the largest, most vicious-looking wolf was going to be Scarlet's opponent. He could see it on his grandmother's face that she intended to make her daughter's fight as difficult as possible.

Scarlet's opponent was almost twice the size of her,

broad-shouldered and snarling. Scarlet did not cower in the face of her, though despite his confidence in his true mate Brine couldn't help the sickening thump of his heart. He gritted his teeth, determined to keep his nerves hidden deep inside him. The last thing he wanted was for Arwen—or anyone else in the pack—to notice his weakness.

To Scarlet's credit, she walked into the ring with all the grace and poise of an ice dancer, a feeling of complete, familiar calm emanating from her. Brine was not surprised by this. He had long since determined that anything that could give away her emotions was somehow absent from her scent. He had no idea if Scarlet was actually terrified but was merely excellent at controlling herself ... or if she truly felt nothing and was a shell of her former self.

Brine did not relish the idea of the latter.

Then his mind replayed their altercation in the bath for the hundredth time that day, rekindling his hope that the girl he had known from his past was still there, her emotions not so completely suppressed and mutilated by his grandmother that she could not still be saved.

Brine shook out of his head to focus on the fight that would determine his and Scarlet's fate.

The snarling, gigantic wolf shifter that was Scarlet's opponent adhered to tradition and bowed to Scarlet when she did the same. "May the best woman win," she said, a victorious, gloating glint in her eye giving away the fact the wolf believed that woman was surely herself.

Scarlet maintained her soft smile. Brine wished she would only show it to him. "May the best woman win," she repeated, before kicking off her boots and tossing them out of the ring.

Then the fight began.

At first, Scarlet and the wolf circled each other, sizing the other up. Since Brine was supposed to be paying attention to all three bouts happening concurrently, he saw out of the corner of his eye that the other two fights were beginning in a similar manner.

Then the wolf launched herself at Scarlet, and the fight *really* began.

Scarlet deftly rolled out of the way, pulling a dagger out as she did so.

One blade?

His mate went in with only one knife? It was horrifying. Was she insane?

He made sure his bland mask was in place and resisted the urge to surge forward to the perimeter of the fight. To stop himself, Brine began slowly walking around all three fights, though at all times he was concentrating solely on Scarlet's.

A chorus of gasps rang in his ears when the wolf grabbed at Scarlet's dress. Her claws slashed though the skirt, seeking purchase, but because the material was free flowing, all Scarlet had to do was cut away the section of her skirt that the wolf had in her grasp to free herself.

If Brine had thought a lot of Scarlet's legs were on display before, it was nothing compared to now. A low growl hummed in his throat when he spied Tarros all but salivating over the sight of so much exposed flesh.

Ignore him. Get control of your emotions or you'll doom her.

But that was far easier said than done. Brine had to shutter Tarros out of his line of sight in order to put him out of his mind.

Scarlet's opponent had flown into a flurry of rage. Her

attacks kept missing no matter what she did. Scarlet was small and fast, slipping beneath the woman's legs, dodging punches and kicks and slashes from claws and knives alike.

"Try and hit her!" someone in the crowd roared.

"Stop dodging!" cried another.

But Brine knew fine well what Scarlet was doing. She was wearing her opponent out—a classic strategy for dealing with a larger foe. Brine noticed, at the front of the crowd, that his uncle and the sandy-haired wolf, Mourne, were nodding almost imperceptibly. They approved of Scarlet's strategy, that much was clear.

Does Scarlet have more friends here than she thinks she does?

Up until now he'd have believed not a single member of the pack was redeemable. He studied the crowd. There were more wolves cheering for her than he expected. It was then that he realized...

She was loved by the people.

After five tense minutes of parrying and dodging, Scarlet struck out like a viper. Her opponent howled in pain, blood blossoming across the bodice of her dress. Scarlet had hit her liver.

"Give up," Scarlet bit out, wiping sweat from her face. But she was too close, and the wolf was angry. She slashed out and caught Scarlet's forearm, ripping the sleeve of her dress and cutting into her skin.

Scarlet didn't even flinch.

"As if I'd surrender to a wench like *you*," the wolf spat, though her face was growing paler by the second. The damage Scarlet had inflicted wasn't fatal—not if it was treated soon—but it was an excruciating wound to suffer through.

Brine knew. He'd been stabbed in the liver before.

Twice.

Dully, Brine realized one of the bouts had finished. A few moments later, the second one did too. The only opponents left fighting were Scarlet and her foe.

The crowd was going insane, the smell of blood in the air whipping them into a frenzy.

Arwen was watching with intense interest, her black eyes shining as she kept her gaze trained on Scarlet. Brine had to wonder whether she wanted Scarlet to die.

Just like my trial. What is her aim in making us face what appears to be certain death?

The wolf shifter was breathing raggedly now, her movements slowing and growing clumsy. She got in another swipe at Scarlet, this time on her left shoulder, but Scarlet had allowed her to do so in order to drive her dagger right into the wolf's shoulder, barely two inches above her heart.

The wolf sagged to her knees, defeated. She knew she would die if she kept going.

"Yield?" Scarlet gasped, kicking the wolf to the floor. Her opponent yelped pathetically.

"I—I yield."

A heavy silence covered the courtyard. Then—

The roar that erupted from the crowd was deafening. It practically blinded Brine, it was so loud.

Scarlet was visibly heaving for breath and fighting to stay conscious as she forced herself to bow to the raucous audience. Brine was immensely proud of her; his heart was racing at the mere idea of naming her as his bride in a matter of moments. But there were two other winners who stood beside her and, not wishing to make it obvious that his choice would be Scarlet in order to spare the two wolf shifters' feelings, Brine maintained a neutral visage as he stood before the three of them and appeared to consider them each in turn for the role of his partner.

"So, who will it be?" Arwen asked from Brine's left-hand side, her inscrutable eyes watching Brine like a hawk as he assessed his potential brides. Brine did not respond, choosing instead to walk back and forth in front of the brides as if he were inspecting them.

Then, when he found himself standing in front of Scarlet, he stopped and stared at her. Her chest was still heaving, her dress in tatters with blood and sweat covering her skin. The braids she'd woven into her hair were coming undone around her face, waves of ginger and cinnamon and pine emanating off it and filling Brine's nostrils with their intoxicating scent.

She'd never looked so lovely.

What was the point in putting on a farce for the sake of the audience? Scarlet was *his*.

He tossed her over his shoulder—she cried out in surprise—and walked away without a single word. The crowd went wild, but Brine didn't care about that.

He felt his grandmother staring him down as they left, but Brine couldn't find it in himself to care about that either.

Even if it was just for an act, Scarlet was his. She was his bride. She was his mate.

Even if just for a moment, and even if it were false, Brine allowed himself a fleeting moment of happiness.

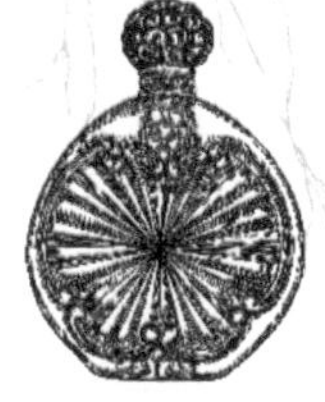

Chapter Thirty-Five

Scarlet

A small cottage had been prepared upon the grounds of the Betraz Estate for Brine and Scarlet. She was grateful for this—it was certainly an upgrade from her tiny attic room in the manor proper—but her stomach bottomed out at the sight of the pretty front door covered in creeping vines and purple flowers. She knew what would happen once they crossed the threshold.

Not only that, but there were also guards at the door, witnesses to what would come next.

"You're dismissed," Brine said brusquely.

Heat filled her cheeks and relief seeped down to her bones. Maybe she wouldn't be made a spectacle after all. His arm tightened around her legs, and she found herself annoyed that he still hadn't put her down.

"Why did you dismiss the guards?"

"I don't want an audience for what comes next," came the gruff reply.

She was grateful for it. She didn't want them there. When the two men were sent on their way, Brine opened the door with a creak. He slowly pulled her from his shoulder and she slithered down his body until her bare feet were on the ground. They stared at each other in silence for a moment, neither of them moving.

He politely inclined his head for Scarlet to walk through first.

She turned and faced the door. There would be no threshold carry. In fairytales it had been a sign of luck on the marriage.

This isn't a real marriage. Your life has been nothing like the stories.

Scarlet gathered her courage and entered the cottage, heart hammering in her chest more painfully with every step she took across the hardwood floor. Save for a fire roaring in the hearth, the house inside was dark, but Scarlet could clearly discern the edges of a large four-poster bed that would seal her fate. She turned to face Brine just as he jostled the door closed and secured it.

"You should get some mimkia on those wounds," he mumbled with his back to her.

Scarlet pulled a tiny tub of the salve from her pocket, which had thankfully not been lost in the fight. "Great minds think alike," she said, sitting down on a wooden rocking chair by the window of what appeared to be a tiny living room. Scarlet had to struggle out of the top of her dress, just a little, to apply mimkia to her shoulder, hissing between her teeth when the cooling drug began working on her wounds.

From the corner of her eye, she watched as Brine inspected the room and then ended up standing in the center of the cottage, staring over his shoulder at the fire. Completely blank. She felt a sting of disappointment that he hadn't offered to help with applying the mimkia.

You blackmailed him into this. What did you think was going to happen?

"Um..." she said, replacing the lid on the pot and placing it to the side, then stood. "Brine?"

He didn't respond. It was like he was lost in his own head.

She forced her feet to move and approached him cautiously.

"Brine?" she said, sharper than before.

His head snapped in her direction. The moment she was within touching distance, he came back to life as if Scarlet had pressed an *on* switch.

For the first time since they were children, Scarlet saw uncertainty on Brine's face. Fear. Confusion. The mask he had been wearing so well up until now had completely cracked.

His silver eyes *burned.*

He was as torn up inside as Scarlet was.

"We've really done it," he muttered, as if someone were around to listen in on them. "We—"

"We had to," Scarlet replied, trying to reassure him. She reached out as if to hold his hand, then stopped herself. Despite what they were about to do, it felt altogether too intimate a gesture.

They weren't lovers. They were comrades.

"We just painted targets on both our backs." He cursed and ran a hand through his hair. "So stupid!"

"The targets would have painted themselves on our backs eventually, no matter what we did." Scarlet was surprised by the strength of her voice, and how certain she was. But it felt true in her soul. The two of them would be targeted at some point in their lives, sooner or later. It made sense for them to take action first—to take their own fate in their hands.

Plus, Arwen had been coming for Scarlet for years. This was nothing new.

Brine looked like he was about to lose it and had no intention of moving from his spot. But they didn't have time to dawdle. Arwen could ruin Scarlet's carefully laid plans any moment.

You're going to have to take the lead.

She squared her shoulders and walked toward the bed. Goosebumps broke out along her arms as she started sloughing off her tattered, but still beautiful, dress.

"Wait, Scarlet, stop," Brine barked, stricken.

She glanced at him over her shoulder to see Brine. He looked *pained*. His claws had lengthened, and tension radiated from him.

"The time for waiting is through. Come." Her voice was strong but slightly husky even in her own ears.

He took one step toward her as if he couldn't help himself and then another, closing the distance between them, though he kept a respectable distance from her. In the moonlight filtering through the window, and the crackling golden light of the fire, her midnight wolf looked almost a shadow.

"Arwen will have me pulled from this house at any moment if we don't consummate our bond. If you don't mark me ... I'm not risking that—not for anything." Her pulse pounded harder as he took one more gliding step toward her. He snarled, causing the hair to rise at the nape of her neck. "Don't you snap at me," she chastised him.

"I'm not," he hissed between clenched teeth. "I'm just... thinking."

"Well, stop it. We don't have time for that. I'm doing my best here." She held her hands out, the dress slipping farther down, catching on one of her breasts. "You could help me some. This isn't easy."

Brine took a breath, which Scarlet echoed as embarrassment threatened to drown her. She was sure he wasn't an innocent but she sure was. It was mortifying to have to convince him to come to her.

Then a thought occurred to her. Maybe he didn't care for her body. Just because he reacted to her scent didn't mean he had to like anything about her.

Scarlet picked at her dress. "I know I'm not a beauty but…"

Brine cursed and she squeaked when he closed the distance between them and roughly tore the dress from Scarlet's body. One second she was clothed, and the next…

She was entirely naked in front of her childhood sweetheart. The boy who'd left her behind.

Scarlet didn't dare meet Brine's eyes as he drank her in.

Her breath caught as he ran his fingers down her neck and shoulder. "Beauty is thy name," he murmured.

She yelped when he took her in his arms to gently place her upon the bed. She was trembling and couldn't stop. She'd tried her best to prepare for tonight, of course she had. She'd heard that what was to come would be painful. Horribly painful. The best thing to do was not to move and take it obediently.

Scarlet slammed her eyes shut and crushed the duvet in her hands.

It will be over soon.

She felt Brine climb on top of her, pressing his bare chest to her own. She shivered as he settled between her thighs, his breathing ragged as he held his face millimeters from hers.

This is it, This is when he'll—

"Open your eyes, mate," Brine whispered. *Begged.* She hadn't even realized she'd closed them. And he had asked so lovingly, so urgently, that Scarlet found herself helpless to obey.

She peeked up at him and for a moment he just stared at her. He pressed a fraction closer and brushed his lips against hers. It could hardly be called a kiss. It was only when Brine repeated the action that Scarlet's mind became sure she hadn't imagined it. But there Brine was, his mouth just barely upon hers, soft and pliant and *adoring.*

Like she was precious.

More than that: Scarlet could see true emotion in Brine's eyes. It wasn't just that he lusted after her. Longed for her. Scarlet could see, on full display, the feelings she had witnessed the very first time they had been reunited, when Brine had called her his mate.

In that moment, Scarlet truly believed that was exactly what she was.

His.

"We don't have to continue if you don't want to," he whispered, the words water over gravel. She could see in the set of his shoulders, in the trembling of his voice, that Brine absolutely did not want to turn back—not now—but that he would. For her he would, even though it was the exact opposite of what *he* wanted.

"Don't stop."

He groaned and shook his head. "I don't want to take your innocence just because of this deal. We can find another way."

His kindness touched her. She didn't deserve it.

Scarlet wrapped her arms around Brine's shoulders and pulled him gently down to her neck, running her hands through his hair. He was trying to be a gentleman, but she didn't want that. She wanted his passion.

"I want this," she urged, the words tickling his ear. "I do. I swear. I've wanted it since you caught me in Merjeri."

It wasn't a lie to her ever-loving shame. There had always been something about him that had called to her.

It was all Brine needed to hear.

There was a flash of pain where Scarlet's shoulder met her neck, Brine sinking into her skin to mark her. She tensed and exhaled heavily. Now they were bound together legally.

And what came next would seal the deal.

Brine stiffened atop of her as he pulled away, using part of the sheet to wipe away the blood from her mark. He tossed the sheet aside and kissed her cheek gently.

"I won't hurt you, Scarlet," Brine said, as he shifted his body over her. His weight was comforting and warm, as if he was always meant to be here, like this, with her.

"I believe you," she replied, because she did. Scarlet raised her hands to cup Brine's face; he groaned in barely suppressed desire at her touch on his skin. The noise did something feral to Scarlet. Unlocked a part of her that she'd thus far never dared to explore.

Before she knew it, Scarlet crashed her lips against Brine's. He growled in appreciation as she clawed at his back to pull him closer. She ran her hands down his sides as he teased her jaw with hungry kisses. Her fingers met the waistband of his leather trousers.

"Off," she ordered, the word dancing across Brine's cheekbone. "Get this—off. Everything."

He chuckled and pulled back to plant another kiss on her lips. "So my mate is bossy in bed." She blushed hard and a nervous giggle escaped. "Now *that* is an order I'll happily follow," Brine said, kissing Scarlet once more before sliding out of his trousers.

Butterflies took flight in her belly as he prowled up her body, desire burning in his silver eyes.

"There is no going back," he rasped, the hardest parts of him caressing the softest parts of her. "Tell me to stop."

"Never," she whispered fiercely.

There were no more orders after that.

No plots, or punishments, or double meanings.

Only a touch of pain and more pleasure than Scarlet knew was possible.

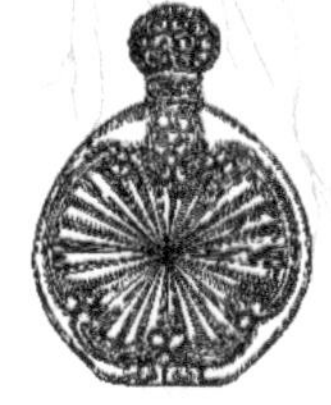

Chapter Thirty-Six

Brine

Ginger, cinnamon, the forest. Peaches. The iron tang of blood and the salt of sweat.

All of these things filled Brine's nostrils. That was why he thought he was dreaming, but when he blinked open his eyes and confirmed that he was, in fact, conscious, those smells did not dissipate.

Then the previous night's events came flooding back to him.

Scarlet.

He turned in the large bed to discover that his mate was still sleeping. Beside him. Her hair was in disarray, her skin covered in flakes of dried blood, the black liner around her eyes smudged and messy. Proof that what had occurred the night before was very much real.

She was his.

Part of him wanted to revel in her soft skin. But Brine didn't want her to wake, not yet. He knew that once he did the spell would be broken. Reality would come crashing back in.

He wanted to live in this moment forever. As if it was just the two of them.

But as consciousness began to clear the last waves of sleep from his brain, Brine began to be overwhelmed by the fact that he'd made a mistake. Because there was Scarlet, her chest slowly rising and falling, her face looking more at peace than Brine had ever seen before, and Brine knew he wasn't equipped to handle the emotions swirling around his chest. How could he give up what he now had with Scarlet? They'd only had one night together. One perfect night, and for what?

Brine didn't even know if he could trust her. Scarlet had given him her innocence, and he didn't know if even that was a ploy to get him on her side. She'd *blackmailed* him into marrying her, after all.

He ran a hand over his mouth, remembering her drugging kisses.

If he wasn't careful, she'd steal his soul.

There was too much at stake for him to risk everything on a romantic entanglement. No matter how delightful she was.

His body cried out at the thought of keeping his hands to himself. Even now he wanted to take her again, revel in his mate's body that fit him perfectly.

He held out a shaking hand, his fingers inches from Scarlet's cheek. There was an errant lock of hair there, slowly moving with every breath she took. It would be the easiest thing in the world to tuck it behind Scarlet's ear, gently wake her with a kiss, and pretend like everything was perfect.

Instead, Brine rolled out of bed and got dressed, though it pained him to do so.

It was only after he finished combing and braiding his hair back, and had begun washing his face, that Scarlet began to rouse from sleep. Her return to consciousness was much sharper than Brine's had been; one moment she was yawning, and the next she was sat fully upright, the covers held against her chest to protect her modesty.

Her large blue eyes were wide and aware as they found Brine's. He rubbed his face with a towel, took far too long to refold the towel properly, then said, "Last night was a one-time thing." He had to get the words out before his resolve escaped him entirely.

But he hadn't expected to see pain ripple across Scarlet's face before she had a chance to slip her usual mask back into place.

Part of his soul shriveled at the sight. He'd destroyed something precious with a few callous words. He knew it in the pit of his stomach.

Stay strong. Thousands of lives are at stake.

Abandoning the covers, Scarlet rose from bed naked to begin picking up her discarded clothes from the floor. In the true light of day Brine had an unfettered display of all the scars that he'd felt litter her skin the night before. Scarlet had been whipped so many times that even with Brine's sharp eyes he couldn't see the difference between the lines of the scars. They'd merged together, crisscrossing over almost every inch of the pale flesh of her back.

"Who did that to you?" he barked.

"Who do you think?" she said without feeling.

God, he wanted to kill Arwen.

Brine continued to watch his mate dress and zeroed in on the bite mark on Scarlet's shoulder. A bolt of pride went through him. Even if it was all a lie—even if he could never sleep there again—Scarlet was still his. All his. Not his grandmother's. Not that horrible red wolf— not Tarros's.

Nobody but *his*.

It was primal. The look of it almost turned him feral.

Brine felt a pang of regret when Scarlet finished putting her bloody, ruined dress back on, tying her tangled hair up over her shoulder with an air of finality.

"I'm taking herbs," she said, focusing on a point right above his head. "There will be no babe from last night."

Brine blinked slowly. He hadn't even thought about that. "Good." The word tasted like ash upon his tongue. He didn't want a babe to be born into this world any more than she did. But it seemed so final.

She nodded curtly at him, all trace of the emotion and vulnerability she had shown him the night before long gone. "I'll keep out of your way, so I expect you to do the same."

Then she headed for the door, opened it, and was gone without another word.

Chapter Thirty-Seven

Scarlet

"You seem to be getting comfortable with your new husband," Arwen purred, linking her arm with Scarlet's on their way to the dining hall. One month had passed since Scarlet and Brine had been wed, and they had fallen into a routine of sorts. They didn't see each other all day—Scarlet acting as servant and spy to her stepmother, whilst Brine was doing only Dotae knew what. But at night Brine had Scarlet strip her clothes so he could hug her and mark her with his scent, so nobody would suspect what the true nature of their relationship was.

They slept in the same bed, skin on skin, like real lovers, even though it was all fake.

At first Scarlet couldn't sleep. She had never shared a bed with anyone, let alone a naked man, and the whisper of someone else's breathing in such close proximity to hers kept her awake into the small hours of the morning. But, eventually, Scarlet found herself one morning waking up in Brine's arms, and after that she found it the easiest thing in the world to drift asleep beside him.

Scarlet nodded minutely at her stepmother. "I know to be careful," she said.

Arwen raised an elegant eyebrow. "Do you? My grandson has a history of hurting his family and leaving people behind. Including me. So you really, truly, *must* be careful."

Scarlet was experienced enough to hide her suspicion over her stepmother's apparent concern for her well-being from her face. Arwen had been easier on Scarlet over the last few weeks, and she had no idea why. Somehow Scarlet didn't imagine it had anything to do with the fact she was married to her grandson.

The shrew was up to something. Scarlet just hadn't worked out what it was.

As they entered the dining hall, she saw that Brine was already sitting down, flanked on either side by two of Arwen's high-ranking pack members. Scarlet, to her humiliation, had to stand among the servants along the wall, her previous position unchanged despite her marriage. Once her stepmother was gone, Scarlet had to wonder if this would continue to be her fate. Still wearing her red cloak, though it increasingly disgusted her, and still serving the wolves who deemed her humanity inferior to them.

Except now she was bloody tired to boot. More tired than she'd ever been before. Living a false life with Brine was exhausting.

She locked eyes with her husband as she made her way to the wall, but though he held her gaze he said nothing at all about the fact she was expected to serve the table instead of sit at it as an equal. Scarlet was so mortified she thought her face had likely turned as red as her clothes, but still Brine said nothing.

How had I been so foolish as to think he would at least try to change my day-to-day circumstances?

She hated herself and felt so stupid. Why did she think he'd act any differently even though they'd been childhood friends? Those days were long gone. Neither one of them were the people they used to be.

The way Brine was acting now simply served to prove that he didn't care, not really. Scarlet had a purpose, and she was already serving it. Brine had no need to elevate her status higher than it already was.

Dinner proceeded innocently enough, with the wolves discussing nothing that Scarlet hadn't heard before. It was only as the dessert plates were cleared away that Brine called her over with a clap. Scarlet did so obediently, though she gritted her teeth when his arms wrapped around her waist and held her close to his body. She hated how his presence enveloped her senses, sending her heart racing and reminding her of their wedding night.

Why can't I just hate him? Why do I have to react to him like this?

Scarlet wished she could turn it off.

"Look how well you have her trained," one of the wolves at the table hooted at Brine, impressed.

Brine let out an easy laugh. "All credit falls in the lap of my lady grandmother, of course."

Scarlet bristled; Brine's arm around her waist grew just a little tighter as if warning her to keep silent.

So Scarlet did what she did best. She kept her head down to listen as a conversation turned toward the diamond mines. The wolves always forgot she was there when they talked like this. They viewed Scarlet like a piece of furniture rather than a living, breathing person. It was what made her such a good spy, of course, even if it was humiliating and dehumanizing.

As with everything in her life, despite the fact that was very little, Scarlet made do with what she had.

"Thanks to your extra ships, grandson," Arwen murmured, crossing over a black-taloned hand to squeeze Brine's, "our diamonds are now ready to be shipped to the Hinterlands." This was something Scarlet knew, and in truth had been something she wanted to ask Brine about. If he was working against his grandmother, did he intend to stop this? He *had* blown up her last ship, after all. Did he intend to block her entire operation?

She could only hope so.

"Then we will finally have the money for step two," Texel said, a disgusting, anticipatory grin on his face.

Arwen nodded. "I have an agreed-upon cost to fund a larger navy now. Once the diamonds are shipped, everything will be set to have the Hinterlands invade Heimserya."

Oh.

Scarlet kept her breathing even, although this was new information. But since she was sitting in Brine's lap he clearly sensed her minute bodily reaction.

"You're dismissed," he said, without looking at her.

Scarlet couldn't believe what she was hearing, despite the fact that she'd been treated in the same way all night. She could do nothing but grin and bear his further humiliation.

She bowed her head, avoiding eye contact with everyone, and vacated the dining hall. But she lingered on the opposite side of the door. Scarlet could not risk missing out on hearing a single scrap of information now.

"Would it not be easier—and cheaper—to operate from *here*?" a voice asked that Scarlet could not recognize due to the muffling of the door.

Her stepmother laughed like a bell. "Cheaper, yes, but it would prove more difficult down the line. By having the Hinterlands invade Heimserya, the current monarchy will have all of their armies tied up fighting them. They will be weakened. Vulnerable." A pause for dramatic effect. "*That's* when I'll strike. Once we have all the humans enslaved, then we can march on my elven *brothers* and obliterate them. Once we get our hands on their resources, no one will be able to stop us."

Her stepmother's honeyed words went down like a treat with the wolves at the table, who didn't think there was more to the story than reigning supreme over other species. But it was only in that moment that the truth about what was going on finally clicked for Scarlet. Arwen did not care about enslaving the humans of Heimserya—not really—nor did she care about stealing the resources of her old brethren for herself.

This was about revenge, pure and simple. Against the elves for what they did to her.

For all her wicked brilliance, at the end of the day Lady Arwen of Betraz was fueled by nothing but pitiful revenge. Such a human emotion.

Scarlet almost laughed.

I can't let her do this.

She crept away from the doors of the dining hall.

And if the diamond mines were how her stepmother was financing her entire, abysmal takeover...

Then that was where Scarlet would hit her.

Chapter Thirty-Eight

Scarlet

Scarlet suppressed a cough as she felt her way through the mines. Felt, because they couldn't afford to give away their position by lighting a lantern.

She wasn't alone. Jaq, Gus, and Pru were all with her. She should have known she wouldn't have been able to stop them from helping her, especially when she had perhaps not-so-subtly asked them where the best place to get the supplies she needed from the manor were. But there was another person who rounded out the party who had surprised Scarlet.

Mourne.

The enigmatic, unreadable Mourne, one of Lady Arwen's enforcers. Granted, he had never been one to treat Scarlet unfairly, but that didn't mean she considered him a friend or someone she could trust. So when Mourne had overheard Scarlet and her friends discussing the plans, Scarlet thought she'd been caught. This was the end. She was dead.

Instead, something changed the entire course of their plans: Mourne informed them that he wished to help. When asked why, he simply said that he'd never liked the way things were run in the first place, that he was a part of the pack because it had been expected of him from his family, and all he wanted was to create a better province in which he could grow old with his wife.

Perhaps, before her marriage to Brine, Scarlet wouldn't have believed him. She would have thought he was lying to get more information from her. Instead, all she saw was a sincere love for his wife upon Mourne's face, which deeply affected Scarlet. So the shifter was in on the secret, and had in turn proved supremely useful.

They had made their way into the mines with no pushback. They were well ahead of schedule, and all because of Mourne. In return for him risking his position to help them out, all he asked for was should things go south, Scarlet got his wife out of Betraz and safely away across the sea. Scarlet didn't want to think about things going south, but she nevertheless agreed.

If things go wrong, can I save everyone?

They crept deeper and deeper into the bowels of the mines. The air was getting thicker and harder to breathe. Scarlet wondered how on Earth anyone managed to work down here for twelve hours at a time. There wasn't much of a choice she supposed.

Scarlet felt a hand on her back suddenly drag her against the stone wall.

"Stay back," Pru hissed. She was the smallest, and the quickest on her feet, so it made sense for her to be at the front of the party to act as lookout.

Everyone shrank against the wall with Scarlet as her friend scanned the area.

Jaq was behind her, hand on her shoulder steadying her as they slowly retreated into the shadows at Pru's insistence, everyone breathing in perfect irregularity as two wolves swinging a lantern rounded the corner and, blissfully, did not look down the shaft to their right as they passed.

Scarlet's lungs burned as she held her breath. That was the second time they'd almost been caught. She didn't want to think about how quickly they would have been captured had Mourne not been on their side, informing them when the various guard shifts occurred.

Eventually, they reached the weakest part of the mines. A fault line ran beneath the bedrock for at least half a mile, more than big enough to ensure the entire system would collapse if a series of explosions were let off.

Silently, and with shaking hands, the group set up their explosives. Scarlet had made them in her workshop that afternoon, fighting the adrenaline in her system so that she didn't accidentally blow up the manor instead of the mines.

After they set up the charges, they returned the way they came, until a light could be seen at the end of a distant tunnel, signaling their escape from the mines.

Scarlet made eye contact with Mourne through the dim light. "Ready?" she whispered.

He nodded minutely. "For years."

Scarlet set the trigger that would begin the chain of explosions approximately one minute from now ... and paused. She could hear voices. Familiar voices. One she hated, and one she wished she did, but didn't.

Her stepmother, and Brine.

"Scarlet, don't," Jaq urged, picking up on the voices moments after her.

Mourne tried to drag her back toward the entrance. "Leave them. They're part of this. We have to do this for the greater good."

She was going to be sick. Panic filled her.

"I know you care about him, Scarlet, but the others are right," Gus pushed. "We need to set the charges off, and we need to go. *Now*."

Without waiting for Scarlet's admission or approval, Pru took the trigger out of her hand and pressed the button. Scarlet stared at the group around her, aghast.

No one was supposed to get hurt.

She couldn't let Brine die. Not least because he wasn't working with her stepmother. Regardless of what he was doing, he wasn't part of this. She had to save him. If that meant saving her stepmother, too, then—

"Go without me," she said, bolting toward Brine.

"Scarlet, come back!" Pru cried after her, but it was too late.

She had mere seconds before the first charge was set to blow the explosives. Twenty seconds, tops, to get out of the mines. Could she make it?

She'd have to.

When she turned the corner and spied Brine in conversation with Lady Arwen and Bright, Scarlet's vision tunneled until all she could see were the eyes of her husband.

"*Out!*" she yelled, waving her hands above her head, desperate for them to understand the gravity of the situation. "This place is set to blow! Get out!"

Brine's eyes narrowed at her. "Scarlet, what—?"

"*Get out!*" she screamed, grabbing his arm and dragging him back with her. She could only hope that his uncle and her stepmother were following close behind.

That was when the first explosion went off. A deep rumble shook the ground, vibrating up Scarlet's legs and sending her teeth chattering in her skull. She couldn't hear anything but ringing. Salt filled her nose, pulverized rock.

The second charge went off. The third.

They were going to die.

Above them, increasingly larger quantities of rubble pounded down on top of them. If they didn't get out soon, they would be buried alive.

Just as Scarlet thought daggers were piercing her lungs, she saw the light at the end of the tunnel, and then tripped over her feet in her desperation for fresh air and freedom. Brine's strong arms wrapped around her and carried her the rest of the way.

Several minutes passed before Scarlet became truly cognizant of what was going on. She was lying on the grass outside the mine, Brine collapsed beside her with his hand on her forehead. All around them was chaos. The entrance to the cave had collapsed. The entire system seemed as if it had sunk deep into the ground.

Scarlet's vision was red, but she sat up and darted her head to and fro, looking for her friends. Mourne and Gus were nowhere to be seen. But Pru and Jaq...

Several wolves had them in their grasp, their claws digging into her friends' arms until they bled. Scarlet opened her mouth, a moment away from screaming for them. But Pru shook her head. So did Jaq.

Scarlet's blood ran cold. Her friends being caught was not something she had planned. In truth, she hadn't wanted to think about them failing.

Now they were doomed.

Beside her, Brine was asking if she was okay, for her to lie back down. Scarlet knew what she had to do. Her friends would die for this, and not swiftly or painlessly. Though she was shaking, Scarlet got to her feet and fled to the manor before anyone could stop her. When she got to her workroom an hour later, she hauled out drawers and boxes and tossed their contents to the floor, knowing what she was looking for. She had only been working on it a few weeks ago, after all.

And then she saw it. The sleeping, numbing poison that she had only just perfected. It would numb the pain of anyone who inhaled it quickly. It would send them into a euphoric state before they fell asleep.

Her friends would feel nothing of their deaths.

When Scarlet rushed back outside, her friends had been dragged to a central plinth in the main courtyard in front of the manor. All around her was pandemonium, shouts and jeers and yells for the two traitors who had attempted to destroy them all.

Scarlet's stepmother took her hand when she saw her, a look of genuine affection and appreciation on her face for once. "I know it took courage to save us at the expense of your friends," she said, stroking Scarlet's face fondly, "but it appears I've trained you better than I ever thought. You saved us, so you get the first blow. I'm sure it will be satisfying, given how your friends betrayed you."

Scarlet's stomach bottomed out. If it wasn't for the fact her friends were relying on her, she would have vomited all over the stones in denial. But she shook some composure into herself and ignored Brine when he reached over for her as she walked onto the plinth with heavy steps.

She couldn't do this.

When she came face-to-face with Pru, glorious, beautiful Pru, who had been friends with Scarlet from the very first day that she'd been brought here, Scarlet wavered.

"Do it," her friend whispered, her eyes glistening with tears but unafraid. Beside her, Jaq held a similar expression on his face. Resolute. Right from the very start they had known what they were getting into when they agreed to help her—no, *demanded* to help her.

Tears burned in her eyes.

She couldn't diminish the choices they had made of their own volition by failing them now. So Scarlet dipped her hand into the powder beneath the cloak, grabbed hold of a hefty pinch, then slapped first Pru and then Jaq in the face. Small smiles curled their lips when they realized what Scarlet had done, knowing that she wouldn't let them suffer.

"I love you both," she mouthed, feeling like she was breaking apart on the inside.

Scarlet forced herself to walk backward off the plinth to take her place beside her stepmother to watch her friends die. In her mind, she retreated into a secret box, finding herself back in the memories she shared with her mother. Pitifully few, and it turned out not enough, to hide from the sight of her friends being ripped asunder by a pack of wolves. Dris wailed somewhere in the crowd.

Scarlet did not know how she found herself back in her little cottage scrubbing at her hands as if they were covered in blood and washing them might rid herself of her guilt, but that was how Brine found her.

A vase crashed against the wall to her right, pulling her back to the present.

She slowly turned around to face her husband who looked like he wanted to tear the world asunder.

"Just what," Brine growled, expression murderous, "the hell was that?"

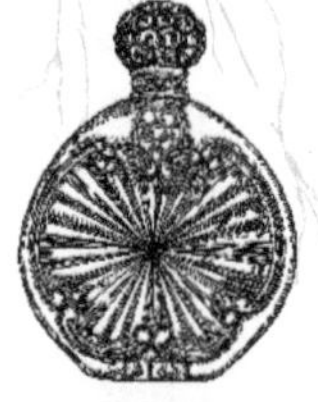

Chapter Thirty-Nine

Brine

"What have you done, Scarlet?" Brine asked, so angry that his voice didn't have the energy to be loaded. It was cold and quiet and still, despite the vase he had only just thrown across the room. Slowly Scarlet turned from where she had been washing her hands. Her skin was ghostly white when she faced him.

"I don't know what you mean," she said, that same hateful calm on her face that had been present when she watched her friends die.

Die for her. He could see it so clearly now.

"How long have you been plotting?" he demanded. "I saw you with your friends before this, Scarlet. You were working with them, weren't you?" He ran a hand over his mouth. "I can't believe you were so coldhearted as to kill your friends just so they wouldn't reveal your plan!" Just what kind of a creature had he married?

One your grandmother created.

Scarlet looked like he'd slapped her. "Excuse me?"

"You killed them to keep your secrets."

Some color returned to her face as her eyes narrowed. "I'd never do such a thing."

"I don't believe you."

"Then clearly it won't matter what I say in my defense!" she exclaimed, taking a step toward the door. "I will not explain myself to the likes of *you*."

"Me? *Me?!* You've drugged me, you've done everything my grandmother has bid of you, and you blackmailed me into marrying you."

She laughed but it was humorless. "And you're the saint? I am your servant. Not your mate. You are doing Arwen's bidding as much as I am. But what makes you worse is that you escaped her and yet *you* came back."

"I can't trust you," he growled. "I can't believe a single word out of your mouth. You're a liar. Just like her."

Scarlet recoiled, disgusted. "We're done here," she muttered, making to leave. But "done" was exactly the opposite of what Brine was. He grabbed her arm and slammed her against the wall. "Brine, what the devil are you—?"

"What exactly is this?" he asked, procuring a pouch of white powder from the inside of Scarlet's cloak despite the reproach in her eyes. He held the powder before her so she could be in no uncertainty about what he was talking about. To his satisfaction, a small frown colored her brow.

He'd caught his little poison mistress in her lies.

"Put that away," she uttered. "It's dangerous. One breath and—"

"You admit that you killed them," he said, nonetheless carefully pocketing the poison. "Before they could admit that they were working with you." Revulsion spread through his veins. Scarlet was just like everyone else around him. A villain through and through, only out for herself.

The moment the poison was safely out of reach, Scarlet bodily pushed Brine away from her, surprising him enough that he took a step back. Her eyes were a brilliant, blazing blue. "You don't know anything," she spat. "You don't know anything. You don't get to judge me. All you can do is leave me *alone*."

Scarlet made it halfway across the house toward the door, taking advantage of Brine's stunned silence, before he recovered quickly enough to leap over a low chair near the fireplace just in time to slam the door shut again.

She was not leaving until he got answers.

He dragged Scarlet back into the middle of the room even though he wanted her gone, out of sight and out of his life. But he couldn't help it. She smelled so bloody good.

So like *his.*

"Where did the sweet little girl who fed me a peach and told me everything was going to be all right go?" he asked, closing the distance between him and Scarlet until his arms were wrapped around her and there was nowhere for her to go.

Scarlet didn't move for a long moment, save for the shaking of her shoulders. Then, slowly, she turned in Brine's arms to face him, eyes full of tears as she tremulously said, "I'm right here."

Then she began to cry. Not the pretty tears of someone feeling sadness, nor the stage tears of someone overcompensating for a lack of grief. No, this was real sorrow, real pain. For once Brine could smell her fear—could taste her emotions.

She was in excruciating, heartbreaking pain.

His arms tightened around her.

"Tell me what happened," he urged, his words gentle as he whispered into her ear. "Tell me who you lost today."

"I l-lost my friends."

"Tell me the truth. For once, let us be honest."

Brine could do nothing but hold Scarlet, easing them down to the floor as she explained between sobs what she had done, and who had paid the price for it.

"I spared them pain and yet you consider me the villain."

His body flashed hot and cold. He'd accused his sweet, broken mate of being a murderer like his depraved grandmother.

"I'm sorry." He meant it from the depths of his soul.

He could not believe he'd ever thought that Scarlet could be evil—that he'd come into this house without trusting her with every bone in his body. Even though, from the beginning, something larger than himself had told Brine that every word out of Scarlet's mouth was the truth. Not for everyone else, but the truth for *him*.

"I may be many things but I'm not a monster." She looked up at him with big, sad blue eyes that tore at his heart. "I know we're not friends, but I can't believe you thought me capable of such a horror."

He began kissing away her tears. "I'm a foolish cold wolf. I'm so sorry."

Brine jerked when her plush lips found his own, the tang of salty tears on his tongue but deepening the kiss nonetheless. Scarlet wiggled in his lap and straddled him, winding her fingers through his hair.

"Need you," she murmured between kisses. "Help me

forget."

Brine wrapped her legs around his waist and rose, carrying her to the bed. He knew he wasn't the only one who felt this deep, unrelenting urge to connect between the two of them. She bit at his jaw, destroying any self-control he had.

He stripped them both like a man possessed, desperate to touch her.

She arched beneath him, and he tossed her legs over his shoulders, destroying his vow to never touch Scarlet again.

It had been an impossible vow to begin with.

Chapter Forty

Scarlet

Scarlet found herself once more smuggling people out of Callmai. Only this time they were friends.

Because his brother had taken the fall for the destruction of the mines alongside Pru, Gus and his wife were no longer safe. And though Mourne had managed to evade capture and suspicion by integrating back into the wolf pack, he had privately insisted to Scarlet that his wife and family escape Betraz. If he was going to continue working in the shadows for Scarlet—Scarlet, not anyone else—then he needed to know that the people he loved were taken care of.

Though the destruction of the mines had ended in personal tragedy, Scarlet was more grateful than words could describe to finally have a true ally on her hands.

"Take good care of them, will you?" she told Ari after they'd entered the pub through the back entrance, having just endured a tearful goodbye with her friend.

Ari laughed lightly, a sincere and trusting sound. "When have I never taken care of the refugees, Scarlet?"

Under normal circumstances, she would have fired a quip

back at her friend. But, considering what she had lost, Scarlet pressed her lips together and said nothing. She hadn't even had it in her to whisper reassurances to the people she was sending off, choosing instead to escape into the pub proper to drown her sorrows in a pint of ale and the anonymous murmuring of the crowd. It was in this way that Scarlet found herself sitting at the bar, cradling a cup of spirits and wondering why it tasted bitter in her mouth.

Barely five minutes had passed by before Scarlet caught an oddly familiar sight out of the corner of her eye.

A flash of copper hair. A pair of fox ears.

The fox shifter who had been helping clear the bodies after Brine's trial.

What is he doing here?

She picked up her ale, expertly weaving her way through the pub until she was within hearing of the shifter's table. He was sat with an oddly feline man, who had a rakish kind of countenance which Scarlet almost felt like she should punch. She assumed he was a cat shifter.

Scarlet sipped on her drink, careful to appear as nameless and faceless as the rest of the crowd. Which wasn't hard; she had been training all her life to appear invisible. At first the two men talked about nothing of importance, laughing about the feline's latest bedroom conquest—Scarlet was not surprised—and the latest guards in Merjeri the fox had evaded—again, not something that came as a surprise.

But then Scarlet heard Brine's name mentioned, and she leaned forward intently. "Things are all going on schedule in Betraz," the fox murmured. "Once Brine has gotten rid of his grandmother and taken over her territory, the Dark Court will..."

The loud banging of the front door granting entrance to a pair of brawny sailors cut off the rest of the conversation, but Scarlet had heard enough. The ale that she'd drunk twisted in her stomach as if it had fermented badly. She thought she might be sick on the spot. Abandoning her drink, Scarlet escaped the pub without bidding goodbye to Ari, gulping down fresh, salty sea air as if she had never breathed before.

All this time Scarlet had thought Brine had come back to Betraz to help. To save the people of the province. To dismantle all the harm that Arwen had caused.

Instead, he was going to pick up where his grandmother had left off.

For the Dark Court.

Scarlet didn't bother to stop the tears from falling as she made her way home. What was the point? She had been a fool. She had let her guard fall around the wolf shifter she cared far too much for and shown herself broken and vulnerable in the process.

She'd entrusted her heart to someone who was just as corrupt as her stepmother.

Chapter Forty-One

Brine

That night, Scarlet was behaving oddly. Well ... odder than usual. The last couple of days the two of them had eagerly gotten lost in each other. They'd stayed up late into the night, naked and embracing and talking about nothing at all until the sun came up. They made an effort to return from their daily duties early, and skipped dinner in the manor just so they could spend more time together.

Brine was grateful for it, despite how their sudden closeness had come about.

Of course he knew what Scarlet had been doing that day—ensuring that the rest of her friends could escape unscathed—so he figured that had something to do with the way she was currently acting. Awkward. Quiet. Avoiding Brine's touch and his conversation. She didn't even eat when he offered her supper in the cottage.

When night fell, and they got ready for bed, Scarlet could not look Brine in the eye. She did not ask Brine about his day and, when he asked about hers, she gave him curt, one worded answers.

Something wasn't right.

Lying in bed, it seemed as if Scarlet hardly dared to touch him.

No cuddling. No caresses or kisses.

"What's wrong, Scarlet?" Brine asked, no longer able to take the awkwardness stretching between them. He'd never minded silence but hers put him on edge. Plus, he had never been all that patient. "What's happened?"

"I don't know what you mean," Scarlet said primly, which was at once both frustrating and also the longest answer Scarlet had given Brine all day. But it told him nothing.

"Just tell me what's wrong," he insisted. "Maybe if you tell me about it, I'll be able to help."

"I don't think so, no."

Brine reached out for Scarlet's blond hair, but she pulled it over her shoulder and turned away from him. He scowled, running a hand over his face and then through his own hair in exasperation. He thought they were past these evasive answers that told each other nothing.

"Why won't you just tell me?" Brine asked again, sitting up despite the chill from the evening air. "Can't you be honest with me about this?"

She said nothing.

He frowned. "Is it your menses?"

Scarlet glared over her shoulder and he held his hands up, inhaling slowly. No blood.

"Stop scenting me!"

He huffed. "I wouldn't have to smell you if you'd tell me what's on your bloody mind."

She twisted and looked Brine in the eye. It was then that Brine realized she didn't *need* to answer this question. Not out loud, at least. Her rage bled away, leaving empty eyes. It told him everything he needed to know.

Even now, Scarlet held too many secrets she wasn't willing to share.

"Fine," he said, rolling out of bed and yanking on his trousers, then his shirt and his boots. "If you wish to speak to me when I'm back, I'll be all yours."

His wife did not attempt to stop him as he left the cottage, slamming the door behind him. He thundered through the forest, a fierce anger bubbling beneath the surface of his skin. He hated feeling this way, especially in relation to Scarlet. Why was it, with every step he took forward with her, he ended up a mile back?

Don't think about it, Brine repeated to himself, knowing such a mantra was impossible to follow. But he was meeting Pyre and Damien tonight, so Brine schooled his expression, shook out his shoulders, and continued through the thick, midnight-black undergrowth of the woods until, finally, he came across the chosen clearing. His friends were sitting beneath a pine tree, swigging from fire whiskey and murmuring to each other in conspiratorial tones.

Pyre looked up in surprise when his fox ears picked at the sound of Brine's arrival, moments before the wolf himself came into view. "You're early," he said in disbelief. "Shockingly so. Something wrong in the marital bed already?"

Brine wanted to slap the smarmy grin off the fox's face, but he resisted. That was what Pyre wanted after all, a reaction. "I had nothing better to do," he said gruffly, crossing his arms over his chest. "Why did you need to meet tonight anyway?"

It was Damien who answered: "You'll be happy to know that your feline best friend has seized another of your grandmother's trade ships," the dragon said, sounding impressed despite himself. For whatever reason, Damien and Chesh had immediately liked each other, even though both of them were difficult men to understand. Brine figured it had something to do with the cat's rakish, daredevil attitude and complete lack of danger awareness.

But Brine hadn't traveled an hour through the woods to ponder his increasing circle of friends. "That's good news," Brine said, trying to piece together where the conversation was heading. "What do you need me to do now?"

Pyre got to his feet. "News will travel fast that Old Mother's ships have been seized. As soon as she's aware of what's going on, our window of opportunity to close in on her will be gone. You need to take your grandmother out … tonight."

Tonight?

Brine couldn't fathom *tonight*. Tonight was right now. Tonight wasn't the future.

But he had come to Betraz with a job to do. He had not come here to find a mate and wed and pretend that everything was all right when everything was very much the opposite.

He steeled his nerves and nodded. "Tonight it is."

Chapter Forty-Two

Scarlet

Usually Scarlet would not appreciate being roused from her own bed—especially not when she'd been able to fall into an early sleep—but tonight she was grateful for the distraction. For Brine had not returned after he stormed out, and Scarlet didn't know what to do about it.

Should she confront him about what she'd heard in Callmai? Or should she remain silent and see if he would tell her about it himself?

Not for the first time, Scarlet had to admit that she didn't know what to do.

What she *did* do was answer her stepmother's call to help her get ready for bed when the summons arrived. Very late, as usual, the woman having no doubt entertained a small party of guests until the middle of the night. It was her usual way of spending an evening, so Scarlet was used to being awoken to help her.

Even if she hated it.

Tonight, though, she was almost grateful for the work. . At least aiding Lady Betraz in getting ready for bed would likely tire Scarlet out and allow her to fall, mentally exhausted, into her own bed once her stepmother no longer required her help.

She slogged her way through the manor, heavy of heart.

Arwen was uncharacteristically quiet when Scarlet came upon her chambers. It was unnerving. Immediately, it put her on edge. What was she up to?

Her stepmother having secrets was never a good thing.

"Come, come," Arwen called out impatiently after a long moment of silence, indicating for Scarlet to join her in front of the mirror on her large, silver vanity. "Comb my hair."

Scarlet dutifully complied, padding across the room on silent feet to stand behind Arwen. With a careful, gentle hand she began combing through Arwen's long, lustrous hair before changing the black-tooth comb for a sinfully soft horsehair brush. Scarlet brushed and brushed until her stepmother's hair began to shine in the dim light of the fire.

"My mother used to brush my hair," Arwen mused. Scarlet kept her mouth shut and listened. "She used to make me wash my face ten times a day and brush my hair a hundred times before bed." Arwen's dark gaze grew distant and almost *pained*. "She was never convinced I was clean enough or perfect enough."

Scarlet's strokes slowed as she watched her stepmother lost in her own mind. Just what kind of woman had raised Arwen? Her hatred and animosity toward her people was deeply disturbing. Just what had happened to her stepmother to make her this way?

In a way, she almost felt bad for Arwen.

Who hurt you?

"How are you feeling, Red?" Arwen asked, after a few

minutes of surprisingly not uncomfortable silence passed between them.

Scarlet blinked slowly. When had her stepmother ever cared how she felt?

She focused on brushing Arwen's hair. The mundane task was helping to calm Scarlet down and set her at ease, though now she wondered if that had been the point all along. For Arwen had never cared to ask Scarlet about her well-being before. It was an unusual question to ask.

Just what was going on?

"I'm fine," Scarlet lied, knowing her stepmother could not do anything with that answer. And she would never reveal anything of her true feelings to the woman.

"You aren't tired?" Arwen pressed. Her pale, dark reflection in the mirror gave nothing away of her intentions. In truth, neither did Scarlet's. "Have you been sick lately? Feverish? Nauseous?" Scarlet shook her head after each question. Arwen raised an arched eyebrow. "And what about ... your menses?"

The brush in Scarlet's hand froze. It was all she could do to stop it from crashing to the floor.

Over the last two or three months, Scarlet had been too busy to even think about them. She'd been taking herbs since she started her monthly bleedings—even before she knew that she would be chosen as Brine's bride—but it was true that she'd been super tired and irritable lately.

And sick.

How often had Scarlet thought she might vomit? How many times had she passed it off as a physical reaction to the horrors all around her? What if it *hadn't* been a reaction to anything external—or, at least, not every instance? What if it had been internal?

It's not possible.

She had been giving the herbs to women for years and they'd never failed any of them.

She's trying to play mind games. Don't trust her.

A howling gust of wind enveloped the two of them through the open window, a chill running down Scarlet's arms no amount of warmth would temper. She placed the brush on the dresser and backed away from her stepmother. "All finished, my lady. Good night."

"I'm not finished." Arwen swiveled to face Scarlet, a triumphant smile twisting her lips. "No need to run away, dearest."

Scarlet was no longer able to maintain a neutral expression. "Dearest?"

"Of course, daughter of mine."

Bile burned at the back of her throat. She caught a glimpse of herself in the mirror. Her face was pallid and horror-struck. She took another step toward the door. "You are not my mother," she said through numb lips.

"No, I'm better," her stepmother purred. Grinning, Arwen rose to her feet, pushed back her stool and stood. "Look how strong I've made you."

"You've done nothing but try to break me."

"And yet, you're still here." A pause. "Carrying the heir to all of this."

"No. I'm not." She would know, wouldn't she?

"You're pregnant, my dear," Arwen said.

The words were a curse in Scarlet's ears. An impossible curse. "No," Scarlet mouthed. "No. I can't. I don't believe you. I—"

"Why, because of your tea?" Arwen pulled out a box of loose-leaf tea from the top drawer of her vanity, shaking its contents in front of Scarlet's face to show her the proof that her preventative herbs had been swapped for something else. "This stuff?" her stepmother taunted. "I have been replacing it for weeks now."

Scarlet gagged. She thought for sure she'd be sick, covering her mouth with both hands as if that might be able to hold the nausea back. "Why?"

"Because it suited me, darling."

The sound of a scuffle, then a full-blown fight, rang in her ears. Scarlet and her stepmother both turned their attention to the closed door.

"Just what is it—?" Arwen began, her query interrupted by the door being thrust open.

Brine barged in, chest heaving, eyes flashing.

"Sorry to interrupt," he growled, a bloody sword in one hand and a dagger in the other, his wild eyes shining with the promise of death, "but I have some overdue business to attend to."

"Brine?" Scarlet's voice was barely audible around the hands she still held to her mouth, but it was enough to stop the man she loved in his tracks. He faltered by the door, his murderous expression broken in an instant to be replaced by confusion.

"Scarlet?"

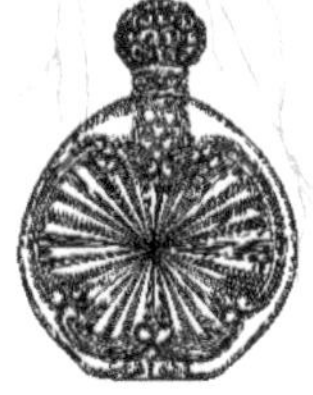

Chapter Forty-Three

Brine

“Are you all right, Scarlet?” Brine demanded, the moment he realized the woman he loved was in a room he planned to paint red with blood. She wasn’t supposed to be here. She was never supposed to be here.

Scarlet didn’t say anything. She merely stared at him, wide, glassy eyes betraying nothing.

“What have you done?” he hissed at his grandmother.

Arwen closed the distance between herself and Scarlet, gently touching a hand to her red-cloaked shoulder.

Brine growled, lifting a sword to point it directly at his grandmother’s throat. “Don’t you dare touch her. Your time of terror is up, Old Mother.”

“Oh ho ho, that’s where you’re wrong.” She laughed, the sound lovely and ugly in equal measure. Arwen ran her hand down Scarlet’s arm, who did nothing to push her away. Brine wished Scarlet would do *something*. Say *something*. “Tell me, grandson, have you never wondered why you saw my precious Red inside the Merjeri manor?”

Brine faltered.

She is telling lies to throw you off. She can't have known you were there. She can't—

"You think you're clever, stupid boy, to try and step out in front of me when in truth I have been hundreds of steps ahead of you. You think I don't know what you've been up to all this time?" Her grip on Scarlet's arm tightened, so hard that Scarlet winced. "You're still that scared little boy who betrayed his family."

"Let her go," Brine demanded, the sword in his hand shaking. "I won't ask you a second time."

Arwen gleefully ignored him, running her long black nails through Scarlet's golden hair. It was clear she knew that so long as she had a hold of Scarlet, Brine wouldn't dare lay a scratch on her. "All this time you were just a sad, lonely, desperate boy I could manipulate. Did you really think your feelings for my lovely Red were that easy to hide? I've known since you were *children.* Why do you think I kept her alive all these years?"

He steeled his spine even though his legs wanted to collapse beneath him. "You lie. She is a human convenience. She's not my mate."

Arwen smiled. "No, no, who is lying now? Your bond is so deep, I picked up on it the moment you set foot in these halls. Even as a pitiful child, you were doomed to fall for her. Of course, I sent Scarlet out to Merjeri manor to lure you back to me. Did you think you were safe in the Dark Court?"

Brine turned his attention to Scarlet. "Did you know?" he demanded, staring her down. "Did you know about this?"

Please deny it.

Scarlet opened her mouth to speak but no sound came

out.

He was the biggest fool.

Brine took her silence as an admission of guilt.

None of it was real.

He wanted to rage at this betrayal, though in truth he realized it wasn't a betrayal. Had Scarlet ever verbally been his? Had she truly ever told him her intentions?

Was this sense of betrayal also his own doing? Had Brine fed himself a lie so tantalizing he eagerly lapped it up even when all the signs around him pointed to the contrary?

A chill ran down Brine's spine when his grandmother's hand moved from Scarlet's arm to settle on her belly. "Have you noticed how sweet her scent is now?" the monstrous woman crooned—to Scarlet's belly rather than to Brine. "How lovely? How innocent? How *young*?"

For a moment, Brine didn't understand the implication. But then he did, and a wave of understanding sent him crashing to his knees. It was all he could do to keep a sword trained on his grandmother.

She cackled, no longer even trying for the semblance of a lovely sound. It was ugly, vicious, and broken. A true villain's laugh. "Did you really think I'd allow you back into the pack after your betrayal?" she crooned with vemon. "After you fled from me? What I needed from you, cowardly boy, was an heir. An heir with my blood and Scarlet's running through their veins that would ensure my line would inherit the Duchy of Betraz. Someone I could shape and train in my own image. And you handed me one on a silver platter! It's all thanks to Red, of course. I trained her well, too. I—"

Brine didn't hear what Arwen said next. Blood was

rushing, pulsing, roaring through his ears, across his vision and through his body. He leaped from the floor, a howl ripped out from his lungs, and he attacked his grandmother.

Chapter Forty-Four

Brine

Brine didn't think, he simply acted.

With his sword in one hand and his dagger in the other, he launched himself at his grandmother. But Arwen was expecting it, and deftly moved to the side. Scarlet, too, was quick to get out of the way, though Brine would never have hurt her, even now when he felt utterly betrayed by her. By her collusion with his grandmother.

By her acting as the woman's spy and assassin.

By her pretending to be in love with him.

By carrying his child, not for love but for power and influence.

The news that Scarlet was pregnant should have been happy news, but instead it wrenched Brine's heart out of his chest. She had truly been working with Old Mother the entire time. Working against him, getting what they wanted only to toss him aside.

Scarlet and his grandmother would be the ones to be tossed aside instead.

"I thought you were faster than this!" Arwen goaded,

swiftly procuring two short swords from beneath her vanity. Why had Brine let her dodge to get there? She was a formidable opponent with no weapons at hand—he remembered that vividly from his childhood—but with blades...

This wasn't good.

"I'm just warming up," Brine snarled.

His grandmother laughed humorlessly. "You come in here covered in blood, blades in hand, and you're telling me that you're only warming up?" Arwen dodged another blow, spinning around with lightning speed and precision to land a blow against Brine's left forearm. He glanced away from the worst of the attack, though her blade still bit into the flesh of his arm. Brine gritted his teeth against the pain. Arwen carelessly flipped her long hair over her shoulder and asked, "Tell me, grandson, how long have you wanted to kill me?"

"How does my entire life sound?" Brine replied, getting close enough to distract with his sword and get in a jab with his dagger. It was to no avail; his grandmother grabbed his hair, her talon-like nails scratching his scalp, and slashed his chest. Like the first attack, it was barely a flesh wound, but it was still the second blow she'd gotten in on Brine when he'd so far not managed to land a scratch on her. She was toying with him, Brine knew, like his vendetta against her was a trivial matter.

It only fueled his desire to see Old Mother take her final breath.

Brine tried desperately to strike Lady Betraz while she painstakingly got in blow after blow, slice after slice. He landed a couple of cuts, but she didn't seem fazed by them at all. By the time Brine had a spare second to direct his attention to Scarlet, who was watching, panic-stricken, by the window, he was a bleeding mess and panting heavily.

And then it dawned on Brine.

He was going to lose.

Better to go down in a fight than with your tail between your legs.

Brine sincerely did not wish for this to be the end of things.

If only I weren't fighting on my own. But alone was what he was; his grandmother and the woman he had sworn was his mate had made sure of that.

And then there was a presence at the door.

A tall, foreboding figure, broadsword in hand and a molten look in his eyes.

Bright.

"Here to finish your nephew off?" Arwen asked, a crazed grin on her face when she realized how much more fun it would clearly be to watch uncle dispatch his own flesh and blood nephew. She waved toward Brine. "I must admit this is getting rather boring."

Brine swung his gaze from his grandmother to Bright and then back again.

So this was it. This was truly the end.

Bright attacked his mother, an enraged howl filling the room

"You really shouldn't have killed my twin, my other half," the older wolf snapped, the blow from his broadsword hitting dangerously close to fatal. Arwen yowled in pain, clutching at her stomach, but darted back just quickly enough to be able to continue fighting despite the blood pouring from her wound.

"You wolves are all the same," she said, venom dripping from her gaze as she tried to work out her next move. "Stupid, vulgar, disgusting things."

"So why does it look like you're shifting?" Bright fired back. He launched another attack. Brine was still too in shock and exhausted to rejoin the fray. Arwen parried the blow. "How large your eyes are, mother."

But what Bright had said was true. Before Brine's very eyes Arwen's pupils contracted to slits, her irises turning amber. "Silence!"

"How tall your ears are," Brine needled, shaken out of his shock.

Her elven ears grew fatter and longer, covered in bristly fur the color of her midnight hair. Her shoulders quivered, her back bent awkwardly as her body elongated and changed shape. The switch was grotesque and clearly against Arwen's own will. Through her leather boots the points of deadly claws poked through, destroying the material and scratching up the floor.

She shrieked at them.

Out of the corner of his eye, Brine saw Scarlet making a slow and steady journey toward the door, out of the fray. Brine wished she would run off and never return, safe with their baby but out of his sight forever.

"Why, grandmother..." Brine said, turning his attention back to the fight. A feral smile spread across his face as he took a step toward the monster that was Arwen. "What big claws and teeth you have."

"Go to hell, the lot of you," she seethed, leaping for Brine in a frenzy. But Brine and Bright were both ready for her, and together they jabbed, slashed, and parried their way around

Arwen, boxing her in until there was nowhere else for her to go.

The final blow was nothing special. A careful slide into her heart, Brine's dagger going in to the hilt, and that was that.

The life drained from the woman's eyes, and she tumbled to the floor.

Brine felt nothing. Not even satisfaction.

He'd help slay the monster from his nightmares yet there was no relief.

Bright spat on Arwen, revulsion shaking his entire frame.

Brine could only stare at his uncle. "I had no idea you hated her so much … all this time."

"She killed your father," Bright muttered, not looking at him. "My brother. My *only* brother—what else would you expect from me, Brine?"

"So why didn't you kill her sooner?"

"For the same reason you hadn't done so yet. For the same reason you ran away all those years ago. I lacked the strength, and the people to support me. The moment you returned, I knew her days were numbered. So thank you, Brine. I—"

"Brine," came a soft voice from the door. Brine turned; Scarlet was still there, the most composed out of the three of them. Brine didn't even care to try and work out if it was all a front. The sight of her made him sick.

She'd tricked him.

"Get out of my sight," he growled, unable to look at her any longer. "Stay in the cottage. I'll deal with you later."

He felt Scarlet bristle at his tone, but she remained silent and resolute until she turned tail and fled the room.

"Nephew—" Bright began, but he cut his uncle off.

“No. I just need … some time to think,” Brine said, wiping a bloody hand across a bloody brow for all the good it would do to clean himself up. “Talking can come later.”

It was clear Bright did not agree to this, but Brine didn’t give him a choice. He left the study, in the opposite direction Scarlet had gone, in order to meet up with Pyre and Damien and Tempest. He had work to do; things weren’t over just because his grandmother was dead. But his heart rang hollow and heavy.

Brine had finally won—had reclaimed his home from the woman he had so dearly hated all his life—so why did it feel like he had lost everything?

Chapter Forty-Five

Scarlet

"Get out of my sight."

Tears stung Scarlet's eyes as she fled the manor. The hallways blurred by and her ears buzzed. She stumbled and leaned against the nearest pillar as she cried.

She couldn't believe how easily Brine had believed Scarlet was working against him. That she would get pregnant and use their child against him.

A child.

Scarlet clutched at the stone as she heaved, bile spattering the hardwood.

She never wanted this. How was she supposed to care for a wee one when she couldn't even protect herself or those she loved?

The clash of steel against steel made her straighten. She wiped at her mouth with the back of her arm and began running in the direction of the cottage. Now was not the time for self-pity. Nowhere was safe now.

She needed to get out.

For herself and her child.

The scent of acrid smoke stung her nose, and it drove her to keep moving. Something was burning. Screams and growls cut through the night. It was all out war.

Get your things and run.

Her grandmother was dead, the man she loved loathed the very sight of her, and he was going to take over Arwen's empire on behalf of the Dark Court. Scarlet wanted to be as far away from Betraz as she could before she could get sucked back in.

She'd never be a pawn again.

She burst into the garden and sprinted toward their cottage only to stop in her tracks as she spotted some of Texel's men staking out the place. Her heart picked up pace and she backed away.

She didn't need her possessions. They were just things. If she traveled smartly, Scarlet could make it to Mill's ferry and he'd help her from there.

With that plan in mind, Scarlet crept away from the manor proper, keeping to the thickest parts of the estate. As she reached the perimeter of the grounds, she untied her red cloak and let it flutter to the ground. The air was chilly, but she didn't care. Never again would she wear such chains. She'd freeze before she'd put the bloody cloak back on.

Now she could finally be free.

"And just where do you think you are going, Red?" a sly voice said.

Tarros.

Scarlet clutched at her stomach and wanted to retch when he stepped out from behind a tree just past the perimeter line. He'd been lying in wait for her.

He chuckled and blocked Scarlet's path, a cruel smile

twisting his face. "Going somewhere, my sweet?"

"Away. Leave now before you get hurt," she threatened.

"Someone has gotten a bee under her bonnet. That's no way to speak to your superior."

She gritted her teeth and glared at Tarros. "How did you know I'd be here?"

"News travels fast," he said, making his way toward Scarlet slowly. She stood her ground, unsure what to do. If it had been only herself she would have attacked but now… she had to protect the babe. "So I figured, where would little Red go if her stepmother was no longer around to keep her tethered here? And then it hit me, of course. She would flee like the terrified rabbit she is. But I'm sorry to tell you, Red, that your journey ends here."

"That's not my name," Scarlet bit out, shoulders shaking as her hand found the dagger hanging from her waist. Even with his mangled legs, Tarros was still a full foot taller than her, and twice as broad. She'd have to strike carefully. He could rip her apart if he got her pinned down.

He'd almost done it before, and now there was no dragon to save her.

He wiggled his brows and glanced around the area. "No one here to help you now," he taunted, circling around Scarlet slowly, deliberately. He heaved in a breath. "Why do I want you so? Even now? It sickens me."

"The feeling is mutual."

She felt his mood change.

Tarros threw himself at her, so quickly that Scarlet tumbled beneath him before she could stab at his stomach with her dagger.

The red wolf grabbed at her fist, smashing it against the

ground until Scarlet's grip on the blade slackened. He tossed it carelessly away. With no weapon, Scarlet resorted to scratching at Tarros's eyes, punching his chest, wriggling beneath him with all the strength she could muster. But Tarros's hand flew to Scarlet's throat and tightened.

"You should have let me have you," he snarled, licking the full length of his tongue across Scarlet's face. "You should have given me what I wanted. Then you wouldn't have to die."

"I'd rather—I'd *rather* die," Scarlet sputtered between coughs. But was this really how she was going to go? She couldn't believe it.

Down to her marrow, Scarlet did not want this to be her fate.

"Maybe I'll take my fill of you and then kill you."

Over my dead body.

She got her left leg beneath her and kicked Tarros in the stomach. But he yanked on her ankle, loosening her shoe until it fell from her foot, and dug his nails into the flesh of her calf. Scarlet cried out in pain. She turned her head and bit down on his forearm until she tasted blood.

Tarros howled and tried to shake her off to no avail. He leaned closer and growled. "You're so beautiful, Red," he crooned, almost lovingly, "without your poisons and your cloak and your grandmother to protect you. I always knew you'd like it rough."

He headbutted her and Scarlet released his forearm with a moan.

"I like the way that sounds," he purred as she struggled against him. "Give me more of those sweet sounds."

"Bite me," she screamed, snapping her teeth at him.

"With pleasure." He pulled and tore the corner of her top

away and frowned at Brine's mark. "Such a shame he did that. I guess I'll just have to cover it with my own."

Her stomach rebelled and she vomited violently, splattering his chest and her own.

Tarros snarled, his upper lip curled back as he got in her face. "Do you think your weak little human reactions will save you?" She turned her head to the side, eyes narrowing on his ear. "You are mine. Now be a good girl and—"

She jerked up and bit down on his ear as hard as she could. He jerked away and she spat out a small chunk of his ear, simultaneously feeling proud and ill.

"You little witch. I'll kill you for this." He wrapped his hand around her neck and squeezed brutally.

Scarlet braced herself.

Don't black out. Keep fighting.

An arrow whistled through the air, lodging itself firmly in Tarros's back and protruded from his chest. Then another, and another for good measure. In an instant his eyes glazed over. There hadn't even been enough time for Tarros to realize he had died, his expression still one of vicious, bloody triumph.

His body toppled against her and his hand slackened around Scarlet's throat. She yelped and clawed at it as she pulled in a desperate, life-affirming breath.

"Get off me, get off me, get off me," she cried, attempting to wiggle out from beneath him. But he was too heavy.

Calm down and breathe.

Her hands shook and she gulped air, tears tracking down her cheeks as she sobbed. Tarros was finally gone. He couldn't hurt her anymore and yet… she was shaken to the core.

A few seconds later a pair of hands hauled Tarros off.

Scarlet scuttled backward on her hands and furiously blinked away her tears. Her vision cleared and she couldn't believe who'd saved her.

Standing above her was the Lady Marianne. The duchess of Merjeri, dressed as...

The Hood?

"Why ... why are you here, Lady Marianne?" Scarlet croaked as she climbed to her feet, legs shaking. "Why did you save me? What do you want?"

Lady Marianne held up her hands. "I want nothing from you." She offered Scarlet a smile. "Call me Robyn. Snakes like him"—she pointed toward Tarros's corpse, disgust curling her lip— "have a habit of popping up when you least want to see them. I'm glad I followed my instincts and did a perimeter sweep before going to the manor."

A perimeter sweep?

As Robyn swiftly and with precision removed her arrows from Tarros's back, wiped them clean on the grass and returned them to her quiver, understanding dawned on Scarlet: Robyn was working with Brine. With the dragon shifter and the fox.

Scarlet's stomach dropped. Lady Marianne was part of the Dark Court.

Out of the fire and into the frying pan.

She scoured the ground and snatched up her dagger from the dirt as Robyn faced her. The lady eyed the weapon and then Scarlet.

"I mean you no harm. I want only your safety. Come back to the manor where you'll be protected. I'm sure Brine—"

"I can't go back there," Scarlet rasped, wishing desperately for the woman to understand. "This estate holds nothing for me. I need to get out. *We...*" Her hand went to her belly. "We need to be free. To be safe. I refuse to stay in that prison any longer." She stared Robyn down. "Are you going to be an obstacle?"

To Scarlet's surprise—or, perhaps, not to her surprise at all—Robyn smiled gently, and held up her own hands in a placating gesture. "I'm not here to send you back. I'm not here to tell you what to do at all. This is *your* life, Scarlet. If you need to leave this place ... if you need to leave *him* ... then you have to do what you must."

"I need your word that you will keep silent."

Robyn cocked her head. "You want me to lie for you?"

"You've lied for everyone else, have you not?"

"That's fair. I won't tell anyone that you've gone. But you should know that running never solves the problem."

Scarlet couldn't help herself; she rushed forward and hugged Robyn with a ferocity the other woman eagerly reciprocated. It was only in that moment that Scarlet realized just how starved for genuine, no-strings-attached affection she was.

"Thank you," she whispered into Robyn's ear. She was crying, but no longer in sadness. "Thank you, thank you."

She released the lady and backed away.

Scarlet paused beside Tarros's corpse and kicked him hard and then spat upon his back. "May you rot in hades."

"Safe travels."

"Happy hunting," Scarlet murmured in return before she picked up her pace and left Lady Marianne behind. She wasn't sure where she planned to go, but there was one person who had the answers.

It was time she visited Ari.
This time for her own salvation.

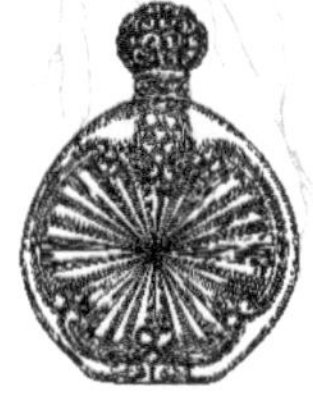

Chapter Forty-Six

Brine

A very long three days passed. Brine did not go back to the cottage. He still couldn't face Scarlet, nor trust himself to act accordingly around her. He knew it was inevitable that he'd have to confront the woman he loved about her betrayal, but he didn't know what he would say to her when he did.

So he threw himself into work instead.

At first Brine was overwhelmed by everything he had to do. He didn't even know where to start. But Brine was not alone, and with the help of Pyre, Tempest, Damien, Robyn and all her Merry Men, Brine began clearing out his grandmother's organization, gutting it from the inside out. Things went even more smoothly when Tempest brought in some of her fellow Hounds to help.

But for every task completed, Brine frustratingly had to face down a new challenge for the position of alpha in the Betraz pack. Even the wolves who supported the takedown of Old Mother were not unilaterally in support of Brine, and there were many who hadn't had an issue with Lady Betraz in the first instance. Brine thought he'd struggle with these bouts—he was still recovering from his injuries incurred during his fight with his grandmother—but with every new fight where he ruled supreme, he gained the confidence to know that nobody was going to beat him.

He was the new alpha, and eventually they'd all come to accept it whether they liked it or not.

After his seventh challenge for the position of alpha, Brine flopped into a winged armchair in the study he had taken as his own, exhausted beyond words. The study had belonged to Scarlet's father, left unused during his grandmother's reign, and suited Brine far more than the study Arwen had used. It had been so long since Brine had been in the study that any and all ghosts of the past—of chasing Scarlet through the room, and she him—were easy to block out.

At least for now.

"Have you ever heard of this thing called sleep?" Pyre murmured from the window, concern plain as day in his voice. Brine was not at all surprised by his friend's presence, nor that of the periwinkle-haired woman beside him.

Tempest smiled grimly when Brine nodded at her, shaking hair out of his face in the process. It was badly in need of a wash and a cut. "Mimkia can only go so far in healing your wounds," she chastised. "So rest, Brine. Then you need to see *her*."

"No I don't." The words flew out of Brine's mouth by instinct. Pack didn't betray pack.

"Do not be a child, Brine, not when you literally *have* a child on the way. Go back to the cottage. You have to give Scarlet a second chance. Have you even given her an opportunity to explain what was going on?"

He shook his head. He felt too betrayed by what his

grandmother had said. "The last thing I want is for her to spew pretty words of poison into my ear," he admitted. "I can't trust her. So how could I trust anything she says? Nothing is different now than it was before. Even the babe was a plot against me."

Tempest crossed the room with three quick strides and slapped Brine across the face. He hissed at the unexpected attack and glared down at her.

"What the devil was that for?" he grumbled, rubbing his stinging cheek. "Just what did I do to deserve that?"

"Because you're acting pathetic and I'm done tolerating it," Tempest said with heat. She flung her arms wide to take in the entire study and the estate at large. "She was a prisoner here, Brine. Why can't you see that? Do you really think she was working against you? Do you truly believe that every look, every touch, every moment between the two of you was false?"

Tempest glanced at Pyre, who stood from the window to join her. He interlaced their fingers together, then held up their joined hands to his lips to brush a kiss over Tempest's knuckles. The Hound blushed prettily, then said, "If Pyre and I had acted the way *you're* acting right now, we would never have ended up together. You have to give people a chance. Especially the ones you love."

"She lied."

"So did you. Did you tell her everything? Did you entrust her with all your secrets?"

No.

He hung his head.

"Go to her, my friend," Pyre urged gently. "You'll regret it if you don't."

Brine knew they were correct. In truth, he had known the whole time but had been afraid. Afraid he was somehow wrong. Afraid that his instincts about Scarlet had been entirely off the mark even when they were children. But now that the words had been said to him, and he'd had common sense slapped—quite literally—back into him, Brine realized how foolish he'd been, waiting three days to see Scarlet. How cruel. She was doubtlessly terrified. Pregnant and alone, with him refusing to believe her. Refusing to listen to her.

"I'm a fool."

"You are," Tempest grouched. "But a loyal one. Go make peace with your wife."

He all but ran from the study.

"Make sure you apologize and grovel, you wretch," Pyre called after him, laughing.

His pulse thundered in his ears as he sprinted through the gardens out to the cottage.

Brine slowed as he reached the small porch and steadied himself. He'd never been good with words. Always too gruff and quick to anger. But now he needed to make amends.

He opened the door and stepped inside. His eyes adjusted to the darkness of the room but she was nowhere to be found.

"Scarlet?" he called, striding into the bathroom.

She wasn't there.

He moved back into the center of the room and spun in a circle. All of her things were still there. Brine inhaled deeply and a shiver of foreboding ran down his spine. Her scent was stale upon the air. She hadn't been there in days.

Brine yanked open the front door and yelled, "Scarlet!"

No sweet, soft reply. Only silence.

Fear squeezed his heart, but he tamped it down. There was a logical explanation.

Where else could she be?

Brine panicked as he bolted back to the manor. He had to cling to the hope that she was, somehow, still around.

Her workroom. She could be there.

He burst into the chamber.

She wasn't.

Where the devil was she?

With her friends perhaps?

The housekeeper. Dris would know.

Brine ran back to the manor and into the kitchen. He moved to Dris and took her hands in his own. "Please tell me you know where Scarlet is."

She stared up at him with furrowed brows. "I presumed in the cottage."

He shook his head frantically. "No. Not for days."

The old housekeeper narrowed her eyes at him. "You've not seen her in days? What kind of mate are you?"

"The worst kind," he muttered, backing away. "Spread the word among the servants. I want her found. *Now*."

He stalked through the manor yelling for his mate, causing servants to skitter into the corners like frightened mice.

"What's with all the racket?" Pyre demanded as Brine reached the entrance hall. Tempest, Damien and Robyn all wandered down.

Brine tugged at the roots of his hair, full-blown panicking. "I can't find her."

Damien stepped forward. "We'll send out a search party. I'm sure she is close. We'll find her."

Pyre cursed. “When was the last time anyone has seen her?”

“The night we took the manor,” Brine croaked, shame drowning him. “No one has seen her.”

“That’s not entirely true.”

He focused on Robyn as she slowly pulled down her hood and fixed Brine with a level stare.

“She left the night of the raid,” she said coolly, her green eyes like hard emeralds. “A red wolf—I think his name was Tarros—was trying to kill her on her way out of the estate.”

His skin rippled and he felt himself on the verge of a change. “How do you know this?”

Robyn crossed her arms. “I was there. He got her pinned, but I arrived just in time. I killed him first. Scarlet left relatively unscathed.”

“So, why ... why didn’t you try to bring her back to the manor?” Brine demanded through clenched teeth. “Where is my mate?”

“It wasn’t my place to tell Scarlet what to do. The poor woman has had every choice in her life made for her. Who was I to tell her not to leave, or to tell you when she left so you could stop her?”

He took a threatening step toward the small woman. “You let her run off in the dark of night with my child?”

“Watch yourself, old friend,” Damien rumbled, taking a closer step to his wife.

Robyn strode up to him and poked him in the chest with an angry finger. “You are a fool. You must know that if you let her explain herself three days ago, she would never have left. Don’t you dare blame me. This is on you, Brine.”

“I get it!” Brine yelled, his voice echoing around them. He

held his head in his hands. "I know this is my fault. I need to make it right."

"You do."

He stared down at Robyn and begged for the first time in his adult life. "You have to help me find her. *Please*."

All at once the frost left Robyn's expression, and she smiled sadly. "Have your wolves search the perimeter of the estate, then. Send some to the outskirts of Betraz. You might get lucky. Her scent is faint but it may still be traceable, if you hurry. But I have to warn you... she looked broken. You must promise to be gentle with her when you find her, Brine. You must promise you will listen."

"Of course," he said gravely. "I just need one chance. One conversation."

Robyn gave him one last look before turning to Damien. "My love, it seems we have some tracking to do. Let's fly."

"I love it when you ride me."

Robyn snorted. "Ever the flatterer."

She turned on her heel and exited the manor, the dragon king hot on her heels.

"They will cover more ground than we will," Tempest mused. "But I have several Hounds along the borders. I'll send word for them to make inquiries."

"Wise as ever, my love," Pyre praised. "Brine, will you send your wolves?"

He ran a hand over his face. "The ones I can trust."

* * *

Three days of nothing. Of silence.

Brine didn't sleep and he could hardly eat.

By the end of the three days there was still no sign of Scarlet. She had become an apparition; all that had been left behind was her blood-red cloak, and a single shoe. Both had been close to the perimeter of the estate, where Robyn had found and killed Tarros.

But no Scarlet. No tangible leads as to where she had disappeared to.

For all intents and purposes, Scarlet had become a ghost.

Brine shifted into his wolf and ran through the forest until his legs gave out. He panted and stared up at the moon until he caught his breath and ran back to the manor.

Once he arrived at the cottage, he shifted back and pulled on a pair of trousers. He lifted her abandoned slipper to his chest as if it were precious. He supposed it was, since it had belonged to his mate. It even smelled like her—just barely.

Brine stepped outside and flung his head back and howled into the dark and murky woods, his pack echoing his pain.

"I'll find you."

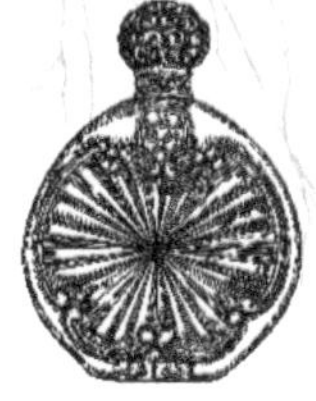

Chapter Forty-Seven

Scarlet

Scarlet blinked, and before she knew it four months had passed since she'd fled the Betraz Manor.

And Brine.

Her heart clenched.

"Get out of my sight."

His words still caused pain to ricochet through her.

She'd settled into her new life quite nicely. Living with Ari was easy: together they moved into a little house along the beach, which was only a few doors down from the pub Ari ran. So close to the dock from which Scarlet had witnessed her stepmother's ship burned to smithereens.

Good riddens.

But Scarlet didn't wish to dwell on such unpleasant memories. She wanted to look toward the future, with a friend and with her child, and with her past firmly behind her.

"*Ah,*" Scarlet uttered, a hand instinctively rubbing against the pressure inside her belly.

"Is the baby kicking again?" asked an elderly man who had

come in to retrieve a small bag of medicinal herbs from Scarlet, a knowing smile on his face. "My daughter is six months pregnant right now. She can't get any rest!"

Warmth spread through Scarlet's body, and she matched the man's smile. "I can relate." She laughed, sealing up the bag before handing it over to the man. But when he reached into his pocket to retrieve payment, Scarlet held up a hand to stop him. "No charge," she said. "If there's a baby on the way in your family, you need every coin you can get."

From the look on the man's face he appreciated the gesture more than he could ever say. Scarlet was no stranger to identifying people at first glance, and from the way the elderly man was dressed—the repaired and re-repaired patches on his jacket in several different materials, the scuffs on his shoes, the uneven shave of his face—it was clear that his family was not wealthy. And yet he held himself happily, and easily, as if he knew that money was not the thing that controlled his life. These were the people Scarlet loved most, and was only too eager to help.

It brought her more peace than she'd known in a lifetime.

Besides, her pirate clients paid more than handsomely enough to allow her to give the small folk her help free of charge.

"You're too kind to us, Miss Poppy," the man said, making his way to the door. When he reached it, he turned to face her once more, an almost angelic smile on his face. Scarlet didn't think she'd ever get tired of seeing that kind of smile on her customers' faces. "You'll let me pay next time, you hear me? I won't take no for an answer!"

Scarlet could only laugh as he exited her shop, which was above Ari's pub. It hadn't taken long to set up a healing apothecary in the Callmai, and word of mouth had meant that, before long, there were often queues outside the door with people seeking Scarlet's help. Her only rule was that her skills were used to help people and not to harm them. It was in this way that she became the official doctor of the pirates coming through the bay.

They accepted that she would not be selling them poisons and other nefarious means to dispatch with their enemies and instead was there simply to help heal them. She was tough but fair on them, and they returned her attitude with nothing but respect.

She'd finally done something her mother would be proud of.

Once upon a time, Scarlet could never have imagined living in Callmai. She hated it so because of what was smuggled in and out of the docks. But people were still people, and so long as Scarlet was helping others thrive on the back of her work then she was happy to do her part.

Besides, just like the old man she had served, the city was also full of people like Ari and the refugees they helped escape the ever-present terrors of Heimserya, and the small folk who were too scared and unskilled to do anything against the people who sought to oppress them. Scarlet could help them without charging a penny just so long as the pirates kept paying for her services, which she was all too glad to do for the sake of the Callmai.

So Scarlet was happy. Even if she wasn't using her real name, and nobody but Ari knew who she was, she had never felt more like herself.

This is what freedom meant.

But once the old man had left, Scarlet buckled against the

little table she used as a reception desk. Though she was happy—truly, she was—her heart still hurt whenever she thought of Brine. He'd tossed her to the side without letting her explain anything. Sometimes Scarlet wondered if she should have put more effort into trying to get him to listen to her. But then she gritted her teeth and firmed her resolve. Why *should* it have been on her shoulders to explain things to him? He had never explained things to her.

He'd sent *her* away.

The damned wolf had broken *her* heart.

Let it go. You must move on.

Knowing that this kind of reasoning was ultimately juvenile and beneath her, Scarlet only felt sadder. But it was too late now. She had to grin and bear it and move on with her life. For her sake and, more importantly, for her child's.

"One moment," she murmured, pulling herself together and standing up straight when she heard the jingling of the bell over the door.

"Take all the time you need," a silky voice said. Scarlet's eyes darted up with a start, for she recognized that voice from somewhere. Looking at the handsome man who had walked into her workshop, she realized he was familiar … in an odd, dreamlike way, as if he were from another life.

Her skin prickled and she eyed him. Where had she seen him before? Where had she heard him?

You're being paranoid.

Scarlet pushed her unease to the side in order to serve her new customer. "How can I help you?" she asked briskly.

A slow, feline smile spread across the man's face as he took in Scarlet's swollen belly, flashing sharp canines.

A Talagan?

"Who's the happy father?"

Scarlet's eyes narrowed and she shook her head. "There isn't one." At least in Callmai, no one usually gave her trouble for being a single pregnant woman.

"You aren't mated? Someone as lovely as you?" The man shook his head in what appeared to be genuine dismay at Scarlet's circumstances.

She bristled and planted her hands on her hips. "No. What of it?"

He held his hands up. "Nothing lass. Just trying to compliment you.'

The man met her eyes, she realized he wasn't meaning to upset her. There was something feline about his yellow eyes and slitted pupils—something that screamed *shifter* at her.

A cat?

"So no man in your life?"

"No," Scarlet said, simply, wondering where the man's line of questioning was going. She didn't feel uncomfortable by his presence, after all, and he wasn't looking at her in any kind of lecherous, desirous way. So why was he asking her if she was mated? She dipped her fingers into the sleeping powder she always kept at her waist.

"I don't think that's true," he said, his smile growing wider. Like a cat that ate the canary. "Your mate is, after all, looking for you."

She stiffened.

And then it hit Scarlet.

She did recognize this man, from the day that she spied on the fox shifter.

He was a friend of Brine's. A member of the Dark Court.

Bloody hell.

She knew this day would happen. She just hoped it would happen after the babe was born.

Scarlet had no time to waste. Without a second glance at the man, she bolted through the back door of the shop, down the stairs and to the main floor of the pub. As usual, the place was heaving, but the moment she locked eyes with Ari the woman looked at her and, without a word, abandoned her work to hold her friend's hand. With the utmost tenderness, she kissed her friend goodbye.

"The far left, remember?" she whispered into Scarlet's ear, when Scarlet embraced her. "On the docks. The far left. And here," Ari added on, pulling out the bag Scarlet had stowed away beneath the bar, packed and ready for her to leave at a moment's notice, for months now. "You'll need this."

All at once Scarlet's fragile happiness was shattered into pieces.

It was time to run. Time to start a new life where she'd be safe.

"I love you," she told Ari, meaning every word of it.

Her friend broke into a grin. "I know. And you'll still love me on the other side of the world, so *go*. And write often. I wish to know what the fire sands are like."

"I promise."

And so Scarlet had no choice but to flee the bar, the bag in her hands and the baby in her belly the sum total of everything important she was allowed to take with her, and hope for the best. She didn't see the cat-eyed shifter on the cobblestone street as she made her way across the pavement and toward the docks, but she had no doubt he would have long since left to alert his friend.

To tell Brine where she was. To get a hold of their baby.

Not our *baby*, Scarlet sniffed, blinking back tears as she fought the stitch in her stomach to reach the boat that was her safety and her salvation. *My baby. Not his.*

She'd have to start anew in the Southern Isles, and hope it lasted longer than four months this time.

Chapter Forty-Eight

Brine

"I found her!"

Brine dropped the tankard of beer in his hands, not caring that it clattered to the floor and splashed its contents across the grubby wooden planks. To his left, a couple of pirates scowled, but one flash of Brine's wicked curved dagger was all it took to send them on their way.

Brine could do nothing but stare at Chesh as he threaded his way through the crowded pub, out of breath and excited. "You found her?"

It didn't seem possible. He'd been looking for her for months. His mate was a tricky little vixen. She'd covered her tracks well.

Chesh nodded, then pulled Brine back through the throng and out into the freedom of the salty sea air and cobbled streets. "The rumors were right, she's here," he said, speaking in an undertone even though against the wind whittling past his ears Brine could hardly hear him. There was a pub on the other side of the city, hidden close to the docks but out of sight of them, which Brine had always personally preferred frequenting in the past, but he hadn't visited the establishment for months due to his new position as pack alpha taking up so much time. *This* was where Scarlet was rumored to have been living. Brine had wanted to visit the pub the moment he heard the rumor, but Pyre had pointed out that Brine's presence would likely scare her away.

So Brine had left the investigation up to Chesh.

"You don't have long," Chesh urged as they reached the docks. "I spooked her on purpose. She's headed to the ship now."

Brine growled beneath his breath and barreled headlong toward the leftmost dock. It had taken all of their wits and planning to organize the ship's routes to lure Scarlet out—for her to view it as the *right* ship for her to board should she ever need to escape. Brine hadn't thought it would work, but Chesh and Pyre and even Damien had been sure. Brine had never been so grateful to have such clever—and dangerous—friends.

Tripping over his feet in his haste to leap over the wooden boards of the jetty, Brine skittered onto the ship and just barely avoided crashing into two sailors holding a heavy crate between them on his way to his berth on the floor below deck. The sailors grinned at him.

"You'll get there just before her," one of them said, angling his head back to imply Scarlet was right behind him.

"Thanks," Brine mouthed, doubling his skittish pace until he was crashing through the door of the private berth he always used when traveling. He waited in the dark, behind the safety of a support column, out of breath and with his heart racing painfully.

Get yourself under control.

When he had a moment to think, Brine realized he felt every inch a pathetic excuse for a man. *Waiting in the dark for a girl?* he sighed, hating himself. *Just what have I become? She's fleeing so she doesn't have to see me. Who am I to impose my wishes on her?*

But then the door opened, a beam of light temporarily blinding Brine's eyes, and then she was there. All guilty thoughts evaporated from Brine's mind.

Scarlet was here, in front of him.

She looked more beautiful than Brine could bear. Even when she closed the door, locking it behind her before sagging heavily against it, looking as if she might cry, Brine could hardly tear his eyes away from her round belly and the glow of her skin. Pregnancy suited Scarlet. It brought her to life in ways Brine's grandmother had sought so desperately to stamp out. It made him realize that the Scarlet he had been dealing with this past year had been a marionette, being pulled against her will on strings she couldn't control.

Now, finally free of those strings, Scarlet could be real again.

In every line of her face, Brine could see the little girl who had once saved his life simply by being his friend.

Then, though Brine hadn't moved an inch, Scarlet straightened and stilled. She scanned the room with sharp eyes, and pulled a blade from the pocket of her dress.

"Come out," she commanded, setting fire to the oil inside a nearby lantern as she spoke. "Come out into the light. Now."

Brine was helpless to obey.

Chapter Forty-Nine

Scarlet

Brine had found her.

Scarlet didn't even need to wait for him to step out into the light for her to know he had. The entire berth *smelled* of him; she didn't need a wolf shifter's keen nose to realize that. Brine's earthy, masculine scent—enveloped her senses and made her feel, for one stark moment, that they were both back in their cottage and pretending to be together. Then reality came pounding down upon Scarlet's head. This was clearly Brine's ship or, at least, a ship belonging to the Dark Court.

This had all been a trap.

Fight.

"Stay right where you are," Scarlet said, heart thundering in her throat when Brine slowly, carefully, stepped out from behind a support column and made his way toward her. Dutifully, he did as he was told, maintaining a respectful distance away, dimly lit by lantern light.

It hurt to see Brine, even now. Especially now. His handsome face was twisted with longing that Scarlet wished wasn't there. He was happy to see her, that was obvious, but how could she trust that? How could she trust anything about this man? Everything between the two of them had been built on lies. They hadn't been true to each other since they were children.

Scarlet's hand scrabbled behind her to unlock the door. She had wanted Brine to reveal himself so they could talk things out once and for all, so that she could tell him in no uncertain terms that she wanted nothing to do with him, but now Scarlet knew she didn't have it in her.

Despite his gruff manners, he would say something too lovely to resist, and Scarlet would fall for it, and that would be the end. For the sake of her child and of herself, she needed to remain free of him. He was Alpha. Alpha was to be obeyed and she'd be subject to no one's authority unless she so chose it.

Brine inhaled deeply and shuddered. "Your scent… there aren't words." He made as if to take another step towards but gritted his teeth and stayed still. Brine surprised Scarlet by pulling something out from behind his back that Scarlet recognized. Her red cloak.

She jerked back against the door and shudder ran through her at the sight of it—she thought she'd never see it again. Why would he bring that here?

With trouble, she pulled her face into a sneer. "I'm never wearing that slave collar again," she said, when Brine proffered it to her. "Get it from my sight."

So he tossed it to the floor. "Then we'll burn it."

"Why bring it at all?"

"Because I thought it might bring you closure."

"I left it behind. That was closure enough."

"Fair."

They stared at each other.

"What do you want?" she demanded.

"I want to talk to you."

That was like a slap to the face.

"Oh, so now you want to talk?"

"Scarlet.."

"No!" Scarlet held her hand up. "I wasn't finished. You were only too eager to ignore me last time."

"And that was my fault," Brine said, earnestly taking a step forward before thinking better of it. Checking himself, his shoulders slumped and he remained a safe distance away from Scarlet. "I should have listened to you, Scarlet, and I didn't. Believe me when I say I regret that decision every second of every day."

That was rich.

She scoffed. "Believe you? You can't be trusted! You had so many opportunities to tell me what you were up to, to include me in your plans, but you didn't. Oh, Dotae be good, what do you have now? I—"

For Brine had pulled out another object from the shadows: a shoe. And not just any shoe. Scarlet's shoe—the one she'd lost in her haste to escape Tarros, the Betraz Estate ... and him.

She snapped her mouth closed.

He turned it nervously in his hands. "When I came to my senses—gods, it took me three damn days to come to my senses—you were long gone. I went looking for you. Well..." Brine chuckled bitterly. "I had just about every wolf at my disposal looking for you too, but you weren't to be found. All anyone located was your shoe. So I ... held on to it."

Scarlet didn't want to guess at what that meant. "Why

would you hold on to something so stupid?" she asked, hand still fishing around for the key she had stupidly locked in the door. Just because she wanted to hear what Brine had to say didn't mean she had abandoned her mission to escape. The man was bad for her. She was bad for him.

Brine offered her a small, almost hopeful smile. "I kept it all these months hoping to return it—using it as a symbol of hope to myself that I would reunite with the woman I love. For there was one thing that my grandmother wasn't wrong about, Scarlet. I've always loved you. I hate that she used those feelings to her own advantage, that she twisted the two of us against each other. More than anything I hate it. But here we both are, still alive and in one piece." His eyes moved from Scarlet's face to her belly. "Our child's alive. And *free*. That's more than I could ever hope for. And I have to believe that, now we're free, we can begin to mend what we've so horribly destroyed. Don't you want that?"

This was all too much for Scarlet.

She wanted nothing more than to wipe out what Brine had just said. That he would simply disappear, and with him any impossible decisions she would have to make. But she knew he deserved something in return for his heartfelt confession: an explanation of why she'd done the things she'd done. And a kind rejection, at the very least.

"I can't go back to you," she said, not having to feign the sadness in her voice. Her heart broke to see Brine's hopeful expression crumble, a stone mask taking its place, but she had to continue. "I won't be like my mother, locked away and complicit while you commit criminal acts for the Dark Court. Living like that literally killed her. It almost killed me. That's not the life I want for myself or for my child. I can only hope you understand this, Brine. Let me go."

"I can't," he rasped.

"Don't make me hate you," she whispered, tears burning her eyes. "You know what Arwen was like. Don't steal my freedom. Please if you care for me at all, let me go."

Brine said and did nothing for a long moment. It stretched so long, in fact, that Scarlet was beginning to think he was incapable of formulating a response, and that the correct thing for Scarlet to do was to simply turn around and leave. But then he whistled, and the door opened from the other side. Scarlet leaped out of the way, a cry of shock on her lips, at the mismatched group of people who emerged to fill the cramped space of the berth.

Scarlet recognized them all.

There was the tall, broad, domineering dragon shifter, and the fox shifter, and the cat-eyed man who'd come into her shop and forced her to flee her new home in the Callmai. But then there was the Lady Marianne—really named Robyn—and the periwinkle-haired woman who had sneaked into Betraz Manor to gift Scarlet the dress she had worn the night she became Brine's bride.

Scarlet backed away from them carefully. "What's going on?" she asked, suspicious and wary. Her hand tightened on the knife she still held in her hand, for all the use it would do against so many people.

Brine waved a hand around at his group of friends. "Scarlet, please meet my pack."

"Your pack?" Her eyes rounded. The Dark Court. "I'm leaving. Don't you dare stand in my way."

"I won't keep you hostage but please let them explain things. Please, do me one last favor and listen. After that you can leave and, if you never want to see me again, then ... I'll understand. This will be the end of things, if that will make you happy. I will let you go."

"Listen? Like you did for me?"

"I was wrong," he said gravely. "Don't make the same mistake."

She swallowed down her bitterness and stared him down.

It was as close to a clean break as Scarlet could hope for, so she nodded her head slowly and loosened her grip on her dagger. "Okay. Explain."

It was the periwinkle-haired woman who spoke. "My name is Tempest. I'm a Hound."

Scarlet narrowed her eyes. The Lady Hound? "*The* Tempest?"

"The very same. I used to believe the Dark Court were nothing more than a criminal organization. No better than damn King Destin, if I'm honest." Tempest's lip curled in disgust at the thought of the late king. Scarlet's heart softened in understanding. Here was a woman who likely had—if not an identical story—a very similar life to Scarlet herself.

"But I changed all that," the fox stepped in, bowing graciously, tipping his silk top at at Scarlet.

"So humble, Pyre," Tempest bit back, but she was smiling. She turned her attention back to Scarlet. "But, yes, Pyre was a major part of the reason I found out what was really going on. He's the head of the Dark Court, which is not, in fact, a criminal organization, but a group of spies and soldiers tasked with destroying the increasingly troubling mimkia trade spreading throughout Heimserya ... and beyond."

It seemed like a fairytale.

But the group took it in turns to regale Scarlet with the operations they'd taken down so far—up in the mountains, in the capital city, in Merjeri—and though Pyre and the cat—Chesh—enjoyed embellishing their stories for the sake of entertainment, it was clear they were all telling the truth.

When they were done, Scarlet realized the only two people in the room who had remained silent through it all were herself and Brine. She caught his eye, knowing he hadn't looked away from her even once during his friends' explanations, and heaved out a sigh.

"This is all ... a lot to take in," Scarlet finally managed to bite out. And it was the truth; her mind was reeling. She needed time to think. "Thank you for your revelations. I'd like to leave now."

Before she had a mental breakdown.

Despite the fact Brine had promised that she could, she still expected him—and the rest of his friends—to lock her up. But true to form, the wolf cleared a path to the door and signaled for Scarlet to leave.

"I hope this is not the end," he murmured, maintaining eye contact in a way that sincerely hoped that Scarlet would stay. Was she really going to walk away from him?

At that moment in time, she had no other choice.

Heart heavy, Scarlet walked through the open door and out of Brine's life.

And it about killed her.

Chapter Fifty

Brine

Having to let Scarlet walk away without running after her was one of the toughest things Brine had ever done. But though he didn't follow after her on the ship, that didn't mean he'd forever left her side.

Or at all.

Over the following week, Brine shadowed Scarlet to make sure she was all right. He knew she could more than fend for herself—had done so for all of her life until now—but even so, Brine didn't feel right unless he was there, ready to protect Scarlet and their unborn child at a moment's notice.

He was desperate to touch her. To hear her voice. To see her smile at him.

It was tearing him up inside that he could only be within the circle of Scarlet's existence from a distance. But he'd take what he could get, if the alternative was to be cut out of her life entirely.

Every day she wore a new bright color. Never red but always vibrant. Like her soul.

Eight days after Brine had first started shadowing Scarlet,

on a warm pleasant evening—the sun painting the horizon with deep red and purple streaks and casting the Callmai in a beautiful glow—Brine lingered closer to the door of her little house than he had ever dared linger before. He didn't mean anything by it; he only wished to get a glimpse of Scarlet through the window before retiring for the evening.

It was therefore to his surprise when Scarlet yanked open the door, stared pointedly at Brine, her blue and green dress flowing around her bare feet.

He swallowed thickly and stared at his mate, waiting for him to send him away.

"Come in, then," she murmured, stepping aside to let him in. Brine could hardly believe his luck. He knew that if he questioned Scarlet's hospitality then she would simply tell him to leave, so he stumbled over the threshold into the cottage, reveling in the warmth on his face from a roaring fire in the small living room. Scarlet closed the door behind them and gestured for him to sit down.

Once settled by the fire, Brine thought Scarlet was sure to say something. Instead she was resolutely silent. Brine had never been one to begin a conversation. An awkward quiet stretched out between them, punctuated only by the crackling of the fire. Scarlet was glaring at him, but Brine didn't want to be anywhere else in the world but here. She leaned against an old wooden table. His mate was luminous, even with a frown on her face, her swollen belly reminding him of everything that he wanted and so dearly hoped he hadn't lost.

"I'm happy here," Scarlet finally said, cleaving the silence in two as if she had shouted when in reality her voice had been barely more than a whisper. "I can't go back to my old life—not even for the side of good. I understand what you're doing with the Dark Court now, I really do, but even they have to make sacrifices that I can't stomach any longer. So I want to be here. This is my home now. Here, with our child. But if you want to—and if you're willing to put in the effort—I'll let you see them. I don't..." Scarlet's gaze fell to her hands fidgeting restlessly in her lap: the one sign that she was nervous about Brine's thoughts on what she was about to say. But then she gulped, steadied her hands, and brought her eyes back up to lock on his. "I don't want our baby to grow up without a father, though that's exactly what *will* happen if you prove to be anything less than the most doting parent a child could hope for."

Brine couldn't believe his ears. He got to his feet, the wooden chair he'd been sitting on scratching against the surface of the floor as he did so. "Please tell me that every word you just spoke is true," he said, closing the distance between them to stand in front of the woman he loved more than anything. "Tell me I am not hallucinating right now, Scarlet. Tell me that you are not lying."

Scarlet continued to glare at him so Brine took a step back. Her hands curved protectively over her belly. "I wouldn't lie about this, Brine. But it doesn't mean we have to be together. I understand why you couldn't trust me before, and that our past may make it difficult for you to trust me now. You can think what you like about me. But when it comes to our child ... I will always be true. I hope you can believe that."

He did.

"That's where you're wrong, Scarlet," Brine said, wasting no time in gathering Scarlet against his chest. She gasped in surprise. How had Brine resisted this for so long? So many precious seconds, minutes, days and weeks and years wasted not being with the woman his heart cried out for with his every waking moment—and most of his sleeping ones too. "I *do* trust you, Scarlet. I want to be with you. The child ... *our* child ... is an added gift I never expected to be granted in this life. I never thought I'd be a father. You don't understand how precious all of this is to me. How important."

She was giving him everything he'd been looking for his whole life.

Against his chest, Brine heard Scarlet stifle a sob.

"Do you—do you mean that?" she asked, her voice unmistakably wet. She glanced up at Brine when he bent his head low to take her in, her lashes thick with tears. "Tell me you're not the one lying now, Brine. I don't think my heart can take it if you are."

He held Scarlet's face between his hands, tenderly stroking her cheeks. Scarlet closed her eyes and leaned into the touch, her previous sob turning happy. "If this is your home now, Scarlet, then it's my home too," he said, meaning every word of it. "My home—my heart—is wherever you are. So if you'll let me ... and I hope you'll let me ... I'll happily spend the rest of my life here in this house, with you and our child. Pirates be damned."

"You would truly leave Betraz behind?" she asked again.

"I would," he said seriously, searching her eyes. "But my love, are you ready to leave Betraz behind? To leave your people behind?"

Her gaze wavered. "I've given so much."

"You have. I'm not asking you to give more. I'm asking you if you truly want to give up your province."

"I... don't know."

He cupped her cheeks. "You don't have to make a choice now. I've already put Bright in charge. He is working with Prey and Damien to weed out those who were loyal to Arwen. Chesh is taking care of her fleet of ships. It will take time but soon, Betraz will be a place of peace and equality for all."

"You want me to go back."

"No." He shook his head fiercely. "I want you to have everything you want. I don't want you to have regrets. You deserve everything and more."

"Can I think about it?"

"Your wish is my command, my love." And he meant it.

Scarlet let out a laugh—the most beautiful sound Brine had ever heard—and crept up on her tiptoes. He thought he imagined the touch of her lips against his at first. The soft and fluttering kiss was practically a ghost. But then Brine yielded against her lips, and Scarlet against his, and Brine deepened the kiss into something firmer. Resolute.

A promise between the two of them that they were both here, together, and that was all they wanted.

"I love you, Scarlet," Brine whispered into her mouth long minutes later, when they finally parted from their kiss for a moment, breathless and entwined.

Her lips twisted into a smile beneath his. "I love you too."

He lifted her upon the table and knelt on the floor lifting her foot. Brine pressed a kiss on her left ankle reverently.

Once upon a time, Brine would have wanted nothing more than to live in this moment forever. Now all he could see was the future: his life beyond this moment.

For the first time in his life, he couldn't wait to live it out.

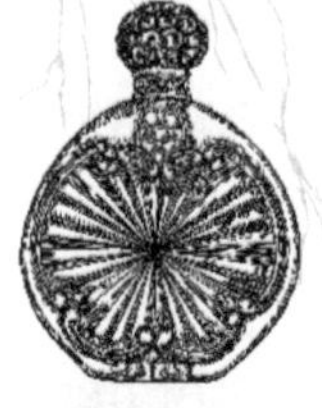

Epilogue

"Faster!"

Brine growled beneath Scarlet, his black and grey fur tickling the insides of her thighs. He threw back his head and howled before putting on a burst of speed.

She laughed as the wind tugged at her hair and cloak as Brine darted through the trees in his wolf form. She'd never moved so fast. Scarlet glanced over her shoulder, catching sight of a slinky black blur that was gaining on them.

Grabbing some of Brine's fur, she leaned forward and tucked herself against his back, barely peeking over the top of his head between his ears.

"Chesh is gaining on us!"

Brine doubled his speed as they broke from the trees and ran headlong for the beach, his paws digging into the sand.

A feline hiss sounded behind them that made Scarlet's hair raise at the back of her neck. She looked over her shoulder and stuck her tongue out at Chesh.

His eyes feline eyes narrowed and he yowled, trying to catch up.

The leopard was a sore loser.

Scarlet turned around right before Brine loped into the

waves. She screamed as a wave crashed over them. Releasing his fur, Scarlet pushed over the sandy bottom and stood, wiping the saltwater from her eyes.

Large warm hands settled on her hips, and she tipped her head back to meet sparkling grey eyes.

"Are you alright?" he mumbled.

"I'm fine."

He frowned, his palm cupping her round belly. "That was a rough dismount."

"It was just a gentle wave. Nothing more."

Scarlet popped up onto her tiptoes and pressed a kiss to his whiskered cheek before facing the beach. Chesh sat on the sand, his black and tan spotted tail, whipping back and forth across the sand.

She cupped her hands around her mouth. "Don't be such a scaredy cat! It's just a little water." He growled, baring long canines. "No need to be sassy."

His fur began to ripple and Scarlet spun around and leaned against Brine's chest, eyes closed. Chesh had no compunctions of shifting infront of anyone.

"I am always sassy," the feline called, his voice carrying over the waves.

Her mate brushed his hand over her wet hair. The babe rolled in her stomach. Brine stilled as he always did, barely breathing. His hands reverently brushed over her belly, feeling their child move as if to reassure himself that it was real.

"He's active today."

Scarlet rolled her eyes. "What makes you so sure our wee one is a *he*?"

Brine smiled wolfishly, making her heart flip. "Or she. I

don't care as long as they're healthy." He bent down and kissed a fleeting kiss to her lips and then down her neck to her mating mark.

"Heaven help me," Chesh whined. "Don't you dare start up *that.*"

She sniggered and slipped out of Brine's arms. He held his hand out and she laced her fingers with his as they waded through the water back to the beach. Her cloak dripped water onto the sand, the liquid quickly drying up.

Scarlet arched a brow at Chesh who'd thankfully put on some pants although he'd left them unlaced like the heathen he was.

"You're awfully grouchy today," she observed. "What's got you in such a state?"

"Ari," Brine muttered under his breath.

Chesh hissed, his feline ears flattening atop his head before he crossed his arms. "She's a troublesome female."

"Just because she didn't fall for you charms doesn't mean she's troublesome."

The feline harrumphed. "She hasn't spoken to me in three days."

"What did you do?"

"He flirted with one of his former conquests," Brine supplied.

Chesh glared at him. "I did not flirt. She came to *me.* Plus, why should it matter? It's not as if I'm mated or courting anyone."

"But you want to be," Scarlet stated. She'd seen how Chesh had been looking at Ari over the last few months.

"She's doesn't want me. Why waste my time?"

"If they're worth waiting for, you wait," Brine replied

resolutely. "Have you tried speaking with her?"

Scarlet snorted and elbowed her mate in the ribs. "Speak with her? You're one to talk. You make rocks look downright chatty."

"I speak with her all the time," Chesh exploded, throwing his hands in the air. "She just gets mad and storms off."

"Trying to seduce Ari is not the same as asking about her life or what's on her mind," Scarlet retorted.

The feline sighed. "It doesn't really matter anyway. If she was meant to be my mate, it would have happened already."

Brine pulled Scarlet into his side. "It's not some magical bond. Mates scenting only shows physical compatibility. A relationship takes real work." He glanced down at Scarlet and smiled. "But it is so rewarding."

"Oh yeah?" Scarlet whispered.

"Yeah," he murmured before swooping down for another kiss. "Marriage to you is the best life ever."

About the Author

Thank you for reading THE WOLF
I hope you enjoyed it!

If you'd like to know more about me, my books, or to connect with me online, you can visit my webpage https://www.frostkay.net/ or join my facebook group FROST FIENDS!

From bookworm to bookworm: reviews are important. Reviews can help readers find books, and I am grateful for all honest reviews. Thank you for taking the time to let others know what you've read, and what you thought. Just remember, they don't have to be long or epic, just honest. <3

Afterword

Hello there!

Aaaaaaah!! It has been such a journey to get here to 'the end' of Brine and Scarlet's story. I'm so incredibly happy with how this novel turned out.

When I first started this story, it was because I wanted to write a female villain. I usually stick with men when it comes to that role. No reason in particular, only that it comes naturally to me. Arwen was one of those tragic but vile cretins that I just *had* to write. It worked out perfectly since this was in part a *Cinderella* retelling (you NEED an evil stepmother). In fact, I've dabbling a little bit with a story of of how she is banished from the elvish kingdom... but I digress.

Next, I love a grumpy MMC. Brine has been one of my favorite secondary characters from the beginning. I knew I wanted someone who was sunny for him, but not all rainbows. When Scarlet walked across my page two years ago, I knew he'd found his match. Someone to tie him to his dark past but also someone who needed a little bit of saving despite her strength of character.

Now we come to our dear Scarlet.

I have a confession... Cinderella ranked low on my favorite fairytale list. Part of the reason was because it felt like she just rolled over and let life happen to her, like she never fought for what she wanted. So Scarlet was born. A girl born to nobility who is enslaved and abused by the very woman who should protect her. By giving Scarlet found family and her province to care for, it was enough of an incentive for her to stay, even when she could run at any time. In effect, she wore mentally chains - which for anyone who has survived abuse of any kind - this is half the battle.

So what's the theme of this book?

Breaking free.

Finding the strength to love despite the chance of being hurt.

And fighting for what you want.

I'm immensely proud of the final product and I hope you love it as much as I do. This book has touched my heart in so many ways.

So what comes next in this world?

If you haven't guessed, I'm moving onto Chesh's and Ari's story next. I'm not sure if it is going to be a new series in the Twisted Kingdoms world or another standalone. It all depends on how the muse moves me.

Love,

Frost

www.ingramcontent.com/pod-product-compliance
Lightning Source LLC
Chambersburg PA
CBHW020338310726
48979CB00015B/2416/J

* 9 7 8 1 7 3 6 7 0 9 0 9 2 *